Death Cracks A Bottle

"I'm sure it was suicide," said Noni. "He sometimes had a most peculiar look, a wildness about the eyes."

Her sisters looked at her without a word. Peculiar looks, wildnesses about the eyes, were not a subject encouraged among the Heavan girls. Nine now dead but one living had been the family's contribution to private asylums over the past fifty years. All Heavans were peculiar, some were barmy, and a small but significant percentage were downright crazy. It had started with Nicodemus Heavan in 1824 who placed boy apprentices upended in opened barrels of claret under the impression that it improved the bouquet. A vague man, he never got round to taking them out; in those commodious days it was hushed up and he was beaten, burned on his shaven pate and douched with cold enemas until he succumbed in a famous private madhouse in Norwich. But the rot had started. Even Noni seemed to realise that she had committed a vulgarity.

"I don't suppose he could have beaten the back of his own head in," said Nord.

"These cunning men can think of everything," said Noni, whose opinion of the sex became more profound and dogmatic each year.

WALKER BRITISH MYSTERY

Other titles in the Walker British Mystery Series

KENNETH GILES

Death Cracks a Bottle

WALKER AND COMPANY · NEW YORK

First published in the United States of America in 1970 by the
Walker Publishing Company, Inc.

This paperback edition first published in 1985.

ISBN: 0-8027-3119-8

Library of Congress Catalog Card Number: 70-97466

Printed in the United States of America

10 9 8 7 6 5 4 3 2 1

I

THE GREY LIGHT from the ceiling window bounced on to the shiny, waxy surface of Mr. Smart's small desk. It was rather good for paper work, but Smart, whose imagination tended to run riot, always fancied that it did not reach his feet. A puritan streak of self denial made him resist the temptation to peer down between his knees at the coir mat underneath. One of the junior boys, Arthur, held out a wicker basket which Mr. Smart, who believed out of kindness it was his duty to teach youngsters something of method and business principles, ignored as he slid open the drawer near to his left knee and produced his day book marked 'breakages'.

"Description first." He held his ballpoint over the virgin page marked August Ninth.

"Old Armadillo Port, four bots."

"What?" Smart, despite himself, peered into the basket wherein reposed the jagged fragments of four bottles with the coloured labels limply holding together some of the remains. Like flesh over a shattered skeleton—Smart had one of the graveyard thoughts which tweaked him now that he was sixty.

"The King's Solera, Very Old Amontillado Sherry. Delightful Cheery Fare for the Connoisseur."

"Sherry, not port," he said testily.

"Tastes the syme, Mr. S., and the nymes get that confusin' like."

Smart wrote. The King's Solera was a rather dubious production—doctored white wine really, he thought—produced in a small village on the Costa del Sol for the tourists: all part of Mr. Botting's new plan. Not for heaven's sake Colonel Jolyon's Number One, though it could not be, the twelve thousand precious bottles at forty-seven-and-six each wholesale being in a locked bin, the master key of which he had on his chain.

"They were all shattered?" he asked.

"Eh?"

"Broken into tiny weeny bits?"

"Yus, sir, little tiny weeny bits over the floor. We 'ad to mop it up."

Mr. Smart had had forty years of combating the thirst of the warehouse and cellar workers, at one time fierce, relentless jousting, but over the past ten years a quiet deploying of his arms—spy holes, spot checks and new methods—against the perpetual thirsty enemy. "Mop it up indeed!" Mr. Smart well knew that the small mop kept for that purpose would be wrung out into a wooden bucket and then strained through fine copper gauze by old Mrs. Frankly, doyen of the lady bottlers, and never quite sober on any of many occasions when Smart had seen her.

He finished his note. Ordinarily he would have told Arthur to go and put the shards in the wire bin kept for that purpose and thence resume his warehouse duties, but he dearly wished to ask the boy a question. He took his time in pulling open the drawer, trying to find suitable words.

"The p'lice just come, sir," said Arthur more respectfully than was his wont.

"Take care they don't take you away with them," smiled Smart.

"It weren't me what bashed his skull in, Mr. S." Arthur took up his basket and went out of the door which led to the long lino-covered landing.

Smart looked at the sheet-metal partitions which comprised two sides of his room and which in times of stress made him feel uncomfortably like some containerised merchandise being invisibly carried Christ knew where. At one time this, the attic floor, had been one large room with six male and three female clerks under the presiding eye of Mr. Smart who, the desk with the side drawers his badge of office, had been responsible for the invoicing of orders, monthly billing, banking and stock-taking of Heavan Ltd. Now machines, operated by two frighteningly capable ladies in overalls, did all this in the New Office Block. He'd been lucky, he supposed, in that he had inherited all the odd jobs the machines could not do, such as answering irate telephone calls. The remainder of the floor, with its little naked electric light bulbs tied on to the mouldering gas fixtures, contained four desks and various filing cabinets at the spartan disposal of the travellers when they 'came in'. Not that this topsy-turvy shifting had been abrupt or one of Mr. Botting's sweeping changes; the machines, starting with small adding and invoicing contraptions, had gradually crept up the stairs and into the old attic; but it had come as a shock when they had, as it were, taken over and marched the whole shooting match down below into the operating-theatre atmosphere of the new building.

His skilled ear caught sounds from the stairs. A heavily built person was ascending the lino-covered risers. Each squeak was an old friend to Smart as he rapidly went through a catalogue of travellers. Perhaps George Rumly, a man who truly lived for his work, his great mahogany face mirroring his unrivalled knowledge of the fortified wines; but, no, George was at the Bear in Devizes for tonight.

He swivelled his chair and watched the door open. For a moment he thought it was George, but this face had a shorter moustache. A rich, husky voice said, "Mr. Smart? Police here. Can I come in?" The last was a formality, for a six-foot, comfortably bellied body had accompanied the moustache through the door.

"Sergeant Honeybody, sir. From the Yard, called in by the Chief Constable, touching the distressing occurrence."

Few visitors of sitting-down status ever came into his office and Smart looked around rather blankly until his eyes found the bentwood kitchen chair, invisible from familiarity, standing in the corner. With his rather shambling movement he hastened to put fourteen copies of *The Economist,* at least seven unread he remembered guiltily, on the floor and cart the chair over.

"Thank you, sir." The chair groaned under the Sergeant's weight.

"I understand you found the deceased gent, sir." Honeybody had produced a wad of stapled flimsy sheets. He did not wait for Smart to answer. "No need for you to go over it again, sir. I'll just summarise what I've got you down as saying, and you pick me up if it's wrong.

"On Monday the Seventh, two days ago, you went down two

7

floors, that is two flights of stairs with a landing in between. You reached the floor you wanted below which has a narrow corridor with six small rooms off it. You went into the second room and saw deceased. He had his head through the hatchway to a service food lift. You went up and saw that the back of his head was crushed."

"Yes," said Smart. Oh, God, yes, and that horrible grey mush mixed with the fine, curly white-blond hair. He wasn't going to forget that in a hurry. Already it had codified itself into a dream in colour, as precise as a Chinese play, and Smart knew that it would be years before its nightly visitation faded. He was conscious that the Sergeant had rested his papers on the edge of the desk and was eyeing him with a bland, quizzical look.

"Turns you up, sir, that sort of thing," said the Sergeant, "even when you're used to it like me. I suppose you never saw nothing like it?"

"In the war," said Smart relieved, "I was a gunner. But that was different. I mean you didn't have to look. . . ."

"That's right," said Honeybody, comfortably. " 'Specially somebody you liked a lot."

"I wouldn't say that," said Smart. "He was not likeable. That made it worse, if you know what I mean."

"A lot of trying people about," said Honeybody, "unfortunate blokes who don't mean to but get on other parties' nerves."

"He meant it," said Smart rather grimly. Suddenly he felt inhospitable. The battered little clock on his desk which had been his mother's showed ten past eleven. He wondered if he was wrong in discerning a distinct look of fatigue in the Sergeant's blue eyes. "Usually about this hour I take a little something," he ventured.

"I feel the worms complaining myself," said the Sergeant enthusiastically.

Smart got out his keys and unlocked the only commodious drawer in his desk. He got out the bottle of Bual, two small glasses, one unwashed the other dusty and unused, and the two-pound biscuit tin containing his week's ration of rich slab cake and a knife.

Mr. Smart wiped the dusty, unused glass with a square of

paper, and opened the bottle to pour. "I trust you like Madeira," he said, hesitantly, wondering how far his visitor's education extended, "it's thirty years old. That's not *old* for this wine really, but . . ."

"Very choice, very choice," rumbled Honeybody. "I once had a 1910, but pearls before swine, sir, as we had been guzzling champers. I was guarding some family jewels at the time, a lot of Labour Party folk having to be invited to a reception. The old butler had a nice taste in licker, I must say. Cake? Nothing like a drop of cake with it, sir." The Sergeant's heavy fingers enveloped the slice and maneuvered it under his moustache.

Mr. Smart used to dally with his wine. When, at eighteen, he had joined the firm there had been a Mr. Heavan whose eleven o'clock wine ritual attended by all senior members of the firm had deeply impressed him. All gone of course, like most of the good things. He took up the lid of the tin but realised that the small glass of his visitor was empty and that the cake had disappeared. He set to work to replenish the deficiencies.

"Did any of the jewels get," he hesitated for the word, "swiped?"

"Stolen, sir?" Honeybody rebuked him. "One old faggot swore she'd lost a brooch, but she'd been trying that on the insurance for years. One quiet hint and she shut up. It turned up two minutes later and she said she'd found it in her handbag."

"Surely she was prosecuted?" Smart held confused but radical opinions.

"It's eccentricity, sir, if you're born right," said the Sergeant. "I suppose it was a minute or so before you noticed that the safe door was open?"

"The . . ." Smart jerked back to reality. "Oh yes, the safe. It was open, oh dear yes, I can see it quite clearly, the door pulled back and the pile of folders neatly stacked inside. It was this neatness that looked so funny. I mean . . ."

"I saw a man who had been killed by blast," said Honeybody, "but neat as a new pin, proper little dandy-man, except that his shoes had been ripped off. Incongruously you might say."

"Indeed." Smart replenished the Sergeant's cake and Madeira. "And the keys dangling out of the safe; one key in the lock, the

9

others on a ring, then the chain hanging down with a leather buttonhole at the end," said Honeybody, brushing crumbs off his papers, "presumably took off his corpse by somebody. Taken off carefully, too."

"He used to have a special button sewn on his trousers," explained Smart. "He wore a belt and his pants only had one button."

"Ar," said Honeybody, "zips may be svelte, as the term is, but they bring us a lot of business in the courts, sir. Unbuttoning, now, sir, requires a bit of cogitation as it were, but zipping's impulsive and spur-of-the-moment." His guileless glance caressed the cake and Smart cut another piece.

"Thankee." The Sergeant's great hand was conveying the goody to his open chops when he paused. "I suppose the button wasn't ripped off?"

"Oh, dear, no." Smart wished he could put the cake in the tin and replace it with the wine in his drawer. As it was his week's ration would scarcely last until the next Tuesday, when he purchased the cake at Sainsbury's on his way to work. The wine, not always Madeira, came from his private bin in the warehouse. Old Mr. Heavan had encouraged the seniors to rent a bin apiece at nominal cost. Over the years Smart had acquired a select little collection of odds and ends, bottles purchased at cost during 'clearing out' times. Resolutely he corked the bottle.

The stout Sergeant swallowed the last morsel of cake and drained the remaining half-glass of wine through the crumbs on his tongue. "How did you happen to know about that button, sir?"

"Dear me," said Smart slowly, "I keep forgetting that this is probably Foul Play. I must be absolutely accurate. Let's see. His coat, brown synthetic I believe, had ridden up round his buttocks —he wore his coats on the short side, and I remember seeing the button—it was made of Dutch metal and glinted in the light—just about on his right hip."

"You often went down there?"

"Quite often, Sergeant. I . . . well, I'm the oldest member of the staff, excluding three of the cellarmen. So I'm a kind of walking history book when it sometimes becomes necessary to recall the past. Better me than a morning pawing through dusty files, even if they exist." He gave his thin, wistful smile.

"And what precisely had come up on Monday the Seventh? I see that the local chaps did not ask you."

"Joshua's Ales, Stout and Porter."

"A good drop," said the Sergeant. "Of course, they started here."

"Indeed. About thirty years ago the brewery (they only had three then) had an agreement with us. It didn't last long, but there was some question as to exactly what the clauses were. I was a senior clerk at the time, but in a confidential capacity to the last Mr. Heavan, so I remembered the transaction."

"Nobody else up on this floor, of course?"

"Only me," said Mr. Smart, firmly. "I was in here at eight twenty and here remained at my desk until, say, five to twelve. I had seven telephone calls from customers and made two outgoing ones, all of which I told the local Inspector. Three times I told him." There was a patch of colour on Mr. Smart's normally pale cheeks.

"What they call routine," said Honeybody, "and I've a pair of ruined feet to show for it. The bone merchant at St. Boniface's starts back in horror every time I bare them at him. He says theoretically I can't walk."

"I find a good prolonged soaking in hot sea-salt works wonders," said Smart. "I purchase it in seven-pound bags at the health shop."

"I might try it," said Honeybody, ruminating that when they were over fifty foot trouble always attracted them; he had a store of limericks for youths and complaints about building societies for the twenty-five to forties. Forty itself was a bit of a problem he had always found, politics were best but too tricky by far.

"And a witness, too," said the Sergeant. "This Jasper Smith, is he reliable, sir?"

Smart gave his barking laugh. "He's my witness and you ask me that! For the record old Jas is as untrustworthy as they come, a thief, if you leave anything small around, a liar, pretty much of a shirker and an informer on his mates if there's benefit to him. He blackmails himself into an ample share of the grog which is going."

"I thought he sounded like an old and faithful servant," said Honeybody, impassively.

"That is what an old and faithful servant is, man!" Smart regretted the third Bual as he spoke, but the Sergeant chuckled and said, "How well I know 'em!"

"I've made use of him over the years; like going to a brothel, you feel guilty afterwards," said Smart.

"You do, sir," sighed Honeybody.

"Any bit of ratting needed, you consult Jasper. I must say that on balance he's saved the Company thousands. It was him that prevented us being smashed open one night sixteen years ago. We weren't insured for what they were after—twenty thousand quid in notes. We were due to complete a purchase next day—a cash-upon-signing job and the money was in a tin box in Mr. Hanna's room. Christ!"

"I remember, sir, that the boys who were apprehended and sentenced alleged that they had given Jas Smith seventy quid for a drawing of the premises, a detailed one, but the Judge didn't believe 'em."

Smart shrugged. "He wouldn't throw away his steady job here on a gamble. Like me," he grimaced, "he waits for the pension. And he whitewashes better than a royal commission."

"This whitewashing," said Honeybody cautiously, "a bit unusual, eh? In this day and age it's plastic paint."

Smart gave the smile of a man on well-tried ground. "The Company is an oldish one, Sergeant. The first Mr. Heavan, Not Long Thy Coming his father christened him, started up in 1704. He was the renegade of a Quaker family in the chocolate trade. A sherry and red Bordeaux man, with rich Malaga and Madeira on the side. So we make a cult of being old fashioned. You've seen the advertising, all Regency bucks and crinolined tarts mixed up with Empire furniture swigging down 'Heavan's Clarry Cup, the life of the party'. We're whitewashed as part of the mystique. Not that it isn't a sound principle, whitewash being slaked lime and a fairly efficient bug killer where wine is concerned. It is eminently practical in the warehouse; if wine is spilt, old Jas

Smith whitewashes over in half an hour. That's all he does, systematically whitewashes from top to bottom and then starts again, with time off for patching jobs."

"It takes him all his time?" Honeybody was sceptical.

"He's an artist with the goo," said Smart. "Mixes it himself in a shed out the back from chunks of burnt stone. Slakes it with water so that it burns fiercely—hot water's the secret for smoothness—then adds a modicum of oil, and there we are. Oh, Jas doesn't break a blood vessel, but he's always on the go. It's a big place. This is the original building, the four floors of it, this attic one included. Then there is the big new warehouse with loading and stacking gear, a bay for trucks and vans at the end, and a two-storey—ground and one floor—new office building. Quite a lot of whitewashing."

"All new except this old house, eh?"

"The Heavans accumulated about two acres of land over the years and the underground cellaring grew up haphazard, with sheds and outhouses springing up indiscriminately; not that it didn't *work*. Then in '43 a dropped landmine plus incendiaries hit the old place. This house was unscathed and a good bit of the cellaring, but all the surface buildings went. A holocaust—a petrol tanker went up nearby. All the locals did their patriotic duty in assisting the firemen—they say the village was drunk for weeks after, even the old people hobbling up with bottles to scoop up the stuff that was running out like a small stream. It didn't wipe the firm out; there was a deal of stuff, mostly in the wood, saved in the cellaring, and we'd joined with half a dozen other merchants in a kind of mutual insurance. But it certainly cleared the way for new building."

"So the 'new' part is around twenty years old, sir?" The Sergeant was gently patient, a kind of fact-grinding mill, thought Smart.

"No," he said, "there were temporary huts, Nissen sort of things. We were too busy finding stuff to cram down war-parched throats to worry too much except when the unions came round about the heads and the lunch room. No, the new part was accomplished in one cyclonic burst—five months from a standing start with penalty clauses—seven years ago."

13

"That was when?"

"That was when we got our new Managing Director," Smart's plump mouth could close like a trap, the Sergeant noted.

"Let's see," he said, "Jas Smith, with ladder, containers of whitewash and brushes, started to whitewash the stairs at nine thirty on Monday morning, commencing at the top. He had your door in view from then until shortly before noon and will swear you never left."

"Not too difficult," grunted Smart, "the stairs are narrow and to get down I'd have to squeeze past his ladder."

"I didn't mean going downstairs in particular," said Honeybody, "but there you were safe and snug in this office. What time did you come out, did you say?"

"I have said eleven fifty-five once to you and about seven times to your colleagues. That was when I went downstairs. At eleven thirty I poked my head out and said, 'Jas, I've got to get down below by twelve if I can.' He wagged his brush at me. I did this because Jas is a funny-tempered fellow. I don't say he would drop his whitewash bucket over you, but . . ."

"Nobody came up to see you during the morning, I see?" Honeybody looked at his sheets. They were marked like a producer's cue-book, product of three hours at the other side of the Inspector's desk the previous afternoon. Harry James, his superior, had some theory of not pressing too hard at preliminary interviews. He put the folded papers in his side pocket and prepared to go.

"I suppose this business means a big shake-up, sir?" His voice commiserated.

"That will be a matter for the Board. . . ." Smart's head had begun to ache and his voice was terse.

2

"I TOLD HIM COMPANY matters were strictly a matter for the Board. He was bloody inquisitive," said Mark Hanna, seated in the big, throne-like chair at the head of the Board table, "a bloody, impertinent, inquisitive little mousy man, Inspector James. I told him I had to preside at the Board and the little snipe said he'd 'poke around' if I didn't mind."

Nerves, thought Eldred Keast, watching the florid face. Nerves and bluster when the whips cracked, that was Mark, all his valuable qualities negated by that fatal flaw. He'd always suspected that the story, forgotten now, that he'd heard whispered in half-hints in 1944 was true. They hadn't busted Mark, just sent him on some liaison to Washington. Major Mark Hanna, small-waisted and broad-shouldered then. Only the large, snapping eyes, piratical in style, and the black curls remained.

"No need to bother ourselves about 'em," said Bill Stigg, "they're paid to sniff and worry. Good dogs, throw 'em a bone or rather a quart or so of the Boardroom sherry when they pause for breath." Stigg was in his thirties, long and elegant, a creature capable of endless graceful gestures, his long 'aristocratic' face belying the plainness of his name.

The Chairman ogled him with exasperation. "There are probably people who could inform him that the late bloody lamented was going to hang us, individually and collectively, today. Hang us high as Haaman."

"My dear fellow," said Stigg, "as we spent the entire morning in your office—I don't recall any of us even took a leak—what does it matter. None of us smashed the bastard's head open."

"And we won't improve things by bellowing like this," said Eldred Keast in his colourless voice. "Suppose we get to business. Better get Stiggins in, eh?" Without waiting for an answer, he got up and opened the heavy teak door. The Secretary to the Board was waiting peacefully in the small anteroom, reading a gardening magazine. He was a wizened cockney apple of a man who looked anything between fifty and sixty and was in fact forty-seven. He could deal with figures with a knife-edged intelligence.

"We're ready to start, Mr. Stiggins."

Over the years since he graduated at fourteen (thirteen really, there being some mystery about the exact date of his birth) from East Southwark Central School, Stiggins had cultivated the art

15

of saying little but looking as if about to say more but refraining. This had probably been as useful to him as his unremitting acquisition of professional qualifications by the good offices of correspondence school. He merely said, "Good morning, gentlemin," and seated himself with his impedimenta at the far end of the table. Well below the salt, thought Keast who detested him. A man sensitive to little pointers, he thought that on this morning the Secretary, one right-angled arm well thrust over on the mahogany surface, was thrusting himself up towards that invisible salt-line. A week ago . . . oh, well, Keast's motto was never to look back or remember unpleasant things if he could help it.

"By agreement I shall take the Chair *pro tem.*," said Hanna, looking at the huge, useless green blotter that custom decreed.

"The Minutes of the Board Meeting held on July Eighth," said Stiggins in his hard twanging voice. Keast felt his knuckles turn white over clenched fists below the concealing table. It did not take long. "The Chairman," droned Stiggins, "announced the retirement from the Board of Messrs. Hanna, Keast and Stigg."

Hanna said carefully, like a rogue elephant picking his way silently through the breast-high undergrowth, "I consulted our solicitors after the Chairman and Managing Director's untimely death—got that verbatim, old man?"

"Yes, Mr. Hanna."

"And they informed me that, until the Minutes were approved at this, the subsequent meeting, the resignations referred to were not valid. We should place this statement, and a declaration that the parties concerned withdraw their resignations, as an addendum to your Minutes and then approve."

Stiggins wrote rapidly in pen and ink and read Hanna's statement back.

"You approve the Minutes, gentlemin?"

"Aye."

"There is, of course, the point of signatures, withdrawals and the like."

Hanna cleared his throat. "We shall put it on record that I will personally take responsibility for all disbursements under the Acts until a General Meeting of shareholders."

Keast dropped his gaze. Hanna's overdrafts were common

16

knowledge; last week 'young Dickie'—to distinguish him from his iron-voiced father 'old Dickie' who laid the odds cheek by jowl to the Members' Stand at most race-meetings—had told Keast that Hanna was asking for time still, months after his plunge on the Two Thousand Guineas had blown up over the final two hundred yards. Keast had shared a school dormitory with 'young Dickie'. It was a gesture typical of Hanna, a guarantee backed by at best a rickety overdraft.

Stiggins looked at the wall for a long minute, but then sedately made his note.

"I suppose we proceed on the Agenda that was previously drawn up?"

Mark Hanna hesitated rather too long.

"I move that we proceed to the Agenda," said Keast, his words followed by quick agreement.

There were four routine matters. Then: "The offer from Joshua's Ales, Stout and Porter Ltd. be accepted by this Board and the Shareholders advised accordingly." Stiggins looked over at them impassively. "This was to be a motion from the Chair."

"Are you going to put it, Mr. Chairman?" asked Keast.

"No," said Hanna, gaining decision, "no, it won't be put and therefore should not come into the Minutes. I suggest that we record that the offer from the Brewery is under consideration from the Board."

"Agreed," said Keast and Stigg.

There was no further business and they waited for the Secretary to place the usual pile of cheques before Stigg—whose chore was to sign them as the junior Director—and depart. Instead, the little man wiped his lips with a white handkerchief and said, "A sad loss, gentlemin."

"Ah, yes," Mark Hanna gave something of a start, his black eyes blinking. He felt in his breast pocket and produced a small scrap of paper. He read in an expressionless voice: " 'The Board wish to record their deep regret at the loss incurred by the Company by the untimely death of their Chairman, the late Mr. Cristobal Botting'. Here you, Mr., um, um, uh, take the paper, take the paper and copy it from there."

"I think my Pitman is decipherable, Mr. Hanna." Nevertheless,

Stiggins gave his acid little smile and put the paper in his briefcase before going.

It was one of the signs that Mark was in a flap, thought Keast, when his memory, even for the names of people and things quite close to him, temporarily vanished. In fun he had himself invented some quite apocryphal occasions—Mark on his wedding night had become quite a classic in its way—but it wasn't funny now. Above Hanna's head were four portraits in oils—three of the three nineteenth century Heavans, all with the remarkably pushed-forward underlip and very close-set eyes. The fourth was the late Cristobal Botting, done four years before. "Portraits should be semi-photographic," Botting had said, "and I don't want my soul, God bless it, put on public display." He had got a very capable hack and there he was life-like, head and shoulders, the ribbon of his M.M. on his lapel (one never knew whether Botting was proud of it or not, he used to wear it only on the most in-apposite occasions), and his quite round, reddish face registered its usual kind, enigmatic, pitying smile under the curly, short-cut blond hair.

"It seems to me that we should decide here and now what to do," said Stigg, his voice a bit strident.

3

NONI HANNA POURED out three coffees, her eyes like black-currants peering between white, flabby folds. "I think we should decide what to do here and now. After all it is our affair."

She finished pouring and passed round the cups. So great was her agitation, under the monumental flesh which covered her all over, that she forgot the petits fours.

Most unlike Noni to forget food, thought her sister, Nord Keast, crossing her slim, elegant legs. One had passed the stage of pretending that Noni's trouble was 'glandular'. In fact she ate like a sow, two sows in fact. Not that she, Nord, would publicly admit the fact; they were not that kind of family. The Heavans had always stuck together whatever quarrels they had privately. The fact that Noni favoured brightly coloured horizontal stripes made it difficult. It was all right saying "somebody should tell her," but when it came to the point nobody within memory had ever plucked up courage to *tell* Noni anything.

"I think we should take a very firm stand." Nefertiti Stigg was the fragile, blonde baby of the family, able to walk, if put to it, twenty miles up hill and clap babyish hands at the end of it and swivel her china-blue eyes from male to male. Even at thirty there were signs of the inevitable caricature creeping up, thought Nord, coldly, although she guessed that physically Nefer would be much the same at seventy as she was now, but the gestures and the voice, with its tremulous sliding into contralto, would seem oddly dated.

Nord shrugged, her thoughts back in her own, cool elegant little house rather than in this great, straggling over-furnished place of the Hannas. "What do you want to do?" she asked.

"For God's sake, you know!" Noni's little eyes darted about in agitation, saw the petits fours and a hand descended to the plate. She gulped. "We want to keep the business."

One of Nord's pretences was a disdain for figures, but Nefer had had the chance to make a career as a mathematician. "Once and for all," said Nefer, "there are one million voting shares in the Company. We three control four hundred and fifty thousand shares, our husbands have fifty thousand—as long as we stay married," she said with that grim frankness which often surprised people. "The remaining five hundred thousand are held in trust by the Commissioners in Lunacy."

"I thought that the Commissioners would be more or less bound to sell, these institutions are always out for a profit." Nord nearly committed the solecism of saying 'so Eldred says' before she remembered that they never referred to their husbands by name while in a family conclave.

"They will not oppose the wishes of an old-established company," said Nefer. "Caesar's wives, my dears, in their great red robes and wigs or whatever the Commissioners in Lunacy wear."

"Foolscap folios with red, barking seals," said Nord.

"I do wish you'd be serious," said Noni, diving into the little crunchy cakes.

"Here, let me." Nefer reached over and filled her coffee cup until it slopped into the saucer, taking it black. She looked as though she would like a cigarette, but Noni would not have smoking around her. "The gross income that we get is forty thousand pounds between us, including the husbandly shares."

(Typical of Nefer, thought Nord, that she did not mention that the proportion was: Nefer forty-five per cent; Noni thirty-five per cent and Nord twenty per cent).

"Whereas," said Noni, "our share of the proposed sale, after deductions, would be a bit over four hundred thousand pounds. And what should we put it in? Stocks and shares?" Her laugh was a little bitter. Mark Hanna was always 'getting a little ahead of the ball', in his words, which meant in practice giving up the various things which his wife wanted, in order to make dully unsuccessful, not even crashingly disastrous, excursions into the Market. "And besides," said Noni deliberately letting the words hang unfinished.

There was no need to mention this ever present 'besides' in concrete terms. It was always in the minds of Noni and Nord. Their grandfather, with no direct heirs and by nature remote although still capable in business, had left a will according to some principle of which his heirs had not the foggiest idea. The three girls had been brought up by a spinster sister of their mother. It was, thought Nord for the thousandth time in perplexity, not as if old Nonsuch (the letter 'n' for luck was compulsive in Heavan christenings) had known them well. Only twice could she remember the thin, dismal old fellow, then pushing seventy, ever visiting them, ghastly occasions of dreadful silence punctuated by a few agonised words while Nonsuch sat, disapprovingly it seemed, on the edge of the hardest chair in the room. In his eighties—and he had remained Chairman and Managing Director until he died aged eighty-six—he had seen them not at all. The will had specified that fifty thousand ordinary shares should be held in trust for the husbands of the three girls who would enjoy the income. Until marriage the income went to the girls. In the case of divorce the principal was given to the Church

20

to which the old man belonged as it would be following the death of any of the girls who was childless. In fact none of them had been unmarried. At twenty-three, Noni had married Mark, some kind of very distant cousin who had joined the firm, and Nefer had snapped up effortlessly a most presentable young man while in her second university year.

Old Nonsuch had sent cheques for two hundred pounds and a statement that his health precluded ceremonial occasions. In fact the old gentleman still spent every available hour playing bowls, his only passion as Nord knew. Even when Noni had married 'a member of the firm'—her inevitable cliché—her dreams of cosy tête-à-têtes with grandpa had been fruitless. Mark never saw the old gentleman outside office hours. They had been very afraid, Nord recalled the other meetings over coffee, that the young, pushing, immensely capable Cristobal Botting would inherit. According to Mark's dismal forebodings he and the old man were as thick as thieves outside the office. They had breathed a mutual sigh of relief when the solicitor had not invited Botting to attend the reading of the Will. "Give me a month and I'll serve up his head for breakfast," Mark had boasted. . . .

There was, however, a 'but' about the Will. If all the girls, within a period of ten years, sold their interest in the business the money realised from the sale of the husbands' shares went to them. "For this would mean that the business which has sustained and united our family for so many years had ceased to exist," old Nonsuch had dictated, "and therefore both would be at an end as far as my interest is concerned." A queer will, thought Nord, once again, and even a mischievous one. She put the thought away from her. Nefer had been talking.

It was the old story. They should fee the best kind of London solicitor and insist that business consultants be called in.

"I know you persist in talking down Mr. Smith," said Noni, pushing away the empty plate, "but he knows the county."

In her elephantine way, Noni could be annoyingly loyal. Mr. Smith was the father of a school-friend, a woman nearly as gluttonous, and old Mr. Smith was one of those old-established, half-competent, careful and dilatory lawyers who proliferate in the provincial cities. Nord had once thought of the law as a

21

profession and considered she knew all about the legal profession. She lay back and thought of a recipe she had read for mushroom ketchup.

"Really, Nord," Noni's voice was gravelly, a sure sign that her temper was failing, "as usual in a crisis you're off in a dream world. How you run your little house, God alone knows . . ." she glanced appreciatively round the top-heavy magnificence of her drawing-room.

Nord, who ran her house with the aid of a surprisingly agile septuagenarian from the village who came in for two hours a day, knew from past experience that Noni's plump finger would plunge on to the button of the little box which rested on the coffee table, thus summoning one of the three ever-changing foreign servants she got from a London agency. A sallow-looking woman answered, bringing with her a fresh plate of cakes and more coffee. Noni started to frown as the woman dexterously planted them in place of the used things, but checked herself. It was the gloomy Spaniard, Nord recognised, who had lasted an unprecedented eleven months.

"Fresh cups," said Noni.

The maid removed the coffee pot, revealing the fresh cups behind them.

"That will be all," said Noni.

"I always admire the super efficiency of *your* household." Nord had rarely succeeded in needling her elder sister since she could remember. Not that it did any good. Noni merely gave her intimidating glance which indicated that she knew you were ignorant rather than impertinent, but if you should progress to the latter you would get hell.

"Compliments apart," said Noni, "what if anything are your suggestions?"

"I'll go along with you two."

Both Noni and Nefer registered annoyance. It was always the way, it seemed to Nord, that people would not accept acquiescence; the more you agreed the more they ravened for active participation. You agreed, rather bored, to the sacrifice of a cock, and they insisted you dabbled your hands in the wretched bird's entrails.

22

"How nice!" said Noni, with what passed with her for wit. "Any more great thoughts on offer?"

"Oh . . . what about Mr. Stiggins . . . you know him, Nefer. What does he say?"

"I have pursued Mrs. Stiggins, who has a diploma in political science gained from some university with which one is not familiar." In her comedienne's voice, Nefer allowed the last words to drop an octave. "And assumed my best university manner. Apart from the fact that her Labour convictions mask a rather ugly kind of fascism, I know little of her except that she has two repellent children, both girls. I met her husband once. Short of taking him to bed . . ."

"Please, Nefer," intoned Noni.

". . . which I do not propose to do, there is no possible method of making him talk on any subject."

"I'm sure we should take advice from Mr. Smith," said Noni.

"I did bring up the question of putting the old place up for auction." Nord saw the shocked look in her elder sister's face and hurried on, "I mean if we have to sell it, I'm sure the ancestors would be barracking for us to get the biggest price we can. But apparently the monsters have swallowed so many plump minnows of late that they have mostly got a frightful attack of indigestion and dividend constipation. So there are no bidders, serious ones, except from Joshua's Ales . . ."

". . . Stout and Porter Ltd., that name is engraved somewhere on me I'm sure," finished up Nefer.

"I don't see why the sale is necessary," said Noni, pulling at her prominent underlip inherited from the Heavan side of the family.

"Botting's statement was all right as far as it goes," said Nefer, who suffered under the delusion that a knowledge of maths enabled one to understand balance sheets.

The telephone rang. Noni gave a ritual groan and forced herself out of the chair. She stood beside the small bracket table and answered it; or rather listened.

When she had finished, Noni wore the tight little smile of triumph which heralded a victory but before speaking she regained her chair. "It was Mark," she said, "a hell of a morning with him, poor sweet, having to gather up the reins. But it's settled; they've turned down the offer from Joshua's."

"A flat refusal?" There was a disconcerting flash of hardness in Nefer's Dresden shepherdess face.

"We, they couldn't *say* that. They've just put it off, swept it under the carpet." Noni involuntarily rubbed her hand along the dust coated on the underneath of her chair. It was that kind of house.

"Oh, well," Nefer shrugged.

"The funniest thing happened," said Noni quickly, "although Mark did sound as though his hair was half off. They were having a chat after the meeting finished and Stiggins had gone . . ."

"What about?" Nefer's voice was sharpish.

"Oh, Lord, telling dirty stories or whatever they do. But the door opened and a face came in, a huge red face with a heavy moustache smelling of drink." Noni paused dramatically.

"Well it had come to the right place," said Nefer, her good humour apparently regained.

"My dears, he was a policeman, a big fat old one, one of two sent down from Scotland Yard," said Noni. "They could only see his face but Mark had the distinct impression that he was buttoning his fly. He just said, 'Sorry all, I was looking for the gents'."

"Scotland Yard, eh? I don't think this publicity will do the business any good."

"Oh, my dear Nord, in this day and age!" chided Nefer. "Figures ain't got bourgeois morality any more, thank Marx, and people will think no worse of us for the odd murder."

"I'm sure it was suicide," said Noni. "He sometimes had a most peculiar look, a wildness about the eyes."

Her sisters looked at her without a word. Peculiar looks, wild-nesses about the eyes, were not a subject encouraged among the Heavan girls. Nine now dead but one living had been the family's contribution to private asylums over the past fifty years. All Heavans were peculiar, some were barmy, and a small but significant percentage were downright crazy. It had started with Nicodemus Heavan in 1824 who placed boy apprentices upended in opened barrels of claret under the impression that it improved the bouquet. A vague man, he never got round to taking them out; in those commodious days it was hushed up and he was beaten, burned on his shaven pate and douched with cold enemas until he succumbed in a famous private madhouse in Norwich. But the rot had started. Even Noni seemed to realise that she had committed a vulgarity.

"I don't suppose he could have beaten the back of his own head in," said Nord.

"These cunning men can think of everything," said Noni, whose opinion of the sex became more profound and dogmatic each year.

Nord, whose role at these occasions was to set the pace for going, got up and retrieved her handbag.

"I suppose you can't stay for lunch?" Noni did like people to watch her eating nowadays.

They cooed conventional excuses. Nord hesitated and decided not to ask after Noni's children; a fierce possessiveness made their mother suspicious of even casual enquiry. Nord sometimes wondered if the youngest boy, unusually backward, could have inherited . . . but she always loyally pushed the thought away, thinking that if even she considered the possibility what must other people think. Besides the really mad strain was four generations back.

Nefer drove with a ruthless, calculated competence and she usually collected Nord, who disliked driving, as she had this day. She got into the heavy leather-lined interior of Nefer's Alfa Romeo.

"Not one of the most productive days," said Nefer, winding the chain of her key-ring round her forefinger. "Mark taking the reins indeed. I really think that Eldred and Bill should have a good talk one of these days. If we want a captain for the old ship, it's surely Eldred the unflappable, not Mark who flaps in the smallest force of wind . . ."

It was a pity, Nord had always thought, that one so devilishly clever in some ways, as was Nefer, could be so stupidly transpontine, the villainy crystal clear beneath one-way glass turned the wrong way. Bill and Eldred should put Eldred in as Managing Director, whereupon Bill would join hands with the revengeful Mark. Eventual winner, after the tosses and turns of the Boardroom wrestling match, would be Bill Stigg. As she hesitated in choosing placatory words something caught the corner of her eye. The driveway of the inevitably named Home Farm, badge of the Victorian respectability of the Heavans left to Noni by the grandfather, where no cow had grazed or chicken strutted these hundred years, was lined by depressed cypress in a thick visitor-forbidding fence of greenery.

"Careful, dear," she said. Fortunately Nefer was the kind of person whom you could say things like that to without disturbing their facial control. "Careful, but near the gateway there's somebody very like Nigel."

Nefer bent and turned on the ignition, then put down her window. She drove towards the entrance with her customary skill. "Just glimpsed him," she said, "and you could be right. My God . . . it's him." She thought she had glimpsed the long narrow face, eyes unequally spaced in relation to the nose, which gave it its strange quality, peering through the cypress belt. It was nearly eight years since she had seen him, before he accused Noni of being the Witch of Endor! Noni had carried it off magnificently, encouraging him to play the tenor saxophone he was carrying until, smartly arranged by Mark who had been peering through the drawing-room window, a couple of policemen had arrived with the village strait-jacket.

She accelerated out of the driveway. "I suppose we should warn her."

"Since the other time she always keeps a chain on both outside doors," said Nord. "Besides nobody ever said he was violent to relatives. I'll phone her."

"Escaped, of course," said Nefer. "It's disgusting that they aren't handcuffed or something."

"It's eight years," said Nord, "he could be discharged cured."

Her sister was too experienced a driver to exhibit any emotion, but Nord, looking at her profile, saw the protusion and sudden twist of the underlip which meant that she was very perturbed indeed. Nord who thought she did not care for money, just four or five thousand a year and a bit of capital there when wanted, nevertheless sympathised with Nefer who most emphatically did care for money. A pity that Nefer had not been a man; she would have taken over the whole business long since. Nord knew little about genetics, but thought it was after all an embryonic fluke. However, Nefer's curves were very prounounced and at best an effeminate man, she supposed, would be presiding over the Boardroom.

"After all," said Nefer, "I thought Nigel wasn't a bad kind of stick, in fact he rather liked me."

("If accusing you of being the Great Whore of Babylon and blasting away on a trumpet is liking," thought Nord to herself.)

"You'll phone Noni?" reminded Nefer as she dropped her at her neat cottage three miles further on.

"Oh, yes."

"It would be wonderful if it was found that Nigel . . . I mean it depends how long he was out . . . I dare say the Commissioners would see it our way . . . I must find out what those damned policemen are doing."

4

LOCAL POLICE FORCES rather like to call Scotland Yard for one reason—it often, though not always, relieves their abiding manpower problems. On the other hand the expense of doing so is frowned upon by the regional auditor and a chief constable who is perpetually getting on the blower to London can look forward to an appointment in one of the less salubrious former colonies. All in all, Mr. Gouge, the Chief Constable, himself a career man who had never seen the Guards closer than at their ceremonial changing, had decided to treat Inspector Harry James to lunch. Mr. Gouge received five pounds a week fixed personal expenses, not subject to audit, but in his mind he quite properly judged that these outgoings were for the entertainment of visiting dignitaries and municipal and national politicians. So, rightly, the seven shillings and ninepence table d'hôte at the Independent Club (a branch of the Conservative Party) and the six shillings and twopence for the half-bottle of Chilean Cabernet came out of his own pocket. You might say, ruminated Mr. Gouge, that his own seven shillings and ninepence was an expense; left to himself it was his habit to be driven to his home to nosh off Mrs. Gouge's housekeeping.

Spearing the last of the stewed rhubarb and deftly pushing the piecrust to the side of the plate, Inspector James guessed his thoughts. It was a recurring trouble which mildly plagued the Inspector who had vaguely generous instincts and was fairly well treated regarding expenses. Sometimes you could offer them a double brandy, though the gap between their stations was such that a captain might often try to lush a general with more impunity.

"That brandy over there looks interesting, Mr. Gouge." Harry stared at a rather grimy bottle of Australian standing amid some dripped-lipped cruets on a service table.

"They use it for this goddamned flaming stuff," said Gouge, stung. "Gets people in. Set any old crap on fire and add another five bob per portion—the catering's contracted out. What's more they add methylated spirit to it so they don't have a failure. It comes under Adulteration of Foodstuff, Section 14, sub-para. 18, but being a member . . ."

"I dare say they might do something better," soothed the Inspector, beckoning the seventeen-year-old boy who was the last member of the staff in the dining-room. In fact they had. Sometimes such youths made gross undercharges. The Inspector had on one tour of duty had double Carlos Segundos at the price of rotgut. But here it was not to be; the youth had a grimy card remorselessly listing prices on a string pinned to the hip pocket of his trousers. However, the Inspector saw that the Chief Constable cheered up under his thirty-pound executive suit and seemed to swell and fill its ample curves.

"We might go into the smoking-room and have a chat," suggested the Chief at length. The Oxtail Dumpling Supreme was a bit of a hoist for elderly duodenums and it was only a step, if professional emergency arose, from the local station.

The smoking-room did not smell of tobacco but of dampness mixed with a particularly strong disinfectant. Inspector James waited until the Chief Constable had seated himself and produced a fattish loose-leaf notebook from inside the executive jacket. "I suppose you have made no progress, the time being so short."

"I had two hours," said the Inspector, "spent stooging around the buildings mostly; your fellows did the tape-measuring and checking particularly well, I thought. I just wanted to get the atmosphere."

He refused a small black cigar. "Well-kept place, super efficiency seated on an eighteenth-century base, but that's England for you. Some swilling, I think, you can't stop it in places dealing with grog and after all a good employee should like the product. But no pinching to resell, I'd take an oath. Anything that goes out is invoiced and billed. No graft discernible, so that knocks out graft as a motive."

The Inspector had been discreetly briefed regarding the Chief Constable who came out as a poor sleuth, but a first-class organiser and man of tact. "Cristobal Botting was an intimidating man," the Chief said, "who nobody knew much. Luxury service flat, entertained in hotels, talked a bit too well on anything but a good listener. Enemies galore I would think, though I hardly knew him personally."

"Forty-five," said James, "the time when an ambitious man must make his run. Where was he going?"

"Joshua's Breweries," said the Chief. "Heavans were going to be taken over and Botting was to become a member of the main Board. It's an elderly Board, the fires dying down, just right for a fellow like Botting. He came from nowhere, y' know. Accent was not quite right, the 'o's being a bit funny, but you only noticed it because he talked so plummily and upper crust. The last Heavan, a funny remote old man but capable of looking ahead, brought him from some little company four years before his death; made him General Manager . . ."

"But he was Chairman and Managing Director."

"Old Heavan died eight years ago—I should tell you that there has been a streak of barminess in the family since about 1820."

"Heaven might be a Barmecide feast at that," said the Inspector, absently.

"What? Oh, yes, I see! A Catholic myself! As I was saying, he

29

had three grandchildren—his younger son's children, all girls—as his heirs. But the old fellow owned only fifty per cent of the show—he'd made it a private company in '51 and I believe the business was under capitalised."

"Beg pardon," said the Inspector whose thoughts had slightly strayed.

"Oh, you absorb club gossip. God knows where I got that from. But old Heavan was one of the sane members of the tribe; the other branch had, I suppose one would say, split off in the 1820s when there had been two sons to divide the business. One was potty and was put away; but he had three children who went the same way. To cut it short all that side of the family, in their sane moments, willed the family interests to each other, and it narrowed down until there was one Nigel as the end product. He'd be fifty-three now. I suppose it's difficult to imagine him in 1940. God damn it," agitation overcame the Chief Constable and he looked about until he saw a piece of moth-eaten, satin rope dangling in a corner.

"A coffee, I'm sure you'll join me. Sorry about this place." He seized the bellrope, tugged and looked down at the frayed end in his hand. Far away there was a faint, cracked jangling which carried the impression that both coffee and service had been 'off' for some years. The Chief went back to his chair and shrugged apologetically. "These clubs are like old families; they suddenly go, one year flourishing, the next on last legs. But reverting to Nigel, he had a short-service commission. He was strange, y'know, but the young men then were a bit strange and it wasn't noticed. He'd been tutored in the house of a clergyman since he was about nine and I suppose, with the war coming, the Trustees thought the Services a good way out of the responsibility. He was a fair fighter pilot by all accounts; things were so hectic when he started getting odder that it wasn't noticed. Then he got this thing about musical instruments. He was a fair musician, by the way, the clergyman who brought him up being an authority on church stuff. But he got this fixation on wind instruments, personalising himself with them, and thinking they had a very bad deal from the strings. After all how many times is the soloist a blower? Most of them are pluckers or scrapers or bangers if you see it on

30

the TV, as I do, the wife being keen on it. So it had its logic. Anyway the Groupie was a piano buff and Nigel shot up his baby grand."

"Shot up his baby grand!" The closeness of the room was affecting the Inspector.

"The Groupie and his family were on leave; they lived in a country cottage near the aerodrome. Nigel hurtled down and emptied four cannon shells into the lounge where the instrument was kept. Ruined it, of course, along with some valuable antiques. I understand it was a bit of a problem but it being wartime you could get over most things. Neurosis and a special home. He was a good patient and was honourably discharged in December, 1944, with twenty-seven and sixpence per week pension. Old Nonsuch Heavan wouldn't let him into the business. Mind you, Nigel wasn't much interested although he knew the value of cash. The firm became a private company with his approval. He spent his money on experimental jazz, new blowing instruments—he was deathly afraid of electronic sounds—and," the Chief mopped his wide forehead with the napkin he had inadvertently tucked into his waistcoat, "and he became infatuated with Cristobal Botting in the way that a man of twenty-seven can be a disciple of a man of thirty-four. Botting was the kind of man who if he wanted to could register intelligent, guarded interest in a subject, then rush home and memorise the *Ency. Brit.* on the subject. In the case of young, as he was then, Nigel Heavan, he thought it worthwhile to take three weeks' leave, ostensibly sickness, and do a crash course in musical theory, the history of the composers and rudimentary blowing down a recorder. That's why, on old Heavan's death, Nigel swung his vote behind Botting for Chairman and Managing Director, giving him the proxies. Mark Hanna would normally have got it, of course."

"Was he sane?"

"It is complicated, I'm afraid. Botting in his usual way got to know a couple of goodish psychiatrists. When he held his little receptions—few people but all quite distinguished—Nigel was there. I would say that Botting stage-managed him, but when the girls cast about for evidence invalidating the power of attorney they came up against two medical gents in the mental field who could swear that Nigel was as sane as me—saner because he hasn't got my worries."

"And then?" The Inspector was intent.

"He suddenly went downhill — after a year's interval. He attacked one of the lady clerks in the cellars with an oboe, fought clear and was found menacing his eldest courtesy cousin, threatening to do her in with a tenor sax or something of the sort."

"What was he doing in the cellar?"

"Oh, Botting put one of the rooms in the old building at his disposal. He used to keep various instruments there; God knows how much he spent per year on new ones. Anyway he was certified and put into an institution near Bristol, as a paying patient. As I've said, I barely knew him, but there was gossip which reached us. You know . . ."

The Inspector did.

"It was to the effect that Botting had encouraged him in his madness. At the committal proceedings Nigel raved and ranted against Botting, then suddenly shut up."

"And you've told me all this for what purpose?" The Inspector smiled.

"Nigel Heavan was released from the Institution last Friday morning."

"Oh, God."

"Yes, that's what I said. If there's anything to drive you mad it's these cases with a psychiatric defence—up to your arse in paper work. I ordered the routine check on all relatives, ex-employees over the past five years, and the one on Nigel was among the first phone calls. Quite cured, they said, and, to make sure, he briefed his own psychiatrists to double check, including, my dear fellow, the cove who is retained by Scotland Yard."

Inspector James remembered a stout, red-faced, irritable man at conferences.

"But that is to his disadvantage; he could hardly plead insanity."

The Chief shrugged. "One day when you have got nothing to do for a few hours, you define insanity for me. Discharged as cured. There could be no conditions, but they made sure that he had somewhere to go—an old friend in London. A respectable man with whom he could live for a time while he got himself sorted out. Of course, with his income—about fifty thousand before tax—there wasn't much of a problem. We telephoned the friend in London, one George Potter, finally getting him at his work. Nigel hadn't turned up at his flat."

"Charming," said the Inspector. The Chief, quite within the rules, had dumped it in his lap. The main problem was whether to send out an alarm for one Nigel Heavan 'who may be able to assist the police' or not. Such alarms are used sparsely; press and radio will co-operate only if they know that such requests are not made lightly. And a frivolous call of that kind could start a stream of libel suits. On the other side was the risk of allowing a murderer with a history of mental instability to run free. The Chief watched him sardonically while he dissolved two indigestion tablets on his tongue. They did no good but he always hoped against hope.

He made his decision. "I'll put a general call out at divisional level, sir, but no press or radio appeals. But I think I'll need more men."

"You can have three of my smartest plainclothes constables until you cut through the red tape. Nothing else I can do?"

Harry James dropped him at the imposing façade of the combined police station and barracks and drove the eight miles along the highway to Chudleigh (pronounced Chilly), a straggling but not unattractive village, a further three-quarters of a mile off the road. The local pub, the Good Queen Bess, although over two hundred and fifty years old, was one of those occasional untidy, featureless buildings that went up in the provinces in the eighteenth century. He gave it a close stare because all too often he saw his Sergeant, Cedric Honeybody, emerging from the pub nearest to the scene of the crime. But it was well after closing time and he sighed as he parked his car in the small bay inside the iron gates of N. Heavan Ltd.

A seven-foot wall of quarried stone cut the place off from the outside. Built in the early 1800s, he thought, from local stone blasted out of a hillside, with each piece selected by the masons by its shape and part in the pattern. It stood more by the innate artistry of the building than the mixture of earth and slaked lime which plastered the original joints, most of them modernly smeared over with cement. About two and a half acres, he thought. The original Heavan would have made ploughboys into warehousemen; now the staff mostly came by bus from the town. He sniffed the faintly vinous, vinegary exhalations of the place and looked up at the untroubled blue sky overhead. Not a bad place to be on such an afternoon.

There were nine other cars in the bay, a portly looking Bentley, an old but well-cared-for Cadillac and a rather snazzy Alfa Romeo being the most distinguished. He got out his notebook. The Directors had been closeted in one room, except for the Chairman, which ruled out three of the people who had presumably been closest to him. He looked up at the old house, he thought probably the ancestral home of the Founder, a fairish Queen Anne structure rather incongruously situated in the country but not uncommon. The new buildings were one floor only, except for the Main Office which sported two. A closed system. He looked at the little sentry box beside the gate. At signing-on and knocking-off times a man, an ex-police constable, sat there. He looked round and saw Honeybody.

"Bloody good food at that pub, Mr. James," confided the Sergeant, "and a fine trade. People come for miles for the cooking."

"They know anything?"

"God's in his Heavan as far as the Bung is concerned," said Honeybody, "because you see this place owns the pub freehold. Had it for two hundred years. It used to be called the Old Chudleigh Hut, became a coaching inn, but it was tarted up a bit and given the new name by deceased six years ago. The Manager knows his job, by God, but you might as well talk to a wet sponge. Such lovely people to work with, Mr. Botting was sweetness itself, Mr. Hanna is just a great bundle of joy. . . . Cor! The workers don't drink there much: there's a decent kind of beerhouse a quarter of a mile away with a fish-and-chip place next door. I got nothing, except there's an acidy kind of young barmaid there who might like to talk. Trouble is that she doesn't like Elder Citizens; if we could get a really smart, gamy young constable, say . . ."

"Money is less complicated," said the Inspector. "I'll authorise a tenner and keep your hands on your notebook."

34

"Sir!" said the Sergeant half-heartedly.

"This man Botting," said Harry, "seems to have been a prize indeed."

"Feared and detested by those who knew him, I should say. The man I saw this morning, Smart, a dogsbody and nearly the oldest inhabitant, hated him. If his alibi wasn't cast iron, I'd suggest concentrating on him, but he was in his room according to the whitewasher."

"One Jasper Smith," the Inspector dredged into his memory, "aged sixty-six. An old faithful and come to think of it so is Smart. Collusion?"

"From what they tell me Smith isn't the sort you can collude with. But he's working now inside the cellaring if you'd care . . ."

An old entrance to the cellaring was by the side of the house; a modern, very heavy roll door was up. The steps were narrow—people's feet having been smaller three hundred years ago—and gloomy. The Inspector went first. About the tenth step down his feet flew forward. Training made him act instinctively, buttocks thrust well backwards, head down and shoulders hunched, arms folded across his stomach. He slid down half a dozen steps, then braced his heels and stopped. There was a pain in his leg from an old injury, but he picked himself up. Looking upwards he saw a ladder, and upon the stairs behind him a slime of whitewash. He screwed his eyes and peered upwards.

"Upsy daisy, luv," came a rasping voice, "or 'ave you bin suppin' Boardroom port too much?"

"None of that. Police here!" Honeybody with surprising lightness had scurried down and was rocking the ladder with one massive hand.

"No need to say that, chum. A block'eads's a block'ead even if he wears a cheap suit and not uniform. And if you 'ave me down it's you wot's in the dock, cock."

The Sergeant raised his hands and made a catching motion. "You won't fall, mate, but resisting arrest can cause a bit of damage. You're obstructing us in the line of duty."

The man came halfway down the ladder. He was tall and thin, with short-cut wiry black hair untouched by grey. His face was long, with a jutting chin and a sallow smooth complexion.

"You're Jasper Smith?"

"Funny old name, like the villuns in the old books. Jas Smith, the wicked squire, always at the girls and poor old widders. Anyway I 'ad two hours with the local coppers and 'ave nothing more to add except, as always, God Bless the Squire and 'is relations whoever 'e might be. Ta-ta, cocks. Mind the whitewash."

The Inspector's eyes had become accustomed to the gloom, and below he was conscious of vague shapes. He walked carefully down and found himself in a narrow passage. It led into a dimly lighted vault. His audience had melted away before him and under the naked electric light bulbs fourteen women were bottling wine under the domination of a stout, nuggety old party in jeans. Each lady had a chair, a small manually operated machine like a miniature guillotine which drove in corks, taken from a box, crates of empty bottles, and in her hand a long, red India-rubber tube attached to an enormous cask, tilted slightly forward. Work ceased as he entered. "My," said the lady in the jeans, "we have a visitation," she camped her words, "from the Vicar." Her ladies sniggered, goodhumouredly enough, but with the undertone which the Inspector knew could speedily lead to tarring and feathering. Help was however on hand.

"We're not 'ere to improve your morals, ladies," said Honey-body comfortably entering from the wings, "but to take advantage of you, so to speak."

There was a gale of laughter. " 'Im, take advantage, 'im . . ." the Inspector was not inwardly pleased at the great amusement of a very stout and very old lady who wore a feathery hat and what looked like the original bloomers.

"Now, ladies, we're down from the Big Smoke on exes touching the death of yer beloved Guv, Mr. Bott. All 'andkerchiefs immediately to be dried on the radiator! Can we do you now, luvs, just to check previous statements?"

"We were down 'ere bottling," said the forelady. "Harry and Edwin was doing the lifting" (the Inspector saw two youths), "and Percivaaal"—she drawled the name and indicated a very tall old man at a trestle table—"was labelling. We were doing number twenty, which we're too ignorant to know about but which tasted like a goodish Julienas Beaujolais, 1964."

"Sixty-five, dear," said a stately old lady by her side.

"Any'ow Beaujolais is low; wot tastes they got these days!" said a wizened, nuggety woman with a contradictory air.

"Napoleon doted on it," said the Inspector nervously.

"Thinks 'e's Nappy," said the head lady bottler, grimly. "And 'im 'ardly out of 'em."

Honeybody intervened. "Just quietly bottling all morning with no breaks, eh?"

"We did seven 'ogs before we 'eard the news," said the forelady. "We work to two hundred and eighty-eight bottles per 'og which is as 'igh as you'll ever get. Times was when they gave you as much as ten litres for spoils, but not now, oh, dear me, no. And my name's Mrs. Frankly in case you want to write me down."

Honeybody's small eyes, so alert under their apparent bleariness, were looking at the rubber tubes. "Amazing, ladies, how you turn a tube off and on!"

"A twist of the 'ose," said Mrs. Frankly, "and it's off." With one hand she took a bottle by its neck, inserted the hose in it and within two seconds had it filled to within an inch of the top. She retwisted the hose and set the bottle down. "The 'ose is grooved at the end, sir, so that the air inside the bottle is expelled."

"And all done by gravity, eh?"

"When starting or air-locked, sir, we 'ave to suck at the 'ose strictly in the line of dooty, hating the taste of the stuff as we do." She leered at the Sergeant.

"And so little spilt," the Sergeant stared down at the concrete floor. Each lady had a small tin can at her feet.

"A cup or so a day is all. I don't know wot 'appens to it. The mice prolly, but wot they go for is the sherry wine, sometimes you see them scurrying round yer feet when we're doing Spanish. It's an un'ealthy life, sir, and knots the veins up remarkable, but we 'ave famblies to support and no union to fall back on."

"I suppose," hinted Honeybody with ghastly archness, "that having got a little fluid down from the suckin'—you bein' too refined to spit it out and get consumption—you feel a Call of Nature."

"In there," said Mrs. Frankly, "where I can see the door, it

37

being partly my duty and what I'm paid for so to speak. I can take my alfred davie before a bishop that apart from a working pee none of my ladies nor me got out of here. There's only one door to the carsey and no window owing to it being a cellar. Percival and the lads I will not answer for, though none 'as the guts to say boo, 'ave they, girls?"

A cackle of contempt made the youths somehow fade into the background. Percival stood looking into space, his nose the reddest and most pointed the Inspector remembered having seen, unmoved by circumstances.

"Well, ladies," he said, "you're all "—he was going to be jocose but thought better of it—"entirely innocent of what happened. On behalf of the Yard I thank you with all my heart. Now, could you have a bit of a smoke while I ask Mr. Percival to come with me? I'll take responsibility. Thank you, thank you all, thank you." He swiftly escorted Percival, who came quietly, to the swing doors at the end.

" 'Ang 'im," said one of the ladies, merrily.

"Up by the balls," said another as the swing doors closed behind Honeybody. They were in the gloom of the main cellaring, barrels blackly racked, bins containing bottles; the Inspector noticed that there were prefabricated bays of wire mesh, reaching to the ceiling, each with a padlocked wire-door. Security stuff.

He paused and offered Percival a cigarette.

"Thanks, sir." Percival was dressed in a decentish black suit with a white shirt and green cravat. His accent was superior. He rubbed his chin and poked his red snout at the policemen. "Unnerving, the ladies, heh? Real old battle-axes and anybody who says they've got hearts of gold wants his head read. This is my purgatory, gents, and it's a fact. I had a good education and a randy disposition. Now I'm eighty. Oh, you might not think it, but grog pickles you and if the Devil don't claim you by fifty, the germs gradually give up and the organs harden like old gaspipes. At least four of those ladies, sir, I robbed of their maidenheads in the twenties. They used to hire out punts on the river in those days and it was easy, they being frightened to struggle and rock the craft so to speak. Life catches up with you, sir, and here I am, a mockery so to speak."

"How did you get your job?"

"Well, sir, I was of a roving disposition, served in two wars and —as you may have it on record—a bit of naughtiness in my prime, smuggling and the like—and then, sir, the tax cut off the grog like a gas meter without a coin in it. It was Mrs. Frankly—who, sir, in 1921 was the most luscious red-head you ever lamped. But with a kind of golden brown skin, sir; usually they're freckled, which I never cared for, or a smooth matt like blotting paper. Oh, my dear sirs." The red nose shook like an old pointer ruminating upon some bird long since shot and consumed, but with its memory lingering. "It was Mrs. Frankly, sir, who saved my life by getting me in the bottling. A glass of wine per hour, sir, and my share of the spirits in season, a good glass, sir. It's been the making of me."

"How long ago was this?"

"Seven years, sir, Mrs. F. having just taken over the head bottleship with two deaths from hobnailed livers including the labeller, and not being fussy about the actual money so to speak, here I am."

"How many people down here besides you, the two lads and the ladies?"

"Only six; the heavy part of the job is done by machinery. The barrels come down a chute and there is a big lift-platform for bottles."

Harry passed over a pound note. "For a drink after work," he smiled.

"I'm not too proud," Percival swiftly palmed and pocketed it. "Come behind this." *This* was a monstrous cask, the great-grandpa of all. In the gloom the labeller thumped its flank. "Empty, o' course; they used to use it for advertising and it's still sound— there's a trap door at the side. Now you want to know who did the sod, eh?"

"Too much to want for a fiddly," said the Inspector, "and I suppose you don't know."

"I did two years inside—it was in 1928—but that fellow Botting was like some of the heavy chaps in the Scrubs. Oh, how can I put it? They were never satisfied unless they had something on you; then they'd let you know it. Even some of the screws

treated 'em respectful. Botting used to have that look about him.
There wasn't a drawer in the building that didn't have his great
round face peering in it once a week. He used to come down here
every ten days—a landlord's visit he used to giggle in that fluty
voice of his. Then he usually looked at me and said, 'Let's see
your name is, um . . .' I'd tell him and he'd just smile. Sometimes
I would have sworn he knew about me having been in trouble and
my age. When I was inside the worst of these fellows was named
Fat Alf, though it was mostly muscle. One day at exercise, the
word goes round for a punch-up, though it wasn't called that in
those days. Blokes rolling on the ground wrestling with each
other, some squaring off, and others pretending to be making a
break for it. When it gets sorted out, there's Fat Alf lyin' on his
back with a chisel stuck in his chest. He'd trodden too heavily on
somebody's foot. And my guess would be that Botting did that
very thing."

Inspector James passed another note, this time ten shillings.

"Deflation, eh?" said Percival impassively.

"Decimalisation. Any ideas about what foot?"

"He was jobbed on the Monday morning. On Saturday there
was a bit of fat—overtime to you—and we worked until four in
the arvo. I don't go out for lunch. When you're eighty a soft roll
with a bit of tasty cheese in it's all you want and my landlady gives
me that in a packet. I don't see any point in going out to eat it ;
I've seen the scenery for bloody nigh eighty years and don't miss
it. A lot of the old crows think the same way and sit there eating
cold sausages and gabbing away. I come out here. There are
plenty of stools around because sometimes the barrels are broached
on the spot. It was twelve thirty-five and darker than now because
Old Mat—he's the boss cockie of the cellaring—turns most of 'em
out before he leaves. I'm just passing this cask when I hear a
voice. It says, 'The only bloody way is to do the sod in. You're
the wiz for staff work. What do we do?' Look, sir, it was half a
joke. Or rather whatever the subject was was not a joke; but he
was *talking* half jokingly."

"He being?"

"Well, I suppose even old Judas had to be content with thirty
pieces."

"I can't give you money for telling me. It would make your evidence worthless."

"My word." Sergeant Honeybody had bent down. "There's four nicker lying on the floor. You must have dropped it, my friend. Lucky I saw it."

"Thanks be to God for an honest man," said Percival, taking it. "And I could hardly take money, sir, for doing me bounden civic duty so to speak. It was Mr. Mark Hanna, sir, a very distinctive voice he has."

"Take that down verbatim, Sergeant," said the Inspector. "And the other chap?"

"Too quiet spoken, sir, to hear. And I didn't want to know, if you follow me so to speak. Let's face it, this is the last job I'll have and without plenty of grog the old ticker'd pack up in a week. I folded my old tent and arab'd back to the old ladies who were so busy nattering they never noticed me."

"Is there another entrance?"

"Christ, yes! This is the old part that the jerries copped during the most recent 'un; it was extended and if you walk on it gets more modern and concreted. A nice well-lit flight of steps up to ground level."

"Australian, aren't you?" said the Inspector.

"How do you know?"

"It sticks out a mile."

"I used to iron out the slang a bit, but now I suppose I'm getting childish. Adelaide, educated at St. Peter's, then a remittance man in reverse. They paid me the share of the property—the brothers and sisters—to get the hell out of it. I got here about the day the Kaiser declared war. Funny old life."

"You'd better get back. We might want you to make a statement. Perhaps not."

The Inspector and the Sergeant walked off through the gloom.

"A bad old bloke," said Honeybody quietly.

Australian criminals were the bane of their work; better educated and fitter physically than their counterparts and with a distressing propensity for violence and glibness.

"He'll put the black on somebody," said the Sergeant "so we'd better put some kind of tail on 'im."

"At eighty?"

"He'll have to secure his job. Imperative. Ever heard of the chicken-men?"

"Chicken stealers?"

"No. My grand-dad was a Sergeant up north. That would be, for Lord's sake, back in the 1860s. They had these little, tuppenny-ha'penny travelling shows. Illicit stuff, fighting dogs in pits, ratting contests, even cocks in some areas. But one of the debased side-shows was a man who'd lie in a kind of sty eating a chicken whole, feathers, entrails and all. He wrung its neck and ate it."

"Christ," said the Inspector.

"Not pleasant and it was difficult to find the joker who'd do it even then. So the showman would look for an old, hopeless drunk who lived for his bottle but hadn't got the money. He'd be given two bottles of gin a day and a faked chicken, imitation feathers made out of cheese cloth and the entrails were cold, cooked spaghetti. After a couple of weeks of that, the showman'd sigh and say that the bloke would have to go as he had to have a 'live' artist—that was the name they used. He'd choose a time when the poor old soak was sobering up and have a couple of bottles of gin on the table in his caravan. That night," said Honeybody, "the bloke would eat the chicken, feathers, guts and all. It never failed. Psychology! My grand-dad could lose these trick cyclists."

It was a nasty little story, out of a profession full of nasty little tales.

"You mean that old Percival would do anything for grog?"

"Yes." The Sergeant peered into one of the locked bays. "He can't go on much longer here. Somebody will shop him or some clerk'll get suspicious. I'd say he is dropping two or three notes a week back to Mrs. Frankly. So if he can guarantee himself a bottle of spirits a day, why he'll try for it. He's covered himself with us."

The Inspector sighed. He never had enough men at his disposal. "He'll do it by telephone—if he does. I'll put a man on him tonight, unless he uses his landlady's phone, *if* she has one. Too many *ifs*. Did you see the Directors?"

"Barged into the Boardroom by mistake like. I'd already seen

42

the Secretary, a shrewd little London type I'd say. Not much to be had out of him. Mark Hanna is a big bloke with the darkest eyes I've seen. Fifty-three, as the record says, but well preserved. A huntin', fishin' looking fellow. He went red with rage when I poked my face round the door; hot-tempered man I would say. Then there was Eldred Keast, he's forty-eight but looks older. Tall, quietish. I'd say the women might like him. One of those casual well-bred chaps out of the ciggy ads. Then the young one, thirty-five, Bill Stigg, he'd be difficult to place, sandy-haired and elegant, might be anything at first sight."

"I suppose you had your ear to the key-hole."

"Wasn't one; the late Botting or somebody was smart. A sound-proof door. I had a good look; there's a little anteroom which was empty. Huh!"

They passed two men with a fork truck easing out a barrel. They came into the new cellaring, clean cement walls and fluorescent light. Even the barrels looked new. At the end was a small glass cabinet in which a small, crumpled man sat.

"Old Mat, sir," said Honeybody. "I managed to have a glass with him at lunch time in the rubbidy opposite over as nice a bit of pork liver as I've tasted. He hates wine, sir, so don't try the la-di-da with him."

So the Inspector's greeting was, "And I'll be darned glad to get away from the stench of wine, excuse me for saying it." Inwardly he excused himself to the Trinity of Lafite, Margaux and Latour.

"Don't hesitate," said Old Mat, "the quacks talk of smoking, but they want to think of what that gargle does to your insides. People don't know, but they put stuff in it, chemical stuff, poisons the mice if they get at it when it's new. Good ale, now, that's what made England, that and Argentine beef."

God, a sense of humour, perhaps, thought the Inspector dismally. Humour was the copper's bane and solicitors got fat on it. "I wouldn't say that," he said, "but for a plain man like myself a cut of a joint and a goodish pint does fine. Not that it hasn't been interesting to walk through here."

"Other people's business is," said Old Mat, who was not so

old when you really looked closely at him. About fifty and wiry. "I suppose you'd have witnessed a hanging?"

"Yes," said the Inspector unhappily.

"Is it true that the hangman races down the ladder and tries to finish them off as they dangle? Half an hour dangling and kicking, a mate of mine who was a screw said. Unless the neck comes off completely."

"That was denied before a Royal Commission," said the Inspector.

"Same like I'd deny that the wine was bad for you; my livin' ennit? Same like 'anging is yours. A man's got to keep his nose clean and take the money. I must say that I'd like to see a 'anging, just to say I'd seen one. The wife and me saw a bullfight on the tour last summer, all nice and arranged for us. Cruelty, of course, but you got to see it once, we said."

"I saw your depositions," said the Inspector, looking at his watch.

"Eh?"

"The statement you made to the local police. You saw nothing suspicious?"

"This is as good a cellaring as you'll ever have, though I says it. We're old fashioned but, by God, I know what goes on here. You got to give 'em a little leeway, sir, but then know how to crack the whip. There's not a man or woman, sir, in this cellaring who don't jump if I want them to jump."

"A good place to work, eh?"

Old Mat looked at the Inspector sharply. "It's steady work where you don't get put off. In the twenty years I've been here there's been no sacking for redundancy, which is more than you can say of the factories around. A nice, steady tempo here and good-class trade. The mass-production stuff is done over at the new place at Ockingham, twenty miles away."

"Mass production?"

"Christ, yes, tanker stuff. They fill the tankers in France and they're driven to a ship, then ferried over to Dover. The stuff's discharged into stainless steel tanks and then into the bottling machines. Mr. Botting saw you couldn't stand still. Brand names is what the public want and he made six big names, two sherries,

44

white and sweet white, a cocktail and a dry red. Smart man he was. Dunno what will happen now he's a goner but that ain't my business. But he knew how to make money and take it from me he knew my job as well as I do. Sometimes he'd come out with a word or two and, believe you me, I knew he'd got to know something about any mistake that's been made down here. Once a cask of detergent got bottled for a light wine; the travellers had no complaints at all, but the Boss got to know. 'Do you use much detergent, Mr. Um?' was all he said to me, but I knew like."

"You were here in Old Mr. Heavan's day?"

"In his way, sir, he was a very smart man; but it was a differenter old-fashiondist way, if you take me. But he knew enough to know he was old fashioned."

"And Mr. Nigel?"

" 'E was a laugh, you never saw the poor sod without an instrument clutched in his sweaty 'ands. Sometimes in a case, other times nood, and nasty looking things some of 'em are, too. He even got on to the bagpipes one time, though that's just a nasty noise and not a proper instrument."

"He had a bit of trouble in the cellaring?" Sergeant Honeybody's bass voice had a suitable port-wine velvetness. "A bit of a romp with a girl, eh, which went too far as these things can often do. And then the trouble started, eh?"

"One Dorothy Lanyard, over the right eye with an oboe, and fastened his teeth into her right hand. I know, because the first thing I did after getting Mr. Botting on the blower was to take an inventory. The right eye, and her hand, but no molestation like her clothes torn off that you read about. Old Mrs. Frankly came waddling out before I could make a thorough examination, but nothing a casual glance could reveal. Old Frankly insisted on a bottle of brandy and marched over and took one down."

"I suppose the police arrived?"

"Nothing like that, sir. A private job as it were. He was at Mrs. Hanna's threatening her—although between ourselves a man would have an almighty struggle to overcome that lady—when some attendants were got with a strait-jacket. A private hearing with a magistrate and four head doctors and off he went."

"Is Miss Lanyard still employed here?"

"After that? No, sir, she did the sensible thing and demanded compo. Six hundred nicker the firm gave her, and you ought to have 'eard what the lady bottlers said about that. Made me ears redden and me a grandpa four times over."

"She was not a lady bottler?"

"She had a little office next to me," said Old Mat, sourly. "A new system Mr. Botting put in. They just ran up these inter-changeable metal walls the Boss was so keen on, and put her there. It took a bit of work off me, so san fairy ann. Not that I care for girls around here."

"Young, eh?"

"Twenty-five maybe, dyed blonde like they all are."

"Pretty?"

"Inside these walls I don't even notice," said Old Mat.

"And when she left there was no replacement?"

"The idea was all right," the man said as his telephone rang. He answered it briefly. "See what I mean? Constant little queries from the office, this, that and the other. The Boss thought a full-time girl here could actually save time; but it didn't work well because she wasn't any good. Oh, she sat there all day, but had not the slightest bloody interest or brains."

"Didn't you report her?"

"She wasn't on my staff list, Inspector, and it doesn't do to make trouble. For all I know she might have bin somebody's bit of nookey what had to be found a job." Old Mat shut his mouth firmly and reached for a pile of papers as they departed.

"I've got permission to use the office it happened in," said the Inspector. "Nigel Heavan is out, discharged cured."

The Sergeant whistled. "I heard of it from the men, Mr. James. Something funny, they thought, those that were there in those days. A funny lot, these Heavans."

They walked through the old house's handsome façade and up the stairs.

"No sign of life," said the Inspector.

"This place is all eyes," said the Sergeant. "Deceptive, like. There's always somebody around in the distance, carrying something or wheeling a truck. Deceptive." He pushed open the door.

"The lock was broken years ago, but there's one of those automatic closing doovers."

It was small, but comfortable. Three of the walls were the original brick, covered in yellow paper; the fourth was a metal partition which wisely did not pretend to be otherwise. It was just large enough for a small desk and custom-made chair. Six smaller chairs flanked the walls. The wall safe, still open, was inset in one of the original brick walls and a small table with a tiny refrigerator upon it completed the room, except that slightly to the left of the desk the wall showed an oblong hole, three feet by two.

"The service lift," said the Sergeant, "where he got it. Suppose we make ourselves comfy. I dare say the little old fridge has ice, and," he peered in, "some bottles of Coke, too. And, at lunch, I laid in a half of fine old black rum." Honeybody's hip pocket divulged its alcoholic content.

From his breast pocket the Inspector took a tiny tape-recorder. He spoke quietly into the microphone, pausing occasionally to let the Sergeant take over.

5

ELDRED KEAST MOVED the tape-recorder to the middle of the coffee table. It was his wife's, recordings of baroque music being one of her hobbies. It was the best procurable, a twin to that used by Cristobal Botting; this fact, plus that Nord Keast had taken their three children to a birthday party, had decided the three remaining Directors to meet in the Keasts' small house.

His long, thin hands inserted the tape and he stayed his forefinger on the control.

"We'll play it right through before erasing if it suits you."

Mark Hanna and Bill Stigg nodded, a trifle reluctantly.

"Now," came the fluty tones of the late Mr. Botting, "don't argue with me, and Mark get that blustering scowl off your face. The time has gone when I put up with your scowls, Eldred's well-bred superiority, or The Boy's sullenness. You will each resign from this Board. When we go into the Boardroom there are six routine matters to be attended to, and then each of you in turn shall announce your resignation, so that Stiggins can record it."

"You're mad," growled Stigg.

"Hear him out," said Keast quietly.

"Seven years ago we acquired a line of Continental spirits and liquors which, partly from your assiduous pushing of it, has done well. The company is a Lichtenstein concern made of straw; the office is in Switzerland. It is merely a go-between with a French-Spanish factory on the one hand and us on the other. You three own the company probably jointly. It means that nine thousand pounds per year profit has been transferred from Heavans to your pockets, less we will say the three thousand the company would possibly cost you."

"This is libel!" Mark Hanna's voice sounded guttural.

"I knew this almost as soon as you started doing it." Botting's voice became shriller. "Or rather I suspected it but had no proof. However, three months ago I spent a month on the Continent and found it out in detail. You have a servant named Leiva for the Spanish-French side. I gave him two thousand pounds from my own pocket. You pay him six hundred pounds a year, but he jumped at the sum I offered."

"The crooked little swine," said Bill Stigg.

"Half crook," corrected Botting gently, "a little person content to be little."

Keast remembered that the great, round face had seemed to swell as he said it.

"Now," said Botting, "you are guilty of receiving secret commissions plus four other company law offences for a start. But your Swiss earnings have not been taxed, my dear sirs, and what the Revenue would do to you I do not care to think. It is the good name of the Heavan family which affects me most. Your actions have bid well to bring disgrace upon it."

Keast listened with detached amusement. How nicely had Cristobal hammed his lines, what leers, unrecorded on the tape, had flickered across the fat chops of the man. He heard his own voice:

"I imagine terms are possible, Cristobal. I expect your own little nest might not stand a searchlight. Suppose we forget the resignation bit?"

"I will face any searchlight, gentlemen. I have switched on the tape-recorder to put my position quite plainly. By not prosecuting I put myself in jeopardy, for the sake of my late master and the family I have served."

It was like a bad play, thought Keast, and there was probably some aesthetic lesson to be learned for if you saw the faces, as he recalled them, it was not melodramatic. Botting was quite neatly putting them over a barrel. There was a long silence, so long he had to peer forward to see the machine was functioning. He recalled that Botting had remained quite motionless, his eyes fixed on the one picture—a faded Venetian oil—which the room possessed.

"This, of course," said Mark Hanna, "is a preliminary to your acceptance of the brewery bid, a stepping stone for your own ambitions."

"Mark," said Botting, "you have little business ability apart from your gift as a salesman—worth perhaps thirty pounds a week and well scrutinised expenses. The firm will not suffer from your absence. As far as your wives' money is concerned, they will be no worse off under the new regime if they take shares and over a ten-year period their position will improve. You can hardly imagine that I shall not devote my energies to expansion and greater profit."

"To feather your own nest," Bill Stigg had said, his voice trembling.

"My dear boy, you in common with your two friends were fortunate enough to marry money. Be content with your lot. I do not suppose Nefer is ungenerous—though I must say under the new dispensation you will have to curb that roving eye, you know. But fortunes need managers such as I to look after them. Be grateful for that."

"There must be some compromise, Cristobal," said Keast.

"I am now going to the Boardroom. In five minutes I expect you there and the meeting will commence."

There was a small bleep indicating that the machine had been switched off.

"Shall I erase it?" asked Keast.

He made the necessary adjustments and spun the tape through the machine.

"Better burn the bloody thing," said Hanna, "the very shape of it makes me sweat blood."

"I doubt whether you can," said Bill Stigg.

Hanna got up, his massive head thrust forward between broad, heavy shoulders. "We'll bloody well mangle it so that it can't emit a solitary squeak. Have you any spirit, Eldred? I couldn't bear to waste good gin on the bastard's voice."

Typical of Mark, all flap when the pace was on, all ebullience when it slacked off, thought Keast as he went out of the room and into the tiny closet where his wife kept her painting things. He brought back a stout, commercial quart bottle and handed it to Hanna.

"But don't do it on the carpet, old chap."

Hanna took the spool of tape in his large hand. The Keast house was built round a small interior patio into which the late afternoon sun now poured, the dull, rough-surfaced Ronda tiles soaking up the heat, the tubs of geraniums, a speciality of Nord's, accepting it as their right. "Out here," said Hanna, opening the glass door. He put the spool on the flagstones, poured spirit generously and flicked his lighter. There was a gush of flame and Hanna wheezed as the fiery fumes caught at his lungs.

"Let me do it," said Keast irritably as the flames died down. He tore off a piece of twine from a climbing geranium and saturated it as a fuse. This time the fire burned more steadily.

Hanna bent down, extended and hurriedly drew back his hand. "A cursed quality of persistence, though I suppose . . . I suppose fire extinguishes fingerprints?" He smashed down a broad leather shoe.

"What the devil are you doing, Mark?"

Like guilty schoolboys was the cliché, but it did not prevent Eldred Keast, like the others, from joining in the nervous start and jumping round. Her twelve stone filling her tailored suit majestically, large but slightly fallen bust resting placidly on her corsets' edge, Noni Hanna gazed at them from the glass doorway, her protuberant underlip wrinkled as she spoke.

"Hush," said Keast, "we schoolboys have to verify what the textbooks tell us about sterilisation."

"No trouble?" said Noni. "I thought Botting had overcome it?" She was lifted from the scent. Since Botting had gone into English-made wine the various diseases affecting the grape must had become a family subject of conversation.

"Come inside," said Keast, wishing that Hanna would not stand like a man without any trousers. "Shinned through the window, one supposes, Non'?"

"Nord left a key at our place last week. I found it after lunch, and called by to drop it back. I remembered she'd be out, so I thought I'd drop it on the table."

"And have a damn good snoop," thought Keast, "instead of plonking it through the letter box."

He got them into chairs and looked at the clock. It was six. "Well, in your honour, Noni, we might force a sherry down our throats."

"Must you men always be drinking?" Noni herself enjoyed her glass, as did all the Heavan family, but it was part of her technique to cast an inhibitory shadow.

"This is good sherry I tried to persuade Botting into taking up." He filled the glasses.

"It is good," said Noni, her broad nostrils flaring appreciatively, "but Botting was perhaps right, the public want well-bottled, well-advertised trash. I hope you boys will not forget that fact. I don't want to see you in cow's-hide coveralls making like ye old-fashioned family vintners."

"The late lamented's policies will be pursued," said her husband.

"He was a bastard," said Noni, "but a very useful kind of beast. Shall you replace him? I take it that the brewery offer is to be rejected for good."

Mark Hanna jerked his chest a little higher as was his wont in playing the role of business baron. "You may take it as just that."

"Suppose they up their bid by, say, forty per cent. What then?" Mark's large head lowered in bafflement.

"Do you really think they might, Non'?" asked Keast who respected the large woman's brains. It was such a pity, in some ways, that none of the sisters took part in the business.

"They are frightened of the monopolies commission making them give up their 'tied' liquor stores," said Noni. "We own about eighty stores, quite legitimately, and nobody could make us give them up. They want the stores plus our know-how, and, God Almighty, with the kind of reserves they have what is another three hundred thousand pounds or so?"

"We've got damned little to offer apart from the freehold properties and know-how, Non'," said Keast. "Plus the brand names that Botting introduced and which have to be watered with prodigious advertising expenditure. Goodwill in the wine trade ... ." He shrugged.

"What we want is a keen young chartered accountant for the managing directorship," said Noni decisively. "You fellows stick to the wine business and selling the stuff."

"Really, Noni?" Mark's voice was a hurt one.

"You can't do everything. You three did the work while Botting sat back and schemed. That's the way our profits increased by some sixty per cent. How much would a good one cost?"

"Well," said Keast, "Botting grossed eleven thousand pounds a year, but there was the share arrangement, you know. Over seven years he made thirty-five thousand in capital appreciation; and of course there were the holidays on business in Bermuda. I would say you start looking at eight thousand a year plus stock participation, such as it is nowadays."

"We want the best."

"You won't get it, Noni. We'll have to vet the promising colts and take our chance."

"I want it done, now," said Noni, "none of your Fabian ways, dear Eldred, and no Williamish tantrums."

"Come off it, Noni," said Bill Stigg.

"It is the famous Stigg temper that worries me," said Noni with massive calm. "When I was first told I'd have taken seven to four you had killed him."

"Really, Noni," said Hanna, "you are in bad taste, to take it at its best."

"You spent the morning in Mark's office, so I believe," said Noni. "Three hours without even visiting the toilet."

"We have cultivated Boardroom bladders," said Keast.

"Old Mat—I once gave his daughter a reference since when he's been as friendly as that kind of a man can be—told me half an hour ago that the Scotland Yard fellows are interested in Nigel. Translated into English, he says the Inspector is a smallish, ineffectual man who tried to be nice, but that there's a horrible great Sergeant who stinks like a brewery and asks nasty questions."

"Were you around the cellaring?" Mark Hanna was annoyed.

"My dear, my habit of prowling around the works—and as its third largest shareholder what better right than mine?—annoys you, but nobody has anything to hide, I presume?"

"You were in the grounds when Cristobal went?" said Bill Stigg, his light tenor voice scolding in tone as it often was.

"Pursue that thought, dear William."

"I mean you're a robust woman . . . putting the shot, wasn't it, that you did in the English team?"

"Of course, you were at a minor public school when that happened, my dear. Yes, I have muscles, but I had no reason to kill Botting, whereas," Noni's small eyes flicked them in turn, "perhaps you might have . . . oh, I don't care as long as it doesn't get in the papers. However, when Nefer phoned me and said she had seen Nigel lurking in my shrubbery . . ."

"Nigel!" It was a chorus.

"Yes, Nigel. So there we are. The police will arrest Nigel and have him put in Broadmoor."

"Charming." The voice from the opening door was a deep bass. Its owner was an unattractive, heavily built man in his fifties, the close-set, light coloured eyes peering in permanent suspicion round a remarkably long nose. "Charming," repeated Nigel Heavan.

Mark Hanna's head went down like a bison prepared to do battle for the herd and Nigel smiled, giving his face a momentary twisted sort of warmth. "Oh, they released me cured, old fellow, no homicidal tendencies guaranteed, not even a yen for musical instruments. All sorts of horrid things done to me, but nevertheless if I take my little pills twice a day I'm guaranteed, as I said, in my right mind. Mind if I sit, and a soft drink if you have one, ginger ale would be just the job. Alcohol, for the time being, is denied me. And how have you all been?"

Keast leisurely opened the small refrigerator and served the drink. He also filled the sherry glasses.

"We are glad to see you, Nigel, though you must remember that on the last occasion you were with us you were threatening Noni with some kind of wind instrument."

"Indeed," said Nigel, "and I think I fancied she was the Witch of Endor, though I do not entirely take that back. A nasty old thing under that bumbling exterior, I believe. Oh, I needed treatment all right. And for that I am genuinely grateful to Botting. Of course he framed me." He looked around at them and laughed. "Oh, I'm not obsessive about it, although it does seem rather logical that Botting, having got my power of attorney, should have me locked up in circumstances precluding me from rescinding it."

"I did rather wonder about that aspect," said Eldred Keast, "although frankly, Nigel, you cannot blame anybody for thinking you were nuts."

"I was in a condition of nervous breakdown when I saw Noni. However that's all over. But as a motive for murder, I'm afraid you can rule out insanity; and for the rest it leaves only revenge, not too convincing."

"I must say you are a perfect bloody nuisance," said Noni, bluntly.

"Now, what have you decided about the brewery offer?" asked Nigel.

"How do you know about that?" said Bill Stigg triumphantly.

"My good fool, shut up. What have you decided?"

"Negative," said Keast.

"I feel, Nigel," said Noni, "very strongly against ever selling. At least we've got something that's kept us going two hundred years, whereas . . ." she shrugged. "And I believe that the brewery will increase their bid. I told the others my reasons."

"I heard," said Nigel, "having been behind that door for a long time."

"How did you get in?" asked Keast.

"I had some idea of seeing Nord. I always considered her the nicest of you, if you'll excuse me. The key was in the door."

Noni, thought Keast, overcome with the thought of snooping at will for half an hour, had forgotten to take the key out.

"Well," said Hanna, "are you for selling?"

"Most definitely not, but . . . oh, yes, there is a big *but*. I suppose it occurred to you that Botting probably fiddled the figures to improve his own reputation? What did you make last year before tax?"

"Around two hundred thousand," grunted Hanna.

"I would say that probably forty thousand represented manipulation," said Nigel. "Oh, and I suppose you know he doctored wine at the new factory? He had a sublime faith in the ignorance of the public. And as you know when the old man found him he was a young chartered accountant with a small, specialised chemical company. Flavourings were his speciality. Cheap Spanish red worth eight shillings retail, my dears, with Botting 'mellowing' it with his essence, and you get our famous line of burgundy retailing at twenty-four shillings. As you know we had—I imagine have—a lot of sales with the hotel trade."

"It can't be," said Stigg, weakly.

"You don't drink it, preferring the more chi-chi stuff, but I doubt whether you could tell. I suppose it still sells well."

"Around two hundred thousand bottles each year," said Keast. "And about the best value on any wine card, or so I thought."

"He had other tricks, I fancy. At the time I went inside he had perfected a way to turn cheapest year-old white into still hock."

"Christ, no!" shouted Mark Hanna, stung.

"Why did you hug this secret?" asked Noni quietly.

"I was not myself," said Nigel. "No excuse! But it was like living a kind of dream—sleeping, waking and drunkenness seemed all run together. Botting knew that, damn him. Anyway we do not sell; and Noni is right about your wanting a first-class man. We'll have to clean up the dirty bits of business before he settles in. You'd better look into the fakery, Keast."

"I certainly will!"

"What's a spare key doing in the front door?" Nord opened

the door, tall and elegant in spite of the three children pushing her.

"Can you children occupy yourselves elsewhere, say with the TV?" Eldred Keast had risen and swiftly walked over. "Okay, and come in for a minute, Nord."

"Keeping the mad cousin from the small fry," said Nigel, amiably enough. "Glad to see you, my dear. Discharged cured, by the way."

"I saw you this morning."

"Lurking and trying to screw my courage up to see your so formidable elder sister. I thought you saw me."

"I'm so glad to see you back, Nigel." Nord had inherited the wide-spaced pansy-blue eyes of her mother. "No, it's only that the children are strung like wires owing to Botting's murder—kids are pretty ghoulish, you know — and another untoward happening will mean nightmarish howlings in the early hours."

"Mind if I open the door? Where I've been fresh air, including the draughts, were a valued part of the regiment."

"Why don't we sit outside? It's so seldom that we can. Bring the chairs, Eldred."

"Been lighting fireworks?" Nigel peered down.

"It's one of my tapes," said Nord, bending. "Surely the kids . . . It's still warm."

"An experiment," said Keast, "and it wasn't one of your tapes."

Nigel had picked it up and was juggling it on one large palm. It looked surprisingly undamaged. "Destroying the evidence, my dears? Don't tell me that Bill's talents in the way of bawdy songs were taken down."

They all laughed. Keast saw that Noni's small eyes noted the fact that Nigel slipped it in his pocket.

"If you didn't kill Botting, Nigel," she said, "it makes it very inconvenient."

"Sorry, my dear, but I can't turn homicidal to please you."

"Where were you on Monday morning anyway?"

"Not far away," said Nigel. "As a matter of fact I was walking around the fields where I had walked as a boy . . . seemingly the same cows, buttercups and daisies. I suppose I should tell you

56

that it was intended that I should stay with a friend in London. In fact I caught the train halfway there, but suddenly I had a yearning to see old, familiar places, so . . ." he shrugged. "At Cotting Village there's a pub called the Brown Goat."

"Joe Pedlar's pub?" said Keast.

"You know him? Well fifteen years ago I performed a generous gesture. Joe had been in the R.A.F. with me, though we hardly knew each other. But he was down on his luck and, well, the Brown Goat was going, and I lent him the ingoing money interest free. He returned it and has done fairly well. So I bowled up to Joe's and am staying there. No secret. It was he who told me about the brewery offer."

"I suppose you should see the police."

"I've thought of that, but wanted to have a sniff around first. You see, my dears, I would not like to be railroaded back to that place."

"In this day and age people aren't railroaded," said Bill Stigg.

"I am afraid they are. Cristobal had a criminal mind, you know, and criminology was his hobby—didn't know that, did you? He was fond of one case where the police, so he said, took the convenient way of railroading a known maniac for a crime. Saved a lot of trouble. So . . . I do not intend to be shunted conveniently away, and I'm warning you."

It was very hot and very still in the patio.

"We'd better go in," said Nord. "Eldred, you attend to some bits and pieces. I have to attend to the children."

Keast poured more sherry and opened a tin of cheese biscuits.

"Well," said Mark Hanna heavily, "at least there shouldn't be anybody else popping from behind that door."

6

INSPECTOR HARRY JAMES had taken a page from his scribbler and written on it. "Somebody is listening from behind the door. You do it!"

Sergeant Honeybody had developed the useful technique of moving in complete silence. Stretching out a long arm, he seized the doorknob and jerked swiftly inward. The woman behind it nearly fell in. Thirtyish, noted the Inspector, with prettiness that fell not much short of beauty. A doll's face with superb complexion.

"You'd be Mrs. Stigg," he said dispassionately.

"May I enter?" she said with superb effrontery.

"I rather think you should explain yourself," said the Inspector and Sergeant Honeybody walked back and carried over a chair. Nefer Stigg seated herself with due regard to her quite spectacular legs.

"Why were you glued to the keyhole?"

"I'd come over dizzy, sir, and was leaning against it for support," said Nefer with charming impertinence, but she saw the Inspector's light-coloured eyes harden.

"Madam, I am investigating a case of murder and you might can the witty dialogue."

"I'm sorry," said Nefer, "but it was ignominous being caught like that. I was listening. You see I'd never actually heard what Scotland Yard were like when they were carrying on."

"I hope you never find yourself in that position, Mrs. Stigg. You are Nefertiti Heavan, the youngest of three sisters who are the last representatives of one side of the family."

"Yes, the sane side. There is a barmy branch which branched off years ago."

"Nigel is really no relation?"

"Only from a genealogical viewpoint."

"Has he come to see you?"

"My God! Nord, my sister, thought she saw him this morning outside Noni's house. She's Mrs. Hanna. She thought it nonsense when we phoned."

"He was discharged quite regularly last week."

Nefer's relief came out as a sigh. "Then he did it."

"Quite a group of alienists registered him as sane, Mrs. Stigg. What reason had he to murder Botting?"

"Oh, he's mad. He's got a thing about wind instruments."

"I know," said the Inspector, "all about that. Assuming he is

58

sane, he had no motive that I know of. We look for some advantage: Botting's death was no advantage to him. And how did you get in here?" he said sharply. "Everybody knocked off three-quarters of an hour ago."

"Oh, I know the watchman. You see, nothing, except private bins, is locked here. It looks deceptively easy, but in fact during the day somebody would see you carrying things out. And at night there is only one exit, with a watchman seated by an alarm loud enough to wake the dead."

"During the day ingress is easy?"

"Well . . . everybody knows everybody else. Except, of course, a new client might bowl up. Provided you looked like a city gent, that's what you would be taken for."

"I noted that the door to this old house is kept unlocked." The Inspector glanced at the rolled-up plan he had taken from his briefcase. "At any rate the lock of the front door, a part of the original I would guess, seems unworkable."

"Apart from old Smart and his records, Inspector, this building is a luxury. The old kitchen was transformed into a well-faked eighteenth century farmhouse kitchen with modern toilets for trade wine tastings; there are three reception-cum-interview rooms. Then there's this with six offices, four of them used by the Directors as kind of hidey-holes where they can work undisturbed, the other two used for old records. Three rooms on the fourth floor stacked with old promotions material which sometimes comes in useful. Then the top, the old attic floor, with Smart's room and another big one used by the travellers. There's nothing to pinch, virtually. The food and cutlery plus glasses for the fork supper capers are hired by us from the pub opposite which we own. Even the cellaring isn't used at this end except for a few giant barrels and bottling."

"Ah," said the Inspector, "I thought you must be able to get into the cellaring from here."

Nefer shrugged. "Nobody does regularly, the stairs being a bit dicey. In fact, this building should come down, but Botting," she produced a cigarette case and weighed it on her hand, "Botting would have it kept, though he had it gutted and movable partition walls put in. It meant something to him, tradition and what-have-you. I think he was of humble origins, as they used to say. He was a bit impressed by those who were not, under that very hard, shiny exterior."

"We have to reconstruct people," said the Inspector. "Bits here and bits there go to create a talking picture, so to say."

"Unpleasant," said Nefer quietly.

"You get used to it. But everything I hear about Botting makes him into a kind of colourless swine. He must have had human failings. Did he drink, did he bed? Was it boys?"

"A man completely in control of his emotions, Inspector. Ambitious, ruthless. He drank, most people in the trade like their glass, as the saying goes. But nobody ever *saw* Botting tipsy. Mark Hanna, who is a good judge, says that some mornings he 'had eyes like an oyster in blood', another saying, but for all we ever knew he used to go home, lock the door and go on a solitary bat. Women," she gave a little laugh, "God alone knows, but he didn't fondle the stock. Boys no. He had certain effeminate characteristics—high voice, etcetera—but a lot of dedicated studs have just that, believe me."

He would, thought the Inspector, the lady impressing him as something of a connoisseur of male frailty.

"Compartmentalised," he said, "did his playing well way from the office. Ah, well, we'll find out. We do, you know."

She got out a cigarette and lighted it while he watched her.

"Who hated him enough to kill him, Mrs. Stigg? There was a deal with a brewery on the table. Was that acrimonious?"

She shrugged. "The family money was safe whatever happened. I think that dear Cristobal was selling us down the river, but no matter if he did our capital would be considerable. In fact if we took shares and not cash we might do moderately well. Not a killing matter."

The Inspector stared at his scribbler. "No cross words, no bitter quarrels in public, no doxies, no boys, nothing at all. On Monday morning he came into this room at nine. A bit before twelve Smart came in here. Botting had left word with the Switch that he was not accessible. He'd been doing that for the past month, seeing practically nobody. Sometime that morning he stuck his

60

head in that shaft," the Inspector wheeled round, "and it was smashed in by a fancy, three-litre bottle of red Cinzano vermouth."

"I thought you got the time exactly," said Nefer, "in the stories . . ."

"Time of death is ascertained largely by temperature. It should drop one and a half degrees Fahrenheit per hour for twelve hours." He watched her shudder and thought she rather faked it. "But sometimes this does not happen. It is a hot little box of an office for one thing and Botting had a chronic vitamin deficiency which made him abnormally susceptible to cold. He wore a hell of a lot of clothes, ever notice it?"

Nefer thought. "He was not a man I looked at much, but when you mention it he had a stiff, swaddled kind of look."

"So it could have been any time after he entered this room, you see." Inspector James stared at the wall safe, gaping open. "The room tells me nothing. I have statistics, the lift shaft is a rectangle about three feet by two feet, lined with oak. A small wooden platform attached to a cog-wheel still can be made to travel up and down. But for God's sake, why?"

"I did maths," said Nefer, "but my sister, Nord, was a historian. We did a project one summer, the old records, etcetera. The grandfather had it made into a book. It was not a good one. It is surely in that shelf. In brief, it was installed by Nick Heavan, who was grandson of the founder, but the instigator of the firm's greatness and one of the first men to realise the potentiality of port wine when the French imports dried up in the Revolutionary wars. It was Nick who realised the future importance of the coaching inns; he provided 'em with their wines. Some used to brew their own ale, and spirits were a matter of their wits and the excise men. But wine was a problem and the gentry had started to suck with alacrity. Nick had the idea of a printed label stuck on his bottles; the labelling then, if at all, was a bit of paper written on in ink and stuck on with flour paste. He also policed his wines. Those inns he provided had neat little signs hung up: 'Wines by Nick Heavan.' Hang it, hence was the Regency toast, 'May I go to Heaven when I die.' They say at one time Prinny and his brother William—who loved his drop—never missed giving it at dinnertime."

The Inspector reached behind him and tapped the oak surround of the lift shaft. "This kind of stuff brings you closer to it, somehow. And why was it installed?"

"They lived above, in and around their businesses, Inspector. Family, 'prentices, all rather higgledypiggledy to us. You can see old businesses in London where the great-grandfather was born in an upstairs room. But also Old Nick and his partners could call down the shaft to the kitchen for a bottle to be sent up. It was handy if a retailer called in for a crack and a bottle of port with maybe a few cold roast birds to go down their apopleptic throats."

The position of the lift platform was a problem which harried the Inspector. It had been found neatly tucked and unbloodied in the big room on the attic floor.

"You just call down the shaft, do you?"

"The kitchen is the end of the line so to speak. I doubt whether that lift has been used in living memory. It is supposed that somebody shouted so that Botting stuck his head in the shaft and then dropped a bottle?"

"You have an ingenious mind, madam," said the Inspector. "The bottle bounced after impact, slid past the shattered skull, and ended up at the bottom of the shaft, cracked but whole. The filth of ages made a bed for it to fall into. It had been a full bottle. It is quite a good advertising piece, but you can buy them on the Continent. It was part of the publicity and exhibition gear stored on the floor above us, or so it appears from the inventory. He must have been seated where I am. A voice called him from that aperture," the Inspector swivelled to his right. "He rose, travelled the four necessary steps, stuck his head in and said 'Who the devil is that?' Or so the local Superintendent surmised. The various unpleasant stains seem to indicate that his head was stuck in the lift-well."

"You're being very frank," said Nefer, a tinge of unease in her voice.

"It's a very good weapon." The Inspector smiled and Nefer

realised that he really was very young, younger than she probably. "And where were you on Monday morning?"

"At ten I was passing in my car. I nipped in and asked the receptionist in the new office building if my husband was alone. She said, no, that he was with Keast and Hanna in the latter's office, the official one in the new building. I went back to the car and on into town and did a rather ghastly fashion show with a girl friend."

"It's all down in the paperwork," Inspector James read her mind, "but this repetition caper is in the text-book. It wears people down. I suppose you didn't nip up and brain him? Unrequited whatsit or he'd caught you at the till?"

She had one charming dimple and it now showed. "I never done it, sir. About the unrequition, or requisition would it be, it did rile me. I am a woman who chastely appreciates a gentlemanly leer. Otherwise why do I undergo the tortures of dieting and the vagaries of daft fashion designers?"

"Botting did not have a secretary, he used the typing pool. Curious, a tycoon sans secretary."

"Oh, that's rather the tendency," said Nefer, importantly. "Botting used to bone up on *Fortune* and all the crap from Harvard. But he was a clean-desk man. My husband and the rest are by temperament cosy morning tea and faithful personal secretary men. Botting liked movable partitions and tape-recorders."

"I see that the company secretary came here with Botting, or a month or so afterwards. They worked together at a small company manufacturing flavourings and essences."

"Harold Stiggins? I think he was Botting's back-room boy. Cristobal could fire the shot and—give the devil his due—could be bloody impressive. Stiggins looks like a stewed, spewed shrewd prune, but my husband said he thought that in anything involving real finance—deep gnome stuff—Botting would stall until Stiggins had briefed him."

"They entered life in the same rehousing scheme in South London," said Inspector James, "Stiggins being three years older. The same Council School as it was then. Botting got a scholarship to one of the London public schools. A good examination man, the report says: oh, yes, we're so thorough that we found an old teacher at the school. His sex life will be equally solved," he looked at her for a long second but her eyes did not falter. "Stiggins stewed away through night school and was labelled academically brilliant. Somewhere along the line they teamed up, worked together at three places. You could be right about his role."

"I hope Stiggins will stay with us," Nefer's eyes narrowed, "I suppose . . . oh, you wouldn't be interested."

"You mean would he take Botting's place?" said the Inspector. "And that is an idea, indeed. Kill the boss and take his place has been a motive before this." He made a note. "But surely Mr. Hanna will take over?"

She laughed, not very pleasantly. "Mark is pasteboard, all front and no behind. He is in charge of sales and quite a good man at a get-together. Eldred Keast, well he has brains, but he is not at all fond of hard work and likes his comfortable existence with my sister Nord. My husband . . ." she hesitated, "he is a prodigiously hard worker without a brain in his head. Give him a mass of paper work and he'll plug his way through the lot in time, and with no sense of priority whatsoever."

"I see that you are the second largest shareholder."

She nodded. "The grandfather left me most, then Noni and last poor Nord who he took a dislike to. I did well academically. I think it impressed him."

"Did all three of you marry poor men?"

She nodded. "Mark is a compulsive gambler and a very soft touch for a loan. My husband is a grandson of the most impecunious peer in Ireland, which is saying something. Keast, like Mark although younger, came of an Army family. He quit the Service eight years ago."

"Were Mr. Hanna and Mr. Stigg members of the firm before your grandfather died?"

"They were, but only Mark was a Director. In fact there were only he and grandfather on the Board and Mark was a rubber stamp."

"Well," the Inspector got up. "Would you like the Sergeant to escort you to your car?"

"Lord, no," said Nefer, "I am a creature without nerves of that kind. Just switch the stairway light on."

The Inspector watched her as she went until he heard the faint click of the closing door before going back to his seat.

"A proper bitch," said the Sergeant.

"Brains," said the Inspector, "she was first-class at her speciality, a form of maths that I could not begin to understand. I wonder what she wants . . . no children, a very good-looking husband if you like them on the inbred side, money . . . I wonder why she doesn't take over the business. You know, I smell some kind of graft; income-tax evasion, something of that sort. We can't get at the books, more's the pity, without going to a judge, and we can't very well do that."

"You mean that Botting copped somebody with his fingers in the till and they bashed him?"

"About that. But he must have had a woman somewhere and I'd like to know who."

"That Nefertiti is a luscious drop of grub," reflected Honeybody.

"And I'd like to know what she was doing outside that door. Oh, God."

There was a knock.

It was P.C. Trice, one of the two men allotted to the Inspector by the Chief Constable. He looked unhappy. The Inspector had detailed him to watch Percival, the old labeller.

"He hasn't left the premises," said the Constable unhappily. "Unless he went over the wall—you probably could in parts, but what would an old cove like that be doing climbing walls?" He was flustered and irritated and it took the Inspector's coldest glance to restore his customary equilibrium.

The Inspector did not bother to ask whether he was sure. You did not acquire the P.C.'s reputation by not being sure.

"I briefed the night-watchman to telephone this room—he has an internal intercom system—if Percival went out. There's only one exit."

"Do they have a time-clock?"

"No, sir, at least not for the cellar people, who are rated as 'permanent casuals'."

"I'd been about to call it a day," said the Inspector, "so we'll look through the cellaring before going our ways. Get out your torches, and away we go."

The stairs were narrow with the smell of old mice-dung and years of living. They were covered with heavy red linoleum. "Let's have a look at this kitchen," said James as he reached the ground level.

It was quite something, a 'done regardless' job. It looked even more spacious than it was, with a calculated whitewashed coolness. Barrels pyramided along one wall. "I wonder if it is real," said the Sergeant, removing a small brass jug from a hook. He turned the nearest spigot; nothing came out. "Fraud," he said.

"I did hear," said the P.C., "that when they have a 'do' they sometimes put a kind of hose-pipe attachment at the back of the cask which makes it look real."

Beside the huge refrigerator, wisely not camouflaged, was a door. The Inspector opened it and peered down into a rather sinister darkness. He sniffed. There was the resinous smell of old wine. The Sergeant shone his torch down. "I'd better go first, Mr. James, being the meatiest. If anything's broken, don't let them cut it off." He eased his weight on to the top step. The Inspector, who had come to the conclusion that one of the few perquisites of rank was having something soft to fall on in times of danger, went last. He counted sixty-three steps, the temperature dropping perhaps twenty Fahrenheit so that his wet shirt stuck unpleasantly to his back.

"Old stuff," said Honeybody appreciatively, his torch flickering around the casks. "A king's ransom, unbroached. I wonder what grog they contain."

"I think I can see a corpse," said the P.C. dubiously. The Inspector saw that comfortably outstretched between the balks of wood anchoring the barrel was a human shape. His hearing was acute and there was a soft adenoidal snore. In the torchlight old Percival slept happily, flat on his back. Honeybody, who could move very fast, bent over him. "Full as a boot," he said professionally.

In the searchlight it was apparent that old Percival shaved rarely and patchily. He had removed his teeth and placed them on the front page of the *Daily Mirror* which rested a couple of feet away from his head, which was pillowed upon an old coat. "Stinks of the sauce," said the Sergeant sniffing wistfully, "out of there," he indicated an old, cracked china jug. "Cheap sherry," he pronounced.

The Inspector had had more than his share of trying to arouse drunks. Percival was mildly stertorous, but his eyes opened as the Inspector sharply patted his chops.

"All right, all right." His legs kicked in an unavailing attempt to rise.

"Don't get up," said the Inspector. "It's nine forty-five at night, but where you kip is no business of mine. As long as you're all right."

"No stealing, sport," said Percival, "all cleanly come by. Some sherry rolled off a hand truck and Mrs. Frankly had it mopped up as she does. I bought the jug off her for five bob. It hit me so I'm snoring off. No harm done, sport. The watchman knows me. Sometimes when there's been a breakage I get a skinful and snore off. No harm, sir."

They moved off, and almost immediately the snoring commenced. The flooring became smooth and they reached the bottling bay, chairs, piping and corking machines resting, a fruity stench in the air. One lady bottler was evidently an old Marxist, observed the Inspector noting the crumpled book which propped up the fourth leg of her chair. Down here bottling with her thoughts, although hadn't the Marx been fond of his grog?

The steps at the other end of the cellaring were wide and modern. The sky peeped at the upper end.

"It looks as though you can get in and out here easily enough," said Sergeant Honeybody.

"Deceptive," said P.C. Trice. "As I see it any smash would be for the spirits, there being no point in carting away the wines. And in a little village like this . . . the local P.C. is around the pub opposite until closing and believe me, sir, the inhabitants peer through their windows all night."

"The English countryside!" said Sergeant Honeybody. "And they give you six months for running a blue cinema!"

"They've got one now," said P.C. Trice, not without pride.

"Some of the Americans who were stranded when they were doing that religious film are running it. The Home Office will tell us when to knock it off. But they're doubtful because it is such a tourist attraction."

The watchman was a comfortable retired constable who was nibbling away at a length of salami. "I suppose you found him in the cellar pissed, sir? Likes his glass do old Percival and working hockdeep in it all the mortal day adds an edge to his thirst as you might say."

"Does he often sleep in the cellar?"

"Not regular," said the watchman, "otherwise I suppose I'd have to do something in the line of dooty. Only occasionally when there's been a breakage and he Got At It as you might say. He usually snores off until around three-ish and then walks out quite steady. It's four miles to where he lives, but off he goes in that jerky, knees-up-ma-brown way the chronic soakers 'ave."

"Did you know Botting?"

"Know?" Shrewd, brown pig-eyes met the Inspector's. "I would not use that word in connection with the lamented. He was a dark horse. I knew him when he first came, being the village P.C. then. A dark horse, sir, one hand not knowing what the other was doing, and that same hand, sir, doing some funny things at times."

"Girls?" gently probed the Inspector.

"A dark horse, sir. The old guv'nor, Nonsuch Heavan was his full name, was a rare straitlaced man in his way. Mad, sir, like all that family. He used to think he was an Old Greek God, Dion somebody . . ."

"Dionysus."

"That's it, sir. He used to import vine leaves, easy for him. And then he put them in his hair and danced stark naked around that old house of his. The servants had to pretend not to see him. But screwing without clerical benefit he was dead against. Like a rat was the late Botting, sir. Within three weeks he'd seen the danger, sir, and dropped the girls like hot coals, and some were hot I can tell you. No parental control these days." He bit off a morsel of salami and wagged his head in reminiscence. "All except one thin little girl, sir, which I could not understand myself,

68

always having liked something to cushion the fall as you might say. Ethel was the first name, the second I've forgotten as she was a by-blow and lived with her granny, old Mrs. Smith. He stowed her away, sir, over in the town. I happened to be in there two Christmases ago and it being a small world I was visiting a friend and I see the little madam hipping her way out of the next flat. She didn't recognise me. My friend said she was a Mrs. Smith who kept herself to herself. Her hubby was a traveller who nobody saw much, a moon-faced fellow. She'd been there more than five years, so he'd installed her, sir, as you might say."

"Would you write down the address?"

The watchman put down the sausage and reached forward for his notebook. "A modest block of flats, sir, in a working-class district. Two-bedroom-and-lounge kind of job put up by cranes. Here you are!"

"You might as well knock off," the Inspector said to the constable as they left. "We'll drop you home." Sergeant Honeybody eased himself behind the wheel.

"I hope I did right about old Percival," said the constable diffidently.

"Quite all right," said the Inspector. "He did not telephone anybody from outside, therefore it means he contacted them inside. I would say it fits. A coup and then a celebration. Tomorrow make some excuse for being around the cellar during the morning."

After dropping the constable, they drove along the three-lane highway to the city. The Inspector produced his map and navigated. It proved an eight-storey block of conventional concrete, aluminium and glass, already marked by the signs, not of dilapidation but of slight weariness, which soon affects these structures. "Fifth floor, number 12," Honeybody read from the piece of paper. "It's ten and she might be entertaining."

In fact the face which looked at them from the opened but chained door was a sad one. A natural blonde, assessed the Inspector, with a fleshy nose and mouth but attractive and disconcerting large grey eyes over prominent cheekbones.

"We're police, ma'am, and here is my identity card. If you wish you can telephone the local station."

Sometimes they slammed the door in your face and there was nothing you could do about it.

"About Cris?" Her face was impassive.

"Mr. Botting, yes."

"Come in." She eased off the chain.

The Inspector glanced sideways at Honeybody's face. The hallway had a mounted stag's head and was painted a dark chocolate brown. The lounge room had the Queen Anne style furnishings and lamps made out of chianti bottles which rang great peals of memory in his head. And, yes, by God there were bits of drift-wood on the mantelpiece and the Odhams Privilege Books in the special-offer expanding case rested on wall-to-wall axminster.

"It is lovely and cosy," said 'Mrs. Smith' as they were seated. "And I hope you will have a drink." She eyed a mating of TV with grog. "Would you like a gin-and-tonic?"

"Yes, that would be a nice thought," said Honeybody, blandly ignoring the Inspector's glare. His hostess turned off the TV screen and opened the small bar.

There was ice in a patent container and she was pleasingly heavy-handed with the gin.

"Could I tempt you to a canape?"

"No thanks. This is delicious," said the Inspector. "I don't want to embarrass you, ma'am."

"About me being Cris's mistress? Oh, it doesn't embarrass me, my dear. I could have done very much worse. I suppose the old P.C. told you. I saw him leering a couple of years ago. I didn't tell Cris because he would have said 'move' and I'm so lovely and cosy here. That's why Cris liked it. It was what he dreamed of as a boy. He was brought up in council flats. I didn't come forward when he was killed because there's nothing I can tell you, my dears."

"I see," said the Inspector, "he could be himself here, eh?"

"Oh, yes, he wasn't really complicated, you know. He had to be because he had to get ahead and you can't stay still, you know."

"Did he keep any papers?"

"Oh, no, dear, not here. Sometimes he brought his tape

recorder and spoke into it. He kept a couple of suits, casuals, undies and shirts here, that's all."

There was something about her, thought the Inspector. You became very aware of her physically, very aware—he drank the cold gin-and-tonic—and there was a certain uncomplicated feeling you got about her.

"How long were you together?"

"Over seven years. I lived with my granny quite near Heavans. Cris was one for the girls and old Mr. Heavan was against it, you know, so Cris picked me and eventually we took the flat. We never had a cross word, dear, our tastes dove-tailing. He was a very good chap was Cris.

"Was he married?"

"No, dear. He'd have probably got a duchess eventually, very ambitious was Cris, although he didn't really like it, but you have to go up or go under as he used to say. And I was always here to come back to. We went our own ways, dear. No jealousy or where were you last night stuff. I used to telephone him at seven every morning—his 'getting up service' he used to call it—when he was at home and ask if he'd be round. He was very considerate and gentle. Have another; he hated people being mean with drinks and food."

"I'm sorry to have to ask you where you were when he was killed."

"There's a secretarial agency, dear, where I work mornings doing filing and making the tea, being unskilled business-wise. Too many girls get so that they hang around boozing in the mornings, so I've always had a job. Here we are, dear," she went and took a card off the mantelpiece, "go and see them if you want. I was there from eight thirty until twelve fifteen. I read about Cris in the evening stop-press. But could you tell me about his next of kin?"

"He didn't seem to have one," said the Inspector with great caution, "neither can a will be found."

"Oh, he had not made a will, kind of dreading it, you know. But I s'pose his estate owns the furniture, and there's his clothes. I make the payments for the flat—he didn't like to put things in writing."

"I don't imagine you have any claim . . ." began the Inspector.

"I know that, dear."

"Well, you should go and see a solicitor. Off the record I'd advise you simply to shut up." She did grow on you, thought the Inspector, half wishing he was unchaperoned by Honeybody.

"That's what I thought, just shut up," she said. "He gave me quite a lot of money, dear, about eighteen thousand it is. He said if ever he had to run for it it was there for him. On deposit, it is, and every time he was here I had to show him the statement. He didn't trust anybody, but you have to trust one person, don't you dear, I mean in life."

The Inspector was looking at one interestingly muscled thigh which peeped from the little silk pleated skirt. "Unless there's any written agreement, I imagine it was a gift."

"Well, that's one of the reasons I didn't come forward, a gentleman once telling me that the Labour Party tax gifts. How they expect girls to live I don't understand, enough to make you vote for the Tories."

"Any idea who killed him?"

She looked blank. "Oh, men make enemies, dear, part of their nature. He wasn't a very nice fellow, you know. He wasn't a great talker, but over the years I knew he could *get* people and would wait his time before he used the knife. A typical man, you know, one of the clever ones."

"He had people working for him or with him?"

"He despised them. A Mark Hanna, a fat bladder of wind, Cris had a lot on him, did silly things in the last war or something. Then a Bill Stigg, a high-priced stallion with the slowish brains they usually have, that was what Cris said, not me, my dear, with one of the la-di-da families as his background, soup and fish written all over him. Then a man named Keast. Cris hated him so he must have brains. But they are all a lot of dishonest buggers, dear, or so Cris said. Every manjack and jill at Heavans was fiddling away to beat the band. I expect Cris had his hand well in the till. We were working class, dear."

"When did you last see him?"

"On the Friday. He was doing a big business deal with Joshua's Brewery. They were buying out Heavans and Cris was to join their Board. It was very big-time and was to be the making of him, but somebody killed him. He wanted to get really big, dear, and then become in charge of one of the nationalised industries so that he could really make people jump. And he'd have done it, dear, if somebody hadn't hit him. He normally went away about four in the morning. He used to try to go away before people started hanging around."

"There was a Nigel Heavan."

"The loony. Oh, Cris had to have him put away, dear. He got his Power of Attorney and had him put in the bin. Mad as a hatter; thought he was a flute at times. You couldn't blame Cris. I told you Cris didn't talk much but you can't spend all those hours in bed without saying something, can you, and it all adds up. I found him a girl named Dottie—Dorothy Lanyard—a real little trollop, but she was office trained, you know, which is what he wanted. The loony used to wander round with wind instruments, so she got him in the cellar and attacked him." Her face altered as she laughed, no longer sad. "The poor fellow was terrified and blacked her eye with his instrument and ran off."

"Where is she?"

"Out of the country. That was the deal. Cris gave her the dough to open a bar in Sardinia and saw she stayed there for a yearly pay-off. That's where all the tough ones go. But I suppose you know all about that."

The Inspector stood up. "Thank you for the hospitality and help. Should you think of anything further, here is my card. Just phone the local station."

She looked sad as she saw them out.

"I could've made an excuse to leave, Harry," said the Sergeant as he prodded the lift button. "You were giving her looks, but you need all your wits about you tomorrow. There's a nasty smell around this case."

Inspector James gave him a venomous glance, reflecting that she had indeed been a right good sort. He hoped she made the best use of her eighteen thousand nicker.

For convenience he and the Sergeant had arranged to occupy the unused spare double room of the village constable. Convenient because of its direct telephone line to the county police and the ease with which cups of tea and, as happened on their arrival, dishes of braised oxtail were produced without recriminations regarding the time.

Eventually he and Honeybody had a double whisky with the constable and retired to their twin beds. The Inspector lay awake and listened to the Sergeant's snoring.

7

MABEL STIGGINS AWOKE to the sound of her husband's peculiar glottal noise. As he got older he was going to have increasing trouble with his tubes, she thought. A good thing they had left London for a non-smoke area and that he had got in early on the insurance policy. Though men like Stiggins customarily lived a long time. She leaned over the side of the bed with her nail clippers. His father was still around the Cut with his barrow of topped-up apples, which the Stiggins family themselves resembled even to the maggot holes. She'd give him fifteen minutes before yelling. It was progress, she thought, for Harold just got out of bed when yelled at, but his father, according to custom, always flopped his wife one with the back of his hand when yelled at. In these days when comfortable dentures were difficult to get it made life difficult. She thanked Harold's nights at the Polytechnic and her own studies at London University for the improvement.

The Stigginses lived in a house in a building commuter's paradise and Harold's money progressively went into mortgages in the district. It was a pleasant area with a local council which was steadily encouraging the legend that it had been a Tudor Manor.

The children ate in the kitchen, while she and Harold inhabited the inglenook which the architect had fashioned in the living area next to his perilous conversation pit. Mabel was competent and had trained the children to be so. The elder girl shoved the two

74

rashers and eggs through the serving hatch, and the pop-up toaster and coffee percolator did the rest. Twenty minutes after she had yelled at Harold, who merely dabbled with a sponge before applying his electric razor, he seated himself.

"You had too much last night, my dear," she said. "Not like you and with Cris Botting gone you'll need your wits."

"We might be in trouble. Just coffee and toast with Marmite, my dear. Cris kept records, you know."

"You were just the secretary, you told me you covered yourself."

"Close that serving hatch."

She obeyed and looked at him curiously. "They don't listen."

"They're my kids, Mabel, and if they don't listen heredity is crap."

"That sort of thing . . ."

"Shut your trap, dear, I've a knocking head. Botting and me did something years ago, nothing I want to talk about. No, it's nothing that you know about, nothing about shares. We did a job and it turned out nasty. He was always number one; I never grudged him that. But he was a funny one. To hear him talk, little needles, you'd think I'd done it alone."

"Harold, something anti-social!"

"Now shut your mouth, my dear, and forget the Uni. Remember your grand-dad, fourteen years for kicking an old lady when she caught him busting her sub post-office. Atavism, that's your fancy word. We did something nasty. It was all right when Botty was alive, but suppose he left something. I've known people who did, blast his soul."

"Don't talk like that in this day and age, dear. It's upsetting enough for the little one to hear about souls at school without you getting the habit."

"Don't be funny with me."

"Sorry, Harold, but there is a Statute of Limitations. It must be fifteen years . . ."

"I looked it up; what we did isn't limited."

"Christ, you mean . . . ?"

"We had to have some money we needed to put back in the till. That's all you want to know. Ten to one his thoughts died with him, the bastard, but just in case, and if the coppers come

75

around here, don't be smart." His hard little eyes pierced her. "Oh, I know about the eminent professors that taught you, but they've sent down a scruffy little Inspector who is worth ten of 'em if it comes to the point. Keep that witty, educated voice still. I mean it, Mabel. You know nothing."

"You didn't do him? The children . . ." Her voice was agitated.

"I had no reason to do him. He was going to sack Hanna, Keast and Stigg. And forget that one! They'll find out all right without us flapping off. He had them in the gunsight, dead to rights. Probability says one of them did it."

"Have you thought about *you*?"

"Ever known me not? I'll have that bacon." He took it off the chafing dish and chewed.

"You should get Botting's job."

"Me? I need a front man, old sweet. I can't do it on my own, you know that. I'd take the chairmanship with a good front man."

"Have you approached them?"

"They hate my guts. Any ideas?" He looked at her curiously.

"Get off with you! I'll keep my mouth closed as ordered."

"The inscrutable Mrs. Stiggins, that's you." He kissed her.

Stiggins dropped the children at the bus point from which they went to school. While she laboriously placed the breakfast things in the depths of the washing machine and fed the scraps into the automatic disposal apparatus, checked the various other labour-saving machines in her kitchen and switched off the burglar alarms and found that the disposable bags attached to the vacuum required renewal Mrs. Stiggins dreamed of a larger house, herself a Chairman's wife.

The melodious chimes of the doorbell—it was *Bird Songs at Eventide*—made her look at the clock. Nine fifteen. She was never very keen on opening the front door unless she knew exactly who it was, not since that time the police came round when they were in Ealing, although Harold had no difficulty in getting rid of them. She had few friends in the locality, most of the women being shallow-brained.

"Oh, come in Mrs. Stigg. I'm afraid you find me at the kitchen sink."

"I've left mine to the daily."

"I haven't one." Mrs. Stiggins could never quite reconcile her proletarian consciousness to daily women. Her own mother had achieved swollen knees by labouring through the nights cleaning out offices.

Typically the small sitting-room was scrupulously tidy. "I suppose it's too early for coffee, but if you like it's only a question of reheating."

"No thank you, dear. You know it's such a pity we haven't got to know each other."

"I'm afraid my social instincts are a bit atrophied," said Mrs. Stiggins, seating herself and offering the box of cigarettes.

"Thank you! I'm an admirer of your husband's work." Nefer peered at the glowing end of her cigarette. "I thought he was the grey eminence behind Botting."

"It's nice to hear such compliments. Harold is the best figure man in the country, I think. But Botting was good, you know. A first-class organiser and what a personality in spite of his voice. Women liked him, you know?" Her cold, amber eyes looked through Nefer.

"I prefer more obvious charms," said Nefer, curled kittenishly on the big leather chair. "However, as the second largest shareholder I wondered if I could pump you as to how Harold would react to the offer of the chairmanship."

"A bit working class, isn't he, Mrs. Stigg? If you look at Harold you think of gin. He's hardly the personification of gracious living."

"My husband, who has no brains but a capacity for work, has all the graciousness to make you sick rolled up in one cuddly ball. He'd be Managing Director."

Mrs. Stiggins stared at her. "I do owe you an apology, really I do. I thought you were too Oxbridge for my digestion. But—and and this is not denigrating Harold: he'll make your money grow and grow—is Mr. Stigg the organiser that you have to have these days?"

"I shall join the Board," said Nefer, "I can't see anything else for it. And you, my dear, might be an asset, and you could sort of keep a wifely eye on Harold."

"I think I'll have a cigarette," said Mrs. Stiggins, "the first since I read the Surgeon-General's report. Dear, oh, dear. I suppose I could. The children are at school and I could get help, income tax deductible. What would I get?"

"It would only be once a week at most," said Nefer, "say two hundred partly paid as expenses. Wine drinking is getting a womanly occupation so you're bound to earn your keep. I'll be Assistant Managing Director, more or less full-time or until I make other arrangements."

"There are your two sisters and their husbands," said Mrs. Stiggins.

"I'll deal with those problems, but the big one is Nigel."

"The daftie?"

"He put in an appearance yesterday completely cured and with documents to prove it. I'm the only member of the family who he likes. We'll see. How does Harold hit it off with him?"

"I suppose Nigel doesn't like him. Mr. Stiggins prefers Bach and nothing else and I don't suppose that endeared him. Besides he'd be identified with Botting who had him put away. I suppose I shouldn't've said that."

"We'll have to say a lot of things, Mabel, if we stick together. I suppose you have ambition for the kids?"

"Well . . ."

"I think they were all up to something, you know, even your husband I expect. Mine spends too much for what he gets; I suppose that's the hardest part—to disguise it I mean. I didn't mind. I suppose it comes off the income tax."

"Everybody fiddles," said Mabel, "and if you read Marx you can see why, but if they fiddle you do have something on them so to say. It can make it easier."

"I think we should do very well together," said Nefer, "providing we have confidence in each other."

She thought that it was going to be a good session with a lot of cosy understanding, but the chimes from the front door made her start.

"Bless it!" said Mabel, "do excuse me, please."

Stiggins returned, thought Nefer, lighting a cigarette from her butt. She would have to revise her opinions probably. Any man who pretended to go and then lurked at the end of the road meant eventually big trouble.

"I think you know Mrs. Stigg." Mabel's voice was surprisingly weak after her usual aggressive contralto.

"Nigel, my dearie, how nice to see you," said Nefer, doing her kittenish uncurling and two-handed man-to-man shaking act. "It *is* so nice."

"I'm sorry to intrude," boomed the basso which went so incongruously with his thin face, supported in turn by a wrestler's neck and body. "I telephoned at a call box for Harold, but he wasn't in at work and I got this stupid idea of coming here."

"He drops the children at school," said Mabel. "Do sit down and would you like coffee?"

"It comes under the list of forbidden stimulants. A cold milk if possible."

"I'll get it from the fridge."

They watched her go.

"That isn't frank, Nigel," said Nefer. "When you were lying you always scratched your chin like that."

"I was watching Stiggins, Nefer, but then saw you drive up. What is rattling in that shrewd, ruthless little skull, my own love, my little cupboard of charm?"

"I want Stiggins as Chairman, Bill as Managing Director, her on the Board, and I'll be assistant to Bill. Look, Nigel, you don't want it. You could hardly have it, a cured madman on the Board, huh?"

He laughed. "Apart from your personification of a bitch, my dear, I do, I really do, admire your ruthless analysis. I used to think of that in the asylum. Nobody trusts a once barmy bod whatever his certification." He raised his voice. "My dear Mrs. Stiggins, there is no need to hover outside that door."

"I brought your milk."

He got up and took it. "I never knew you, Mrs. Stiggins. As you've been listening at the door, you'll know that my purposes are friendly and that Mrs. Stigg and I had a little affair some years ago. Thank you, excellent milk. I wanted a few words with Harold Stiggins to find out what Stigg, Hanna and Keast are really up to. I encountered a little shiftiness when I met them yesterday. I'll tell you what, Nefer, it's my intention to sell out my shares, but not to any ruddy brewery. I'm going to Majorca, but if the family would buy them over a period of years you would find me generous as far as terms are concerned. But to put my cards on the table I don't want to find my shares worthless because the assets have been embezzled. That's what worried me in the asylum, the thought of Cristobal's great fat hands in the till. No business can stand that for too long."

"It wasn't that," said Mabel, "in fact he was building it up for another stepping stone."

"Something might be worked out," said Nefer thoughtfully, "and if I had proxies for your shares you could rely on me."

"I think we should go and see Stiggins," said Nigel, scratching his long chin. "I fear he may think my enmity to Botting over-spills on to him. It doesn't. He was Cristobal's creature, but so were we bloody well all. You'd better come along if you will, Mrs. Stiggins, as a gesture of goodwill or a dove or what you will."

Nigel drove alone, soberly and steadily so that he arrived a good two minutes after Nefer and Mabel Stiggins. They parked outside and walked towards the new office block. Stiggins was on the ground floor in a medium-sized office of glass. He was addressing a tape-recorder as his hands quickly turned over a pile of papers, thrusting them steadily into an out-basket. His small wizened face twisted in astonishment as he saw them and came over to open the door.

"A lynchin' party so early?" he said in his clipped cockney. "Mr. Nigel, I hope you bear me no grudge."

"None at all," said Nigel, as they walked in. "I'll get to the point. We want a figure man with some capacity for ruthlessness to take the chair."

"Ah," Stiggins paused and pursed his mouth.

"My husband to be Managing Director," said Nefer firmly, "he's a good workhorse and his aitches are impeccable. I will be his assistant which takes care of the brains. And I want your wife as a Director. I understand her, although I don't particularly understand you, so she could interpret as it were."

80

"Ah," Stiggins paid the words over grudgingly. "It might work. There's the question of the emoluments."

"We are not ungenerous as a family. But what's to be done?"

"Botty," said Stiggins, "Mr. Botting strained the figures to the utmost to inflate profit. Oh, it passed the audit, quite legal. But there we are, for a hundred years or so the half of the business has been more often than not in the hands of trustees. Naturally they insisted on maximum drawings." He sighed. "The firm's top-heavy with short-term borrowing, not but what Botty wasn't good with the banks."

"My money has accumulated," said Nigel, "I could advance . . ." He stopped as Stiggins' cold eyes flicked him professionally like a hangman.

"No good in the long run, sir. My suggestion is short commons for two years, maximum retrenching—Botty always thought that didn't look so good, but he had a weakness in his thinking—and then a public issue. Inflation will continue so we'll need, as far as the human 'eart can fathom, a hundred thou to liquidate borrowing. It depends, but a hard two years is indicated. Three, p'raps, according to the advice I get from the City. But, lor', people will always drink."

"And putting things right like doctoring red wine," said Nigel coldly.

"I know nothing of that, but if it's there it shall be put right."

"Give it to us straight," said Nigel. "Is the firm rotten?"

"No," said Stiggins, "no sickness I can't cure." His eyes slewed to the glass wall.

Mark Hanna, a file in his hand, was glaring through. Stiggins touched his temple in a mock salute.

Nefer laughed. "It's all right, I can fix it with Noni. And Nord would not care much. Eldred is a lazy devil."

"Astute, though," said Stiggins, "and looks at me like so much poop."

"They don't *need* you for charm, Harold," said Mabel.

For the first time, Nefer saw his grin, a process which seemingly split his face in two. "You must take me as you find me," he said.

Nefer laughed with him, but her face froze. Treading with the delicacy of an elephant on eggs, the big, florid-faced Sergeant

—what was his name, Honey something—was mincing through the glass doorway.

"I do hope I do not interrupt you folk," he said in his port-wine voice, "but I did wish to see Mr. Nigel Heavan at his convenience. I'm Sergeant Honeybody of the Yard." His small eyes seemed to look at everything in turn, lingering finally on Nefer's legs.

"I don't suppose you'll want my convenience here," said Nigel, getting up. (A powerfully built bugger, thought Honeybody professionally. It would need three men and a wrist dug well into his throat to get him into the police car.)

"I'm in the office used by the late Mr. Botting, sir, my guv'nor being out, but he asked me to see you, sir."

"Well, I've finished here. You'll let me have your thoughts in writing just as soon as possible, will you Harold?"

"Indeed, Mr. Nigel."

Although he had gone across the concrete yard and up the stairs of the Old Building many times, Nigel was conscious of constraint. He had become sensitive to the attendants who had watched him always, never a moment when you could be sure that an eye was not upon you. A powerful swine, too, he thought, with a kind of animal assurance. He pulled his thoughts together; he mustn't think resentfully of people again.

He looked about the office. "This was Botting's when he first came here. His first job just about was to put up the new buildings in place of the Nissen huts."

"Sit down, sir," Honeybody was peaches and cream. "In a sense it's your office, you owning the show."

Nigel gave his short, barking laugh. "Via trustees for seven years, Sergeant. You might say that its proper occupant is a Commissioner in Lunacy."

"Not now, sir."

"No, not now. But how did you catch on that I was here, not that I have concealed anything?"

"Birds always return to their nests, sir, which is what you learn as a copper and saves the pain in the feet. Where there's a pub, sir, there's a policeman whose little spare-time assignment is knowing everything about that pub. And when people come out

82

of an institution they usually stay at a pub if they have no family. In your case, sir, the publican is a friend and real truculent when friendship's involved they say. But the local P.C. pretty soon knew you were there, sir, and when you got there. So that brings us to where you were last Monday morning in a purely routine way."

Nigel laughed again. "I was wandering about the countryside near here. I skirted the old Kingsbury Farm, God knows who has it now, wandered near the river to Turpington, and, God, walked for four hours solid. After getting out you feel like walking in the fresh air."

"I have to ask whether you were on these premises, sir."

"Not within a mile. I was going to see friend Botting, of course, just to watch his jaw drop. He had no idea I was out, but I wanted a few days to adjust."

"It does hit you," said Honeybody.

"It's quite different to anything you imagine. Anyway I got back to the pub around two, took my two little tablets, ate liver and bacon and sat on their back veranda and read until the evening. Then I watched their TV and heard the news around ten thirty."

"Were you shocked?"

"Don't be an ass. I realised my own position. Collar the loony and save trouble. Curiously, Botting always said he knew of a case where you did."

"Interested in criminology, was he now?" said the Sergeant. "It's funny how a certain type of man is. No, sir, we're not rail-roading you, but you knew the place, were near it and you had cause to hate deceased."

"Hate? No more than you hate a boil which has been lanced. Somebody had to put me away, though of course he did it for money, for hard cash as a book I once read had it. The only worry I had was that he might be parasiting the business stone dry."

"You knew this old building as a boy, sir?"

"Of course. Old Nonsuch had lost his family except the three granddaughters who he did not see too much of. I wasn't much of a relation, but I used to spend school holidays with him. I had the run of here."

"People don't realise that they had air-raid shelters in 1916, sir. We're too young to associate them with anything but Hitler's lot, but there were shelters. Being not far from the sea, the local council got a bit of a bug in its head about submarines blasting away and zeppelins doing the village over. A chance for old Neddy Heavan, the gaffer in those days, to do his bit. Any warning and the populace were allowed down the cellars. People in those days were scared of being trapped, so there were emergency tunnels dug. Shored up with pit props, goodish jobs like, especially as it's soft stone around here and easy to work. One of the shafts came out in a field at the back of these buildings. It's owned by the Company, but's never been used except for a farmer who grazes it. Your generation, sir, used to play around it as boys. It's still there and the local police had a look and although it was once covered by wire, it shows signs of still being used. It leads by extension to this building . . . so you see . . . if I were you I'd get me a solicitor and that's the truth. I suppose you have one?"

Nigel looked momentarily blank. "I . . . well, I don't know, it was all taken over. I certainly have money to fee a drove of the swine. But, look, I don't want to, ten to one they'd shop me."

Honeybody half rose and sighed gustily under his moustache. "I believe you, sir, but thousands wouldn't."

"All right, arrest me, damn you!"

"No cause to say such a thing." Honeybody supported his weight by one meaty knee lodged in the curve of the desk. "No cause, sir. It's just a friendly caution. Just as you might say to a piano player who hit a wrong chord."

Nigel, half to his feet, collapsed and laughed. "Playing on my aversion to pianists, sergeant! Good psychology, like kicking a cripple on his stump."

The Sergeant's backside hit his chair. "Lord, sir, nothing was so intended. Although I'm partial to the piano and the harp. The strings seem that melodious to me, sir."

"Sergeant," Nigel's voice had authority in it. "I'm going back to my pub. Good luck to you in your snooping."

"We have to snoop, sir." The Sergeant sat there and watched him go.

8

YOU HAD TO SNOOP, Inspector Harry James had ruminated comfortably as the tender pigs' liver rested lightly on his stomach. He wished that his wife Elizabeth could get it more frequently in their London suburb. His thoughts toyed amiably between his wife and pigs' livers. He had spent an hour on the phone between six and seven, briefed Honeybody, drinking his mug of tea spiced with a tot of whisky, seated in his underwear on his bed, and was now to inspect the late Cristobal Botting's pad. It was sixteen miles away in one of the county's fashionable areas.

The Bonnett Arms roughly occupied the site of an old manor from whence various Bonnetts had gone crusading, their effigies to be seen in the old church which sat wearily beside the river. The new building was vaguely Moorish, but with its large landings and long, air-conditioned and sound-proofed corridors it gave the desired impression of absolute luxury. The Inspector knew that it was lived in by wealthy families who felt themselves unable to cope with property and servants.

The Manager, his name on a very discreet brass plate, had an office on the ground floor which looked like a boudoir, business activity being confined to an inner room from which the subdued clack of a typewriter could be heard. He was not too pleased.

"Oh, you can have the key," he said, opening a small escritoire. "The late Mr. Botting paid three monthly in advance and there is six weeks to go. However, the local fellows looked it over. What I want to know is the next of kin—there are his personal effects."

"He had no kin whatsoever," said the Inspector, "according to a statement he made on several occasions and wrote on a document once which required such information. When the time comes, I should pack the stuff up and send it to Heavans where he worked. Let them worry."

"Thank you, I will."

"What kind of a man was he?"

"We have two kinds here, the gentry and the made-it-them-selves. He was the latter. A bit over-ingratiating I found him, but a perfect tenant. He came in six years ago."

"Women friends."

"Oh. I keep an eye on that as a matter of routine, not but that the flats aren't their homes. Quite a few, I think, different ladies but they were never there when the servants came to clean. No particular regular lady and he seemed to prefer blondes."

"Parties?"

The Manager smiled. "We are as sound-proofed as anybody can get without being totally inarticulate. I have the year's accounts in this drawer, we keep them for that period and I fore-cast your visit." He bent forward. "Give me a man's bills and I'll describe him to you."

"Very good!" said the Inspector.

"You've got to make some romance out of the bloody job. We provide complete servant service, valet, maid, internal cooking, food by food-lift . . ." he paused.

"Gawd," said the Inspector.

"He was used to them! Grilled meat, a bit overdone, with mushrooms or asparagus, was what he'd order in the evenings. We have a valet service, he never used it to my memory. But he used our dry cleaning and laundry service abnormally—a very clean fellow. Used heavy woollen underwear, but got through two pairs a day. And his bill for heavy socks is strange, he must have con-tinually changed them. We put on party service, even provide a cook who does the necessary in the kitchen if required, but that he never wanted. Solitary grills—he looked an over-weight kind. Always out all day including Sunday. A very powerful personality I should think. He did no entertaining here in the party line. We have no bills for liquor, but he was in the trade and the inventory I took showed a very interesting collection."

The Inspector thanked him. He took the stairs up to the third floor, broad, easy ones, between the alcoved statuary. Botting's had been a small unit. Two bedrooms, a dining-room, a sitting-room, kitchen, bathroom and separate shower.

It was curiously lacking in personality even though the main equipment was according to the inventory provided for the

Inspector by the local police part of the hiring. No personal photographs, the books in the sitting-room mass-produced gentleman's library jobs. The second bedroom had been turned into a work-room. Two sides of the room had book-casing and here was Botting's real library, accountancy, company law, market reports, plus, and Harry whistled, four hundred works on criminology, some rather rare. On the desk were ten box files as itemised in the local police report. The flat had been searched thoroughly and there was not much point in trying to recapitulate the work of three trained constables. He settled down to read the files. It was obviously Botting's policy to keep a copy of his most important papers at the flat for a time—for one year it seemed by the sequence of dates. With a trained eye the Inspector read quickly. Botting had interleaved scribbling paper with his own notes in shorthand. He peered and traced over the hieroglyphics with his own pencil. Very imperfect Pitman overlain by bad Dutton. A lot of people never had the patience ever to finish a shorthand course, ending up with a bastard system of their own. He had spent some time at lectures concerning this matter. An expert might translate most of it—providing Botting was always sober when he wrote it—but he could get perhaps thirty per cent. Deceased's opinions of his associates were lurid and crudely expressed. It became obvious to Harry that Botting was manipulating the accounts. 'See Stiggins' the notes frequently said. Then there was the Joshua's Brewery negotiation, with Botting's own meticulous digest of sundry meetings. 'What were the 1939 negotiations? See that stupid effer Smart. Something must have occurred.'

He had filled a dozen pages with his own shorthand before he finished and stretched his cramped back muscles. There was a tape-recorder on its own table. It was switched to 'play' but there was no tape. He consulted the police inventory, none were mentioned. Probably Botting brought tapes from the office, played them and returned them. Nevertheless it worried him. He prowled through the flat. The kitchen was beautifully fitted, Harry thought enviously, and never used. He peered into the big cooker which was as spotless as the day it came from the maker. Over the sink was a rack containing three serving plates.

In the corner was the food lift, but no primitive affair. A white door had set in it a small red light, now dead. He tried it and it resisted his pressure. It obviously only opened when the lift stopped at this particular kitchen. There was a 'breakfast nook' and he thought this was where Botting consumed his grilled dinners. The refrigerator had various soft drinks, a couple of eggs and the remains of a pound of Cheshire cheese.

The wine cupboard, fitted with racks, was in the living-room. It was elaborate and obviously expensive. The Inspector's father had been in the wine trade and he clucked to himself as he looked at the seventy-two (by the inventory) bottles. Some were halves, but all were rare, some uncommercial to the extent that they represented small vignerons whose wares were bespoken by a select handful of customers. The late Cristobal Botting had concentrated upon red burgundies. "My word," gloated the Inspector, looking at one particular hand-written label. But all the time his cold professional eye had taken over command. There was a discrepancy in size, the thick cork floor of the cupboard being about six inches too high above the base. You never knew, Botting might have specified it, but the Inspector reached into his breast pocket for his ingenious little tool kit. He would have to do it the hard way, and he reverently strewed the thick carpet with bottles before unscrewing things. As it turned out the floor was genuine enough except for one small section, three inches high by two feet square. The surface winkled up by means of a small metal insert. It was padded with papers and on top were some two dozen tapes. A shrewd hidey-hole: searchers would get carried away by the wine.

"Stone the crows!" Whichever way you looked at it there was a couple of weeks' work here for one man. He put the bottles back and went back to the workroom with the loot. A thought struck him. Back in the living-room was a small bar and on it he found a half-bottle, opened and recorked, but placed on its side in a wine holder. He knew that burgundies were often stouter creatures than the professionals would admit. He uncorked it and held it to the window light. Only about a third of a glass out of it, strange in itself. There was no evidence of what Botting had done on his last night on earth. He had left Heavans at seven, driving off in his Mercedes. Evidence, but the Inspector looked at the label and weakened. He made his pencil mark at the level of the wine and took it out to the kitchen where he collected the cheese and a plate and a small kitchen glass. He ate and drank as he worked.

No doubt about it, the late Botting had been a consummate scoundrel, though that was a relative word. He thought the motivation might have been power, which often was sanctified whatever the means. His birth was registered on a yellowing certificate clipped to the death registrations of the parents. That was all that was personal. A thousand documents in original or photostat completed the bundle. It was difficult to tell, as background or even addresses were often lacking. But it stood out that here was material for blackmail. No cash information, but a lot of shorthand notes about weaknesses. "A lush, talks around eleven thirty." "Boys under seventeen," "ladies' corsets" and other comments were attached to concrete written evidence.

They'd be sifted, thought Harry, impaled momentarily between the gorgeousness of the cheese and wine and the squalor which his eye perceived, by a small department at the Yard who would duly investigate certain disclosures. It was a kind of unblackmail, not 'Mr. A' in the box, but the exertion of police power. Most of it was statute barred, he thought, or unprovable, in the case of old embezzlements long since covered up. But there was a rape, paid off but possibly resurrectable, and one quite large infringement of the company laws. Grist to the slow grind of God. An elderly Superintendent took such cases and pursued ancient crimes. Many a man who had learned to sleep quietly heard with a start the early morning doorbell.

They were neatly stapled and Inspector Harry James put them and the empty burgundy bottle in his brief-case together with the tapes. The remainder of the cheese went back in the refrigerator and he washed the plate.

"Any luck?" enquired the Manager as Harry returned the key.

"Not a nice man, one fears. However such are the generality of the fish we trawl."

"I did a bit of detection for you as a reward for being a bit politer than the locals. And the thought that you might tone down any publicity."

"Consider it as toned."

"The night before he got it, he was presumably home, but no evidence, right?"

"Quite right."

"Among the luxuries we provide is an occasional attendant at the entrance of the garage area. Sometimes at big parties there can be a jam, so we get a fairly intelligent pensioner, or sometimes two in shifts, to do the traffic control. If I see the cars arriving I go out and get somebody on the roster. The last night he spent here he cleared out at something after midnight but before twelve thirty; he returned at dead on three precisely. The attendant, one of the more intelligent ones, pinpoints it because old Lady Hartletop, who was giving the celebration, was reeling around drunk and thought Mr. Botting was her late uncle. The attendant knew him and thought he looked disturbed; he was an impassive kind of fellow normally."

The Inspector took the attendant's address and left. He drove towards the poorer part of the countryside and found the attendant, comfortable in his shirt-sleeves, seated in his little garden in the sun.

"I make a few bob to help the old pension along by such jobs," he told Harry. "It's easier than gardening and some of the nobs slip you a couple of bob, although I never suggest it. Refusing is another thing with tobacco costing what it does."

Harry offered him his pouch.

"Thanks," the old fellow filled his pipe. "Well there was this old dame Hartletop, fair tanked up and screaming in the horrible way the upper class have when pissed, walking up and down waving as her guests drove off. There were six private cars and seven taxis. The lights were full on and it was brilliantly lit. I held up the outgoing cars for Botting to get in. He just parked his car outside his lock-up garage, I suppose not thinking it worthwhile to take it in, and got out to go into the building. Old Lady Hartletop when she's reached a certain state thinks people are her uncle who perished in the Battle of Jutland. She strides up to Botting—built like a battered old tank is her ladyship—and tries to throw her arms round him. He ducks back and one of her sons grabs the old lady and diverts her attention. But he was fair upset. I'd seen him often, big, stiffly moving man with a great round face and fair hair atop it. He never seemed to register any expression at all. Just looked at you. But he was white, Inspector, and the muscles round his mouth were jerking. I've seen men look like that during the war, when they sensed their time was coming near. And, by God, Mr. Botting's wasn't far away when I seen him."

"That's extremely helpful, sir. Apart from knowing him by sight did you have any opinions about him?"

The old fellow fiddled with his matches. "Thirty-five years in the Army I was, sir, and for the last ten they called me 'the Black Bastard of Northern Command'. It's a tradition, sir, there's always a sergeant who gets the title and the mantle duly fell on yours truly. You get to know men, sir, in that trade and I put Botting down as a wrong 'un. Just on his appearance, Inspector. Somebody once told me that he had difficulty in keeping his hands off the ladies, God bless 'em, but, then, sir, who hasn't?" He stretched stiff legs further into the hot sunlight.

"A tin of tobacco on expenses," the Inspector put a ten-shilling note into his hand and left.

He was annoyed when he went into the office which had once been Botting's to find Sergeant Honeybody absent. The Sergeant's notebook, incongruously neat and finicky, was on the desk. "God damn the fearful old brute," said the Inspector. Cheese and burgundy and sustained mental effort at ten in the morning is a mistake.

From the door the Sergeant's smooth voice made him jump. "Would you please come up to the attic floor, Mr. James?"

The Inspector followed.

"I have come to a little understanding with our co-operative friend Jas Smith," leered the Sergeant as they reached the landing.

"I don't want any more, sir," said Jas, "a man of my age can't stand it."

"I have no idea of what you are talking about," said the Inspector, "except that you want to volunteer help as your bounden duty is."

"Yes, sir." Jas looked a bit grey and the Inspector hoped that Honeybody had not overdone it. They went into Smart's office.

"My nostrils were tickled yesterday," said Honeybody, "while interviewing Mr. Smart. Oil, sir. Three-in-One Penetrating Oil, very efficient stuff. And then, of course, the partition wall is bolted together. In the filing cabinet I found a spanner and a tin of oil. Just watch me. Remember that Mr. Smith saw Smart bending over this filing cabinet!" The Sergeant's left hand worked dexterously. A four-foot section of partition moved a foot away from its neighbour.

"Right," said Honeybody. "He sticks his head in the other room and calls down the lift, and then whoosh, the bottle follows."

"Jesus," wheezed Jas Smith, "who'd have thought the old effer had it in him? And me seeing his arse at the cabinet all the time."

"Here he comes," said Honeybody, listening. "He's been downstairs in the new warehouse."

Mr. Smart looked astounded at his room. The large man with the bushy moustache, Sergeant Honeybody he recalled, a mousy man in a nasty-looking grey suit and Jas Smith.

"My name is Inspector Harry James and you are Mr. Smart. While apologising for taking your chair I must invite you to sit. Honeybody, get him a chair. I may say—and all this can be taken in writing—that you can call a solicitor or if necessary refuse to say anything."

"I don't understand." Mr. Smart sat down.

"And damned if I do." The Inspector smiled and Mr. Smart saw that he was a charmer. "First, what was it that Botting wanted of you—when you went to see him?"

Smart looked hard at Jas Smith.

"Take him on to the landing," said the Inspector.

"He's a bit deaf, but plays a transistor radio while he works," said Honeybody. "Come on, Jas, we'll squat on the stairs and listen to it."

"If you want to make a statement, do so," said the Inspector as the door closed.

"I'm an innocent man," said Smart, a shambling man who watched the Inspector doggedly. "And what have you been doing to my wall?"

"You're an accountant," said the Inspector, "let's proceed

seriatim. I was brought up in the wine trade so I know the jargon."

"Well I'm darned," said Smart and laughed. "I knew your father when I had started out and was the London traveller. I heard years later that his boy had joined the police. Funny, I thought."

The Inspector talked of his father for a few minutes. "And though these personal associations are pleasant, what did Botting want to see you about so urgently the day he died?"

He watched a tongue touch lips. Smart would be a tough adversary, he thought. "Well," the man said, "it's a strange story. It goes back to the thirties when I became a personal assistant to old Mr. Nonsuch Heavan. A strange name and a strange man. He was the last of the 'sane' branch of the family, but, you know," Smart wagged his head, "he was violently eccentric. A good business man, but the shortage of capital was something chronic, Inspector. And business was bad in those days, only our retail shops saved us. Old Nonsuch knew the last of the Joshua family and in short in January, 1939, he borrowed thirty thousand pounds, a fortune then. There was an agreement signed that Joshua or his assigns could at any time buy Heavans for a further payment of sixty-five thousand pounds. Then came the war and everybody drinking all they could get. The loan was repaid in 1945; meanwhile in 1942 Joshua's main office got a direct hit during the day. Old Joshua and his executives all went, plus the files. A rare old mess. That was that. I suppose Nonsuch destroyed his copy of the agreement. As it happened I had the rough copy which they had threshed out—in this very building—and initialled. I showed it to Mr. Botting a month before he died."

"Would it have any validity?"

Smart shrugged. "It fulfilled the requirements of a contract except there was no time clause. That would be a matter for argument. I think that the intention was to tear the thing up after the loan was repaid, but it was a gentleman's agreement. Old Joshua was rather like that, you had to trust his word. I concluded that deceased was plotting to use it to his advantage."

"What did he say?"

Smart gave a small, unpleasant laugh. "It'll be somewhere on tape-recorder. He always had you on tape, one of his less amiable characteristics. He said two things. One that he wanted an affidavit, two that it would mean five thousand cash and the security of a job for life guaranteed by a Board minute. I said I'd think it over. We had various little talks, an expert at pressure was Mr. Botting, and finally I had to see him at noon on the day he died."

"So you removed the problem by dropping a three-litre bottle on his head?"

"Madness."

"We'll see. Perhaps you, sir, will stand at that filing cabinet while I open the door." He looked down the stairs to where Jas Smith and the Sergeant stood. "Get him up the ladder, Sergeant. Right. Now, my man, is that what you saw?" He flattened himself against the wall.

"Yes, sir," said Smith, "Mr. Smart leaning against the filing cabinet. Several times I looked up and saw him."

"Shove him off and caution him to keep his trap shut," said Harry James and watched the Sergeant prod Smith in an avuncular but cautionary way.

As he went back Smart was wiping his wet forehead and looking at the gap in the partition wall. "I had no idea you were that serious, Inspector."

"We found a spanner and a tin of oil in the filing cabinet."

"They were never there to my knowledge," said Smart, rather white. "I had no reason to kill him."

The Inspector shrugged. "Perhaps loyalty to the Heavan family who Botting was plainly planning to gyp. Or else the fact dawned on you that you were the sole possessor of an immensely valuable secret."

"I didn't do it."

"I think I must ask you to accompany me, sir," said Harry formally. He rather liked the chase; the kill always depressed him.

"Only the fact that we have a mutual friend who says you're not too bad prevents me from sitting back and giving Smartie a case for wrongful arrest," said Honeybody. But he was downstairs! The Inspector looked round and there peering through the gap in the wall was a mahogany, cheerful face, heavily moustached, and not Honeybody!

"Christ, George!" said Mr. Smart.

"Half a tick and I'll come round." He was almost a double for Honeybody, thought Harry when he saw him, except he was better dressed with a canary waistcoat and a gold Albert festooned with masonic medals.

"George Rumly, Inspector, one of the travellers." He smelled vaguely vinous. "Perhaps we can all take a pew . . ." he looked around. "All right I'll prop on the cabinet. To cut it short, Inspector, I was all morning in the next room the day the gaffer died. It was like this, I'd got back from Dorset on the Saturday night—I'm a bachelor and I don't hurry home, such as it is. On Sunday there was a convivial gathering. I'd scored a few decentish free samples, perks of the trade, and on the Monday morning, sir, I quite frankly felt like death. Yet corpsed or not Rumly is always up at six ack emma. I passed the watchman as he was going off at seven thirty. Old Joe knows me like a brother and I had a sample quartern of rum as a gift. I went up to the travellers' room. Frankly I thought of conjuring up a few trade ideas and making it an excuse to see Mr. Keast, a man who knows his onions, and that way avoid having to travel. There was nobody else in the room. I sat at the very end, immediately in front of the lift, and got a bottle of Fernet Branca out of my brief-case. I was stunned as a mullet, and that's a fact. What port can do to you it had done to me! My thoughts were on eternity. As it happened I never got the energy to go to see Keast. At twelve, by my watch," he glanced at his brawny wrist, "there was a bloody flap. I got up with my brief-case and went down the stairs. There was a lot of noise and a ladder and whitewash bucket was on the stairs. There seemed to be people on the second floor. But I took the remains of my hangover down and out of the front gate. I think there were people about down in the yard, but I'm just a fixture after seventeen years. I walked to my car, which I'd parked outside not to attract attention, and drove on my way to Devizes. I worked Wiltshire and then, as the details were published, I thought I should come back. I am a man whose spirit is notoriously weak. Or it may be t'other way round. But last night, with the worry of it, there was some conviviality and history repeated itself. I heard you fiddling with that partition wall, but just sat there listening. I beg your pardon because eavesdropping is not my line."

Inspector James looked at him, big, florid and, now he saw him close to, older than Honeybody.

"A relic of the past, Inspector," Rumly read his thoughts, "a survival of the gentlemen of the road—all little cads in Volks today."

"You may have saved me making an ass of myself. I suppose you are certain?"

"I think a jury would believe me," said Rumly with a quiet dignity.

"I should say," said Smart, "that Mr. Rumly is the best in the business of selling wines. Nobody to touch him."

"Botting started the American incentive system," said Rumly jovially, "pep-talks and prizes. I shut my ears and won the prizes. It annoyed the great, red-faced sod. But, believe you me, sir, I could walk out of here and be suited after an hour of telephoning. I stay with Heavans because I get as much as I would elsewhere and Mr. Keast and Mr. Smart are gentlemen, no peering at the expense account. I play fair, so do they."

"Do you know who killed Botting?"

"He was nothing to me," said Rumly. "He ran the firm and that was that. I'm just interested in my massive order sheets and not letting the customer down. Heavans don't let customers down."

"Well," the Inspector got up limply, "I'll send somebody to fix that partition. I'm glad that you're cleared, Mr. Smart, and thank you, Mr. Rumly, for coming to the party."

9

"I wish you had cancelled the party," said Noni in her most bullying way. "It doesn't look right with the police about."

"It's a business party," said Eldred Keast unhappily, "the three-monthly wine tasting. It has nothing to do with us as persons."

"He's right, Noni," rumbled Mark Hanna, a spoonful of cold consommé in mid-air. These Friday dinners of Noni's were a ritual. "Getting the family together," she called it. It was redeemed by the fact that her food, with no expense spared, was outstanding. That the wines were perfect was axiomatic in a Heavan household.

"Business as usual," said Nord, "I can't see we would have made matters better by postponing this do. I suppose we're all going?"

The wine tastings of the House of Heavan were in fact quite famous. Meticulous timing and preparation went into the functions held in the big old kitchen.

"I tested the trade," said Bill Stigg, "discreetly and the wise old heads were in favour of carrying on. Besides we've got three Americans, friends of Botting."

The two maids cleared the table and Mark Hanna served hock as small chickens larded with truffles and steamed over sundry vegetables were served with green peas. For all her bulk, Noni never overdid the quantity. Afterwards, Nord knew, she would go into her dressing-room and wolf sweet biscuits. The chicken was delicious, Noni put a great deal of thought into her meals and a retired chef from the city came in to do the main course.

"I note you didn't invite Nigel," said Keast.

"He's hardly family, not really, and I'm afraid it's going to be embarrassing to the children. Madness is such a problem." Noni was visibly restraining herself at the chicken.

"And yet," said Hanna, "Nefer looked pretty thick with him and Harold Stiggins Esquire this morning. Want to tell us about it, Nefer?"

It was Bill Stigg who turned red. Nefer said with perfect composure, "Nigel, with his shares, wants Stiggins as Chairman. After all, my dear, we must get along with him. It seems best to agree."

"I see," said Keast and there was a nasty little silence.

"If you can't beat 'em join 'em," said Nefer.

"A slogan much favoured by Hitler," said Keast, his pale face set. "He got some important members on that line of theory."

"Now, Eldred," said Noni, hesitant, "we must keep a united camp. This Stiggins is well qualified to keep the books."

"I thought I'd join the Board," said Nefer, quietly. "I think I can deal with Master Stiggins."

"A good idea," said Noni. "I have the children and so has Nord and you're good at figures."

Mark Hanna was looking as if he would choke. "Do I understand," he said heavily, "that it is agreed that we put this little cockney upstart into the driver's seat?"

As usual at such crises his wife looked at him as if she did not really see him. "It seems to me that it's the kind of world where you have to have 'em. I always remember grandpa's chauffeur, a vile little man, but, my God, could he drive and do all repairs, saving a mint of money in the process."

"This is not a bloody car," said Mark Hanna.

"No difference really," said Noni. "This chicken is really delicious and you know the truffles come from Africa? I never knew they grew out of France. A disgusting price, but I dare say the natives have grown cunning."

"They do grow practically everywhere," said Nord, "except in urbanised areas or where they cut down the trees. What did you pay?"

"Three pounds for thirteen ounces and the man said he was robbing himself. You won't find me serving them often."

"Did you ever have them egg and breadcrumbed and fried?" asked Nefer.

Mark Hanna deliberately put down his knife and fork and pushed his plate away. "I suppose as a corollary Bill will take over the Managing Directorship?"

"That's what Nigel seems to want," said Nefer demurely.

"I want all of you to pull together for the good of the family," said Noni. "My two sons will be coming into the business in a few years, and I hope Nord's will be shoulder to shoulder with them. We must think ahead. Do finish your chicken, Mark, after all they were three pounds, the truffles, I mean."

The three men were silent. A pity, thought Nord. Eldred's position meant little to her. His sons might join the firm—she rather thought not, envisaging potential barristers—but basically

98

Eldred was too slothful to do more than the limited and excellent job he did. There was nobody more charming than Eldred; his mind enabled him to get on with almost anybody.

Noni, who had a fabulous hand with pastry even in the heat, had made an apple pie, superb in its simplicity. She handed round portions. The men looked at theirs as though it poisoned them.

"Well," said Hanna, his eyes flashing, "I suppose we should ask our new Managing Director to propose a grace upon our vittles."

"Don't be unpleasant, Mark," said Nefer. "Noni's right. We have to stick together in troubled waters. We all benefit, and we have the power, if we play it right, to control events."

"I do wish you'd eat your pie, Mark," said Noni, "making pastry in the hot weather isn't fun."

"Bugger the pastry!" said her husband. "Bugger the pastry!"

Noni's face flushed, but calmed as she heard the entry of the Spanish maid. "What is it, Juana?"

She took the pasteboard square in her hand, but almost immediately Harold Stiggins appeared in the doorway.

"I must apologise for this intrusion, Mrs. Hanna, but there it is, business waits for nobody and knowing of your weekly functions, but thinking it would be over, I've risked pushing myself in, if you'll excuse it."

"Do you like apple pie?" Noni's great face was impassive.

"Dote, Mrs. Hanna. It's not often you get a prime one today, but don't put yourself out."

"Another chair, Juana. Appetites are a bit pickish today, Mr. Stiggins, but I am proud of our apple pie. We're having some old Malaga with it. But perhaps it is too sweet for your tooth."

"To tell the truth, Mrs. Hanna," said Stiggins, helping the maid with the chair, "I shall have to rely upon these gentlemen for the connoisseur bit. You need education to talk the language which I can't talk. But an account book now, I can make one of those sing, and I quite understand my function. Thank you." He calmly ate the pie with apparent relish.

"Are you going to serve coffee, my dear?" said Mark with poisonous politeness. "If not I think I shall leave."

"It will be served in a minute," said Noni, "and I wish you would stay."

"Delicious, Mrs. Hanna," said Stiggins. "My old mother had a light hand with the pastry; it's inherited, I believe, because the wife hasn't got it."

"It's something to do with the acidity of the hands," said Nefer.

"Delicious!" Stiggins ate with neat rapidity. A maid brought in the coffee.

"Brandy is over on the sideboard," said Noni. Her husband fetched it and poured.

"This is nothing to me," said Stiggins, "I'll have to rely on you fellows for the chi-chi."

Keast winced. "I suppose that it is all settled, in which case we have nothing much to talk about."

"A pity Nigel's not here, so that we can get it settled once and for all," said Stiggins, his wizened face looking at them in turn. "I know it's repugnant to you gentlemen, but you do have to have a financial captain of your ship. And I make no stipulations except that we'll have ruthless retrenchments. Heads will fall, as they have to, people like old Smart and George Rumly."

"Rumly is the best traveller in the business," said Keast.

"You can't stay behind the times, Eldred," said Stiggins. "A great old-timer no doubt, but it costs money to keep him on the road. A boy at eighteen nicker and a firm's car would make the calls. If you look at it coldly you'll see it my way. They either buy the wine or they don't. The personality sales, which people like Rumly make, aren't worth the price when you analyse in depth. Sorry! Botting had the right idea about brand advertising, though, much as it draws a tooth. Don't worry, I'll have extended figures within a week."

"So it is all settled?" said Keast.

"We'll have to have a general meeting," said Stiggins, "in fifteen days' time. I had notices posted to all shareholders before I left the office. We'll have to get another Secretary, but that's no trouble. There's a young colt I know with the qualifications who'll do it cheap because of the experience."

"I think we had better be getting back to the office," said

Keast. "Bill and Mark can come with me, and Nefer can drop Nord."

Mark Hanna got to his feet, but Bill Stigg remained seated. "If you don't mind I'll stay on. Harold will drive me in."

Hanna and Keast walked out to the Fiat which Keast had had tailored to his height.

"We're at the mercy of that little sod." Mark Hanna always intoned the obvious.

"He can be worked," said Keast, "at least for a time. He'll be as sweet as *Malaga Virgen* for, I'd say, two years, by which time his fangs will grow."

"It's being pushed around by them that rankles," said Mark. "You don't notice them for years and suddenly you feel them breathing in your face."

"Indeed. I think it was Hume who made some similar remark." Hanna's large eyes swivelled in disgust. It was this kind of remark which made him uneasy in Keast's presence.

In his unease Hanna made a step which he had not anticipated. "There's a fellow in the cellar who sticks the labels on: he braced me yesterday afternoon in a sly way, saying how loyal he was and how the chats we had down there were sacrosanct."

"Christ," said Keast, and felt the wheel jump in his hand.

"It's all right," said his brother-in-law, "I slipped him ten. Just an old drunk."

Keast bit back what came to his tongue. A quarter of a mile passed by. "Do you mean the old fellow named Percival Somebody who works with the bottlers?"

"That's him."

Keast eased his foot on the accelerator. "He'd better be retired on a good pension. Of course, that's an early delivery into Stiggins' hands. But the quicker the better. You can't trust a drunk with a secret. For God's sake *we* of all people know that."

"Oh, he's all right and who would listen to an old soak?"

"The police will listen to anyone, oh, let's forget it," said Keast.

"I thought you might say that." Hanna flicked sideways his great black eyes.

"I don't think we should talk like this," said Keast, "it's not wisdom or joy."

"I suppose Bill didn't do it," said Hanna. "Convenient if he did."

"We were all out of the room at various times," said Keast, patiently. "We agreed for convenience to say that we were not."

"But if Bill did, how convenient."

"Now listen," said Keast, "it's Nefer who owns the shares. Putting Bill away would solve nothing."

"I suppose you didn't do it, Eldred? After all you were through Staff College!"

"Mark, do not be a fool. Keep your nerve for God's sake."

"Somebody did it," said Hanna. "If we put Bill up for it he'd get acquitted, but it would take the pressure off us."

"He went out of the office three times," said Keast, "but you see, Mark, it is a question of one in, all in. And Nefer is the largest shareholder after Nigel."

"Did you hear the parrot-faced little swine calling him 'Nigel'?" growled Hanna. "Next time he'll be patting my shoulder like Botting used to."

"And you must put up with it." Keast was barely moving the car along, tucked into the side of the lane-way. "I'm very serious about this, Mark. Shut up and soldier on."

"If you say so, I suppose I must," said Hanna discontentedly. "But I wish to God those policemen were out of the premises, I assure you. I slept bloody badly last night."

"Mark," said Keast carefully, "we've known each other these twenty-five years. If you want to tell me anything . . ."

"Good God, no!"

"Then let's keep our mouths closed." Keast accelerated and drove into the yard at Heavans. "That is the Inspector fellow, the insignificant chap. The big man is a Sergeant."

They got out of the car and Inspector James walked towards them and introduced himself. "I wondered if we could have a chat, gentlemen. That is my Sergeant, by the way, Mr. Honeybody."

Hanna wasn't too bad about meeting people with official titles, thought Keast. He boomed a greeting, but Keast saw the shrewd, calculating appraisal in the Sergeant's eyes.

"I blundered into your Boardroom, I'm afraid, sir, and renew the apologising. But it is difficult, you know. We constantly go into new premises and a man gets foxed in remembering where is where."

"Where do you want to go?" asked Keast.

"I'm working, thanks to your courtesy, gentlemen," said the Inspector, "in the office in which the late Mr. Botting died. It is isolated, and we perhaps might sojourn."

"Suits me," said Keast quickly. Mark Hanna was throwing back his head in the old familiar truculent gesture which presaged blustering panic. "We have a party on this evening and though it's organised, I have a few things to do."

"Won't take too long," said the Inspector and led the way, Honeybody in the rear. "I expect you know this office," he said as he seated himself behind the desk.

"Not well," said Keast. "These offices are tacitly our private hide-aways, for the odd think and planning."

"Are all the offices equipped with safes?" The Inspector had removed the solitary painting and the wall safe stood open.

"I didn't know he had one," said Hanna.

"I had better make my position a bit clear," said the Inspector. "My father was in the wine trade and I have some knowledge of accountancy. In fact your Mr. Smart knew my father; and I'm quite sure that this safe would be known to both you gentlemen. Structural installations would have to have been approved at fairly high level for one thing."

"I knew it," said Keast.

"I had forgotten," said Hanna.

"Mr. Smart, who found deceased at midday, also found the safe open. The key chain had presumably been removed from the button on Mr. Botting's trousers."

"We don't seem to be getting anywhere," said Keast.

"God!" Mark Hanna jumped in his chair. From the lift-well came a dim croaking sound and then a crash.

"Sit still, nothing to worry about," said the Inspector. "My Sergeant merely shouted my name down the lift shaft and dropped a quart bottle, the largest we could lay our hands on, after it. Two things emerge. One is that anything shouted from the top floor is inaudible here except as a vague noise, the second is that a bottle makes a devil of a noise dropping down. Facts, gentlemen, for we in the police are all Gradgrinds. There was a traveller up on the top floor getting through a hangover, one George Rumly who swears the top opening was not used. On the stairs below the top landing was one Jasper Smith whitewashing away. So I conclude that the third floor aperture was used."

"Can you hear me, Harry?" howled Honeybody's voice. "I am now speaking from the third floor, just above you."

"Clearly." The Inspector lowered his head and spoke into the shaft. "Can the constable hear you on the top floor?"

There was a pause. "No, sir," bawled the voice. "Just a confused noise he reports. But I've got my head right into the shaft and am speaking directly down. To drop a bottle I'd have to withdraw my noggin. Stick your head in Mr. James, if you don't mind."

The Inspector did. It was like looking down a chimney.

"I can see the shape of your head quite clearly." Sergeant Honeybody's voice ricocheted around the passage. "You slightly turn your head, as he did, and then I drop the bottle."

"That appears to be how that killing was committed," said the Inspector as he resumed his desk. "I suppose it was one of you gentlemen or Mr. Stigg who came into this office, saw that he was dead, took his key ring off the special button he had sewn to his trousers and opened the safe."

"Unwarrantable," whinnied Mark Hanna. "Disgraceful. I'll have the coat off your back."

"I do wish you would spare me the clothing clichés," said the Inspector. "I hear that particular one fifty times a year. You will notice that albeit sweatily and uncomfortably I am still adorned by a coat."

"There isn't any need to be truculent," said Hanna.

"Mr. Hanna, these wretched cases are always sordid. There is no romance in murder. In the case of the late Cristobal Botting the motive was almost certainly pecuniary, as it so often is. He represented a financial threat to someone. And I have no doubt that one of you gentlemen came up here possibly by chance and took tapes out of that safe. Three resourceful men with Service backgrounds. You wouldn't scream at a corpse, seen too many in your time."

Mark Hanna looked complacent. The bloody fool, thought Keast.

"We did not do such a thing," said Keast.

"I have sent a man out—we got four other chaps down this morning—to intercept Mr. Bill Stigg," said the Inspector smoothly. "I have no doubt that he will confirm your story of being together. I must admit that there is some evidence that you all left at various times to relieve yourself. The bladder, gentlemen, is a notorious difficulty in evidence. However . . ."

"It's not unlikely that three men of our age can sit down for four hours without micturating," said Keast.

"I am sorry to harp on it—I understand that stringed instruments are de trop in these premises?"

"Nigel is cured," said Hanna. "No nonsense about stringed instruments—or so he says."

"I got a warrant, I'm afraid," said the Inspector, "to search the room in his pub. There was a curiously maltreated piece of tape. Oh, it was illegible." He saw the relief on Mark Hanna's face. "But—I'm afraid police work is full of that word—deceased was a man who re-recorded. He always took another tape off any important one. I have two men with a small pile of them taking jump-samples. There is one piece concerning his demand for you to resign your directorships."

"That," said Keast, "was half a joke. Nevertheless I don't think we should discuss it. It was a private, privileged matter."

"If you have anything to say to me," said the Inspector, "now might be the time. I must say that it was a nasty-sounding kind of interview and I'm interested to know when it was recorded. I think that the original was taken from that safe soon after his death or in the confusion after Smart's alarm. He took the precaution of secreting copies. Perhaps you know that he was a blackmailer, although not for money."

"Goddamn his soul," said Mark Hanna.

"We keep free from theology," said the Inspector. "Evidence

points to the fact that somebody went into the room immediately above this, bellowed down to Botting and then dropped the bottle. It killed him. I suppose that if it hadn't the killer would have finished him off when he came down the stairs. Do you see what all this means?"

"The floor above has all the display junk," said Hanna. "You've no idea what we get sent to us in a year. Two bloody great plastic horses, non-deflatable, came in last week. And there's our own window-dressing stuff, artificial bottles, etcetera. There are no locks on the doors that I remember."

"You seem to have a poor memory for locks, sir. There is in fact a lock of an old and childish kind which personally took me all of one minute to open."

"You had not permission to do that," said Mark Hanna.

"You must see your solicitor, or go to the local police station, sir, if you wish to complain. There are appropriate forms. I unlocked it as had the local police before me. A path had been cleared through the junk to the lift aperture."

"It would be used quite regularly," said Keast. "I suppose that if there is a key Smart would have it."

"Well, that's it if you have no further comment regarding the tape-recording."

"I'm afraid Mr. Botting misconstrued quite an ordinary business deal," said Keast.

"I suppose you *did* resign your directorships?"

"We are still Directors," said Hanna.

Keast said smoothly, "That's misdirection, old chap. We did resign, Inspector, for we were all fed up with poor Botting. We obviously could not stop him selling to Joshua's Ales as he held Nigel Heavan's proxies, so we decided to bow out."

"All right," said the Inspector, "and thank you."

They had barely gone when Honeybody came through the door. "You must have hit them hard," he said, "from the way they looked."

"Sit down. They must have stood to lose a lot if their directorships went. I'll have to find who the blasted family solicitor is. Or else this man Stiggins should know."

"He's a curious character," said the Sergeant. "The boys have

106

been doing a bloody good job, sir, with the bumf steadily mounting up." He took a pile of flimsy red paper out of a brief-case and put it on his side of the table.

"There was a complaint about one Harold Stiggins, living in Kentish Town, eighteen years ago," grunted Honeybody. "He apparently owned and operated a part-time business which folded up—a company so he wasn't responsible, but the receiver didn't like the smell of things. We got nowhere during one interview with Stiggins. The file was annotated that it was a bucket-shop operation of the unprovable variety, but Stiggins never came on any file again. As for Botting, there never was anything against him, not even a driving offence. But there is just one cross-index item, thanks to the new computer. Listen to this: an illegal bookmaker named Georgie Krock—he paid no tax and gave better odds in consequence—was found dead in his flat in Walworth. He was at a Casino and complained of feeling ill so returned home unexpectedly. Somebody bashed in his right temple with what was probably a spanner. No clue to what was taken, but it was known that Krock could pay out a couple of thousand in greasy notes if necessary and think nothing much of it. But he had an accountant, on a part-time basis, one Harold Stiggins; absolutely no suggestion that Stiggins did anything else in connection with the business other than figure-work. Stiggins was questioned. On the evening when it occurred he was at the flat of the sales manager of the firm where he worked as accountant. The manager was one Cristobal Botting. There were no other witnesses. The local boys finally filed the whole thing. Botting was a reputable up-and-coming company man, so was Stiggins. However there was evidence that rubber gloves had been used about the flat. And, of course, in Krock's complicated business only he and the accountant would know the cash balance at any one time."

"Who was 'on' it?"

"Porterman," the Sergeant mentioned a heavy, methodical Superintendent, "though he was Inspector then. I phoned through to him—he's got that death-and-mutilation up at Manchester—and he says that Stiggins struck him as pretty well a nonentity, but that Botting was a real charmer. He didn't think they were implicated. Deceased had a lot of nasty little irons out—he lent money to a lot of the hard boys around Warren Street."

"It would have been nice if it was him," sighed Harry. "What else?"

"P.C. Crote stopped Bill Stigg as he was leaving the house of Mr. and Mrs. Hanna. He asked three questions. Did any of them leave their meeting the day Botting died? Answer, no. Did he know of the existence of a tape-recording in which Botting collectively threatened them? Negative. What were they talking about at the meeting anyway? Answer, the importation of six million litres of sherry. That is a lot, isn't it?"

"About fourteen million bottles—a lot of money to tie up, but not a record shipment. They were obviously going through the motions of working to the last."

"Nothing else you don't know except that Eldred Keast went to Staff College and is the brainy one of that lot. Brainy but very easy-going is the verdict, none of the greatly-loved killer spirit that makes Empah builders. He stopped a packet in Malaya and went into his wife's family business. He gets on with people very well. He is also a fearful snob, but there we are it's a harmless vice compared with some."

"And therefore the kind of man who would detest Botting, with the kind of brain to manipulate an affair like this."

"He does not look like a killer," said the Sergeant. "Too civilised, I think, except for poison and it wasn't done that way."

"Pity," said Harry, "there are plenty of opportunities here for poisoning anybody over a drink."

10

"WE MIGHT PUMP him over a friendly drink," suggested Mark Hanna. The three Directors were in his office. "Perhaps a few quid, eh?"

"I have had some experience of bribery," said Eldred Keast, "and that fellow is not bribable. But no harm in inviting him—

oh, and that fat flunkey of his—to the tasting. Just one minute," he dialled the desk telephone. "Inspector James? This is Keast. We had omitted to ask you and the Sergeant to the wine-tasting—some rather interesting hocks. It's at seven in the big kitchen, just downstairs from you."

He replaced the hand set. "They'll come, both having a bit of a thirst if I'm a judge. The Inspector says he knows wine—you, Bill, look after him. He gets the best. I'll take the Sergeant, he being a simple sort of fellow. But for God's sake let me do any pumping. I repeat, I do the pumping."

"I was in Intelligence in Cairo," said Hanna.

"If I remember aright it was only Hitler's incredulity that you would send out all that stuff uncoded that saved us."

Stigg looked embarrassed, but Hanna rolled his black eyes and laughed. "I picked my man, didn't I? You are a bastard, you know!"

"Been together nigh on thirty years," said Keast. "Look, this solicitor I phoned is an old pal and I put it on the line which embarrassed him. Will this Inspector or his merry men put us in with the Income Tax or not?"

"And secret commissions," bleated Bill Stigg.

"They are very hard to prove," said Keast grimly, "especially as we are the only surviving Directors. We shall have to cut Stiggins in, but that's for tomorrow."

"I was thinking of that doped wine Botting used to turn out," said Hanna. "Why shouldn't we keep on with it? I thought of going over tomorrow and taking a look at it."

"If I know the late Botting he'd knock the top off the casks and put the goo in himself," said Keast. "We'd need a chemist and once you start enlarging the operation laterally God knows where it would end. You'll have to clean that up, Mark, discontinue the line I suppose, or see if you can do it on price with genuine wine. Oh, here we go." He took up the telephone. Eventually he put it down and sighed. "An old friendship blighted, gentlemen. It'll never be quite the same again. He says that in practice the police do not notify the Treasury of income-tax evasion. Neither do the Treasury solicit information from or give it to the police. Cynically, the Treasury will take tax from crooks who declare their income, and the wise ones partly do, and on balance the tax men feel they have more to lose than to gain. Both sides are pretty touchy."

"But there is always the little informer," said Stigg.

"There is, Bill," said Keast, gently, "but the information so gathered is fairly low-line. The Inspector in charge here, according to my friend, is on the list for a Chief Inspectorship. I think we shall forget it. We will just be very nice to the police in an officer-and-gentlemanly way. Which brings us to the ostensible purpose of this exercise, the final touching-up of the party."

The catering was generally left to Stigg, who was good at this kind of organisation, the actual provisions being left to the pub opposite. The food at Heavans was always expensive, lavish and cold. Twelve varieties of pâtés and terrines had been flown refrigerated from Bordeaux yesterday, the twenty cheeses had come from London by van, and the cooked frogs' legs had duly arrived at London airport and were presumably on their way. Peaches, grapes and passion fruit lay in the kitchen in the gentle embrace of the turned-down refrigerator. The waitresses, engaged by old Mrs. Frankly, the head lady bottler, who though vinous knew her stuff, would be encased in crisp uniforms, the two men chuckers-out—rarely used—would be in the alcove behind the kitchen with the china bin into which people looking bad were invited to spew.

All this Stigg explained.

"The cars all right?"

"At the airport now. I thought we'd see there could be no possible recurrence of that unfortunate happening last year . . ."

An elderly wine-writer had been left marooned and subsequently arrested by the airport police for being drunk and disorderly on airport gin.

"Well, we can leave it to you, Bill," said Keast. "I suppose the tinned stuff is on hand in case the frogs' legs go astray?"

Bill Stigg looked a trifle surly. "I'll check. Smart was fixing it with Fortnum's."

They watched him go out.

"I find it appalling to envisage him as Managing Director," said Hanna. "You saw how he was looking?"

"He must look how he wishes, Mark. If we go on like this I'm sure there will be gross unpleasantness. I mean that if we push young Bill too much . . ."

"I hadn't thought along those lines."

"If it was Bill by himself I might suggest remedial action, but Nigel has aligned himself. And there's the problem of Nefer. Dear, oh, dear. At least Bill denied everything to the policeman."

"So he says," growled Hanna.

"But was telling the truth, I think. At least to us he was. Including the agenda bit about the sherry which is documented."

"D'you think he did it?"

"Nefer is tiring of him. I know her form. But we must not talk like that ever, Mark. We both decided that some years ago. Our position . . ." He shrugged.

Hanna wriggled in his chair. "We'd better get ready to put a good front on things, though I'm dammed if I feel like a tasting. Oh, Christ!"

"Hope I don't intrude, fellows." Stiggins peered round the door. "I glimpsed Bill going into the landscape, but thought you fellows might be here. I'll take a pew. Just as well that young Bill isn't here in a way. We old-heads will have to guide him." Stiggins gazed pleasantly around. "And suppose you call me Harold? Nobody ever said 'Harry', not even the wife though I don't know for why."

"We'd just run over the details of the tasting, Harold," said Keast. "It's an important one because we must get into a masterful position in the middle range of hock, which is a bloody battlefield."

"I know the figures and would as soon be out of hock," punned Stiggins. "It is branded lines in a big way we must be after. Oh, we'll keep the chi-chi part as long as it turns in a passable percentage. I hope we think alike."

"We're interested in the money," said Mark Hanna.

"I shall operate along those lines. There's been a bit of the old tickle, hasn't there? Funny business," he added as he saw Hanna's blank face. "No, no, not now, but I must know it all from the start. You won't find me shy away from a tickle. I knew there was, you know, because I really used to do Botty's close-figure work. If I may say so it wasn't too clever. In fact it gave me a bit of trouble once with an ambitious young audit clerk who

111

wanted to know why we paid more than open market price for some things. But that's forgotten, eh? All sweetness and light."

"I think we shall have a good association," said Keast.

The little man's hard, questing eyes looked at them in turn. "And Mr. Nigel. I'd like us to have clear thinking about him. The sooner he's bought out the better, quite frankly. It does a company no good to have a stigma. But for the present I have these figures for your scrutiny."

Stiggins picked up his small flat leather carrier, opened it and talked for three-quarters of an hour.

What he said was solid sense. Mark Hanna admitted it, Keast concurred.

"So," said Stiggins, at length packing himself up, "we shall get along, although there will be unpleasantness." He paused.

Keast looked at Hanna and said nothing.

"The ladies, God bless them," said Stiggins, awaited an answer for a second and then gathered his things. "My own lady has come in with fresh clobber and I'll be in the changing-room."

They watched him go. "On the whole," said Hanna with pompous satisfaction, "we shall find him a useful blade."

"The cleanest sword in Europe," said Keast, and Hanna ogled him with bemused suspicion.

You really could do nothing with Mark, thought Keast wearily. He really wished he had nothing to do with it, just sat still and took the money. However, one was constantly forced into doing something positive by some cursed economic law which he was too tired to remember. "We'd better go and change," he said.

The changing-room, which contained three showers and toilets plus half a dozen metal wardrobes, had been one of Botting's innovations. He had been a man who was incessantly washing himself, so that Keast had wondered how much human skin could take. But the room was handy for quick changes on sweaty days or when evening dress was unexpectedly needed. He noticed with distaste that like most small men with bandy legs Stiggins favoured long, vividly stripped underpants. He looked like a comedian's version of a jockey as he hummed to himself and climbed into his black dress trousers. Keast got quickly into the shower. When he came out Stiggins was bent before the platform on which the boot

112

polishing equipment rested. "I'm quite looking forward to the 'do', you know," he called. "Botty would never invite me, but I'm looking forward to talking turkey with some of the trade."

Keast chose his white, tropical evening jacket. "Most of them are fancy dans, the innumerable writers and editors who pimp on the food and wine trades. Then there are the people who come because they can consume, with any shrewdness, stuff worth a tenner at a restaurant. The remainder come because they're friends within the trade and we go to their shows. Sometimes I think it's a waste of money. I advise you to stick to the special wine the waitress will serve you; it has the minimum alcoholic content. Some of the others are pretty strong." He dressed quickly and expertly, noting that Stiggins would finish up like something out of a tailor's window. They ended up dressed together, probably by design on Stiggins' part. Hanna was singing in the shower, funking it as usual.

They went into the kitchen where Bill Stigg, at his best, was welcoming the earlier visitors, the ones with a thirst and a capacity for food. Stigg had done his usual thorough job, the old tables groaned under the load of food—the local hotel manager presiding —and the trim waitresses saucily offered dry sherry, their neat little buttocks dimly appraised by the heavy-eyed arrivals.

Keast patted shoulders, kissing an old hag who wrote articles, and saw the plentiful moustaches of the police sergeant whom he claimed in the old two-handed shake. He introduced Stiggins to a couple of earnest men, waved to his wife who was entertaining a woman from one of the glossies, and stood before the Sergeant.

"I hope you are a judge of wine."

"A lot of people it has been my sad duty to pull in have been, Mr. Keast. The man in Dorset who buried children alive—not so long ago though people may have forgotten—was a rare Bordeaux man. I cracked a bottle with him three days before he was arrested. Most hospitable he was and with one of the neatest wine bins I've seen. A poor policeman learns, so to speak, a lot of upper-class vices. I'm afraid I could shock all these ladies and gentlemen, sir. Thank you, I will join you, sir," the Sergeant detached another sherry. "I understand it's mainly hock tonight. Very choice, although I prefer the reds in the usual way."

113

"Some pâté . . . we rather pride ourselves . . ."

"I had a bit, sir, and if I may say the modern way of serving it refrigerated is sadly mistaken. It started as farmhouse cookery, Mr. Keast, when refrigeration hadn't been invented over in Australia."

"I'll make a note of that," said Keast. "I'm sorry you don't like our catering."

"Thanks, I'll switch to hock," said Honeybody as a waitress passed. "It has a funny kind of buzzing feeling over the tongue I always think. We have, you know, to rub against money in our type of work and the better type of crooks always live well. God bless us, why would anybody steal except to have frogs' legs in aspic?"

This was not the conversation he had planned, thought Keast. He chose the light retort. "Women?"

"I never knew a good crook who didn't get it for nothing, sir," said the Sergeant, spearing a hunk of terrine from a passing tray. "It costs them very little, sir."

It was becoming a nightmare to Keast. He supposed it was because he had no authority. Power of life and death, exercised wisely, had he had in his time over sergeants; many a time had he reminisced with them over a condescending drink, but this one was a uncontrollable rogue elephant. A Sergeant who, he suspected, knew his hocks!

"I suppose you're getting along with the case," he ventured.

"That little fellow, my Inspector, who is drinking with Mr. Stigg" (as the Sergeant said it Keast saw that Stigg was being voluble), "well, Mr. Keast, he is as brainy a little bastard in his way as you'll find. It is a business when you get down to it of getting things in mathematical sequence, then it becomes clear. He is a great man for getting convictions in cases of violence. Do you think I might have more of the pâté?"

If Keast thought himself impaled, the more so did Bill Stigg who had taken to resting his weight on one leg. His gambit, "I suppose you'll be making some clear-up in the unfortunate business," had interrupted the Inspector's frown at the pâté. Saturated before cooking in lard and cheap cognac, the Inspector had been cogitating in gloom; and by God he thought that the unfortunate herb, oregano, had been added. Why they couldn't leave the stuff to spaghetti cooks he could not imagine.

"Clear-up," he said absently, "you mean arrest? Of course. I always arrest somebody, what the hell do you think they pay me for? No arrests and there's no promotion."

"But wrong men!"

"Mr. Stigg, I have no doubt that innocent men are now languishing in long-term prisons. You must surely know that the British law implicitly does not declare innocence? It hands down a judgment, sir, including 'not guilty'. I think innocent men have been hanged. There are some on positive record. It is nothing to do with me. I'll have this terrine, miss." It was much better than the pâté he had tasted.

"This is terrible," said Stigg.

"Good, I thought. It's the bacon and preserved goose that gives it the flavour." The Inspector munched.

"I mean about innocent men . . . "

"I like the sherry. God bless you, sir, we are all partly surrounded by tigers. A million to one you'll never be badly bitten, so perk up."

"It's never mentioned in the press."

"Among all the atrocities at their disposal they don't have to bother about prisons. Horrors are ready made and easy to photograph in so many places. Why bother with some poor devil who gets his titties caught in the high-powered mangle?"

"You're pulling my leg!"

"I wish I were, sir. I must say those cheeses look a bit sweaty. I suppose you haven't kept them with a vinegar-saturated cloth over them. Then let them breathe for about an hour. Nothing like it. And I am not at all happy with your statements, sir. Not happy at all."

The Inspector winced as a finger prodded him in his kidneys.

"I know from his look that you are bullying poor Bill." Nefer had tried to look elegant but had ended up, very attractively, looking fluffy.

"I was merely offering to put innocent men away for forty years."

"God, he'd be old!" Nefer's huge eyes widened until they became enormous.

"It's caddish," said the Inspector, "to leave a man alone with his lawful wife. Hell, you see *lawful* becomes ingrained in us. But I should do a bit of polite sleuthing—and wenching."

"In the line of duty," cooed Nefer.

"As I tell my wife." The Inspector bowed and moved away. It was the night of the heavy guns, he thought, as a very beautiful elegant woman bore down on him. It would be Nord Keast, he thought.

"Inspector James," she said, "I have read about your cases. It's thrilling to see you in person."

"I'll get some more of that terrine," said the Inspector, "because I meet lovely women quite a lot but a good terrine is hard to come by."

"I'll get the private-bin hock," said Nord. "Because I meet a lot of nice little men but the private-bin is really something. We even ration it among the family."

They found a small table and Nord dimpled at the Inspector. A very nice piece, thought Harry. "Now what do you want out of the pump, ma'am?" he said after one sip. Fifteen quid a bottle—if you could buy it, he decided. "After this kind of priming I can only be truthful."

"It's just that I don't like this hanging over all of us. Who did it? Was it Nigel?"

"Whenever I eavesdrop," said Nigel, who had come up behind them, "I hear people ask that question. Cannot an ex-madman have charity, dear Nord? After all Keast was trained as a professional killer. Didn't he head some special squad who got through the lines and decimated enemy hierarchy?"

"I have to think of the children, Nigel."

"Sorry," he said in his basso. He had some kind of charm woven into his rather weird face.

"I'm Inspector Harry James."

"Oh, in the end they used to allow me my *News of the World* in the silly house. You got the bloke who murdered that old solicitor. Pity he got off on appeal. Though solicitors are such

116

a tricky lot. From my reading they do more than their fair share of murder."

"They do tend to think of the money angle, which can be a powerful temptation."

"Well," said Nigel, "I had no pecuniary motive, that is for sure."

"To get back to Mrs. Keast's question, I do not know who the murderer was, but I think I know the way to find out. I should arrest somebody tomorrow, the way things are going. The trouble is that so many people could have killed him."

"You haven't finger-printed us," said Nord.

"There were no relevant finger-prints," said the Inspector. "Finger-printing is nowadays a form of identification. It is very rare that it solves a murder. Regarding your husband, if you will excuse me, it doesn't seem to me that on known form passing Staff College helps in the case of planning anything complex, which this was. Your husband is not Northern Irish is he?"

"A local boy," said Nigel.

"He's very clever," said Nord, bristling.

"Do I take it that you are accusing him of murder?"

"You are a swine, as I was told." Nord took her glass up and walked away.

"You have annoyed her," said Nigel. "In many ways she's the best of the bunch. So is Keast in a human way, although completely selfish. I see that your myrmidons searched my room, by the way, and took away that braised piece of tape. I went to the Keast house and found Stigg, Keast and fat Hanna apparently burning it. You see, I come clean. I thought they were fiddling, or had been, and that Botting had caught them with their fingers in the till."

"It was something like that," said the Inspector.

"I've got the biggest stake in this business, Inspector, and I don't mind. When you have money people get at you and you've got to learn to roll with the punch and balance things out. Better a dishonest genius than an honest idiot. Old Nonsuch Heavan as good as told me that when he engaged Botting. Anyway those three fellows are utterly dependent on their wives. It must rile a fellow to be in that position. And Mark gambles, Bill likes a pretty lady, and Eldred"—he went and got a glass of hock for the Inspector and a ginger ale for himself. "Maniacs, ex and all, should not drink take. Where were we? Oh, yes, Eldred. He would not be happy if he had not a private hoard. A kind of affront to his masculinity. I can't understand it, but then I never have had to."

"I'd love to be a kept man," said Harry. "At the moment my wife is in hospital being confined. All I can see is school fees. I suppose that if you are kept *she* pays the school fees."

"I think he did it," said Nigel. "The other two are too stupid."

"What about the women?"

"You are a better judge than me. Noni would defend her own if it came to it. But I must push off and be amiable. I see a few ogling eyes directed at the maniac."

The Inspector watched the burly figure walk away. That was the end of the special bin! He went and filled a plate with frogs' legs, Italian bread and Irish butter.

"Beautiful grub, Mr. James." It was, almost inevitably, Sergeant Honeybody. "And did you by chance try the private-bin hock? Mr. Keast introduced me to it and I took the precaution of nobbling the bottle. Allow me to fill you up. Young lady, I wonder if you'd bring us a generous plate of froggies so that we don't have to exercise our poor old legs?" The Sergeant had a way with waitresses in a rather horrid avuncular manner. He put the bottle on the table. "The labeller, Percival, has been under surveillance. He must have made a tickle because it was three double Scotches at the pub over lunch and he changed a tenner. The constable got it from the landlord. The bank thinks it was issued to Mark Hanna. He likes to draw personally in tenners as some of 'em do."

"Where is Percival now?"

"Down the cellars. Old Mrs. Frankly is behind the scenes looking after the waitresses and on such occasions she keeps the lady bottlers on overtime. They get the overs, you see, so it's part of the game. They're down there," he jerked down his fleshy thumb, "stretching burgundy."

The Inspector knew that statistically more burgundy was sold than ever produced, the red Spanish Rioja being the customary agent for dilution. It was so sanctioned by time that it was hardly cheating unless you went over ten per cent, when it was considered low in trade circles.

"There's a certain amount of coming and going down the cellar stairs," said Harry. The old door was open and figures came and went.

"Most of us are a bit too old for fun and games," said Honeybody regretfully, "at least in the inconvenience of cellaring. It's romance, though, wandering about and tapping the casks. Old coaching-inn stuff in its way—see that old bloke waddling down?"

He was in fact Mr. Gooseboote, the well-known authority on food and wine, a point at which he had arrived after some years of being publicist for right-wing dictators. That job had ceased largely because left-wing and right-wing politicians had become virtually indistinguishable, possessing their own native-born flacks with even less scruples and, to be frank, the sheer geographical proliferation of states, ministers, cabinets and men of power had left Mr. Gooseboote in his late sixties rather marooned on some Munich island. In his prime he had largely been paid in things, the old-time right-wing dictators having been short of ready cash. Grog, pent-house flats, commandeered blondes, gun-point credit at bars and restaurants, had been Mr. Gooseboote's lot, but little cash, so when the day came he had his column, 'Gooseboote on Gracious Living', planned and ready and he did fairly well in his sere years, largely due to a magnificent library which he had pinched in South America. For at one period in his career—an unpleasant one—he had been paid largely in old rice wine, which had commenced by tasting indescribable and ended by burning out his taste buds. But he did well enough and after all it was the alcoholic content that counted. He had the duplicated hand-out in his pocket, given him by the young flack with his first sherry, and all was right with the world. But he had never been down a cellar; on the right-wing—or the left-wing when he thought of it—going down cellars was risky, but now he was in gracious living there might be some atmosphere stuff in it. His mind formed phrases as he descended the stairs. His sense of smell had disappeared one day in Brazil but he could imagine the romantic, aromatic associations of these three-hundred-years-old—give or take a century— vaults. "Fancy and Frogs," he thought, but would that appeal to those young bastards his editor was so frightened of? Why the hell should he have to be bothered at his age with young people! A nice English dictatorship with a newspaper baron connected with it now, that might be the stuff, but Mr. Gooseboote reminded himself that newspaper barons had no use for ageing journalists.

He had reached the bottom of the stairs without thinking. Various people had passed him. He had automatically pressed himself against the wall, allowing them the use of the banister. Mr. Gooseboote, with his aptitude for survival, remembered people who had mysteriously fallen through banisters. The lighting was not very good, he noticed, but it almost seemed that in the first bay was some kind of bacchanalia. Elderly ladies were sitting on stools swigging. Mr. Gooseboote had seen nothing like it since his days in the remoter regions of Peru. "Evening, my loves," he said.

"You haven't never loved me," said a large old lady, "but here's a glass for the sake of old times what never were."

Mr. Gooseboote thought, looking at it in the dim light, that it was probably hock. He gulped it and returned the glass with a thank-you, before making his way further into the dimness of the cellaring between the great barrels and occasional vat. A senseless procedure, reflected Mr. Gooseboote, growing all those acres of grapes and turning them into a dangerous drug. It should be done synthetically. A remarkably dull lot of people upstairs, including Americans. He made a mental note to do a piece on Californian wines, which had greatly improved, so he had been told. He heard a groan. In his life Mr. Gooseboote had heard enough of them to know a groan of pain when he heard one. Nick off, quick, was his first response. Then he remembered that there were two obvious policemen at the party; and the old ladies had seen him come this far. There were quite a number of things in Mr. Gooseboote's life which made him chary of getting in wrong with the police, so he sighed and got out his pencil torch.

An old man lay on the ground with a cask—eight gallons, registered Gooseboote—next to his head. Dying, thought Gooseboote as he bent to see the contusion on the side of the skull. He went back and informed the ladies, who waddled back in some kind of pecking order.

" 'E's been done over with a firkin of sherry," pronounced the head lady. "And it's poor old Percival, firkined at last as you might say." Gooseboote realised that they were all quite soused.

"Ethel, you go get a doctor, a hambulance and p'lice. The rest of you stay here without moving in case you destroy the evidence."

They stayed there watching Gooseboote with alarming, boozed intensity, but years of training enabled him to stand quietly without speaking or even apparently looking. There had been a doctor at the tasting, a florid man who wheezed as he knelt beside the stricken man. He got up after a few minutes and wagged his head. "He's going out fast. Nothing at all I can do. Massive head injuries as you can see." He addressed the smallish man in the grey suit whom Gooseboote recognised as the younger of the two policemen.

"I found him, officer." Over the years Gooseboote had found the best policy was to speak, quickly and with greasy politeness, to coppers. "I had strolled down out of the party to get some background—I'm Gooseboote of Gracious Living—passed these excellent ladies who gave me a drink, then heard a groan and investigated with my flashlight. I then notified this good lady."

"Mrs. Frankly, the head lady bottler," she said through a small cloud of alcohol. "We are bottling on overtime tonight and I had to see that the waitresses knew their jobs. Naturally old Percival was labelling, as he do, but Lord he must have wandered out."

"The bottles were stacking up for him," said a small swarthy woman. "My watch says nine fifteen. He weren't there when I looked at quarter to the hour, Mrs. Frankly."

"Watch-watching I can't abide," said Mrs. Frankly, belching heavily, "with that poor Percival lying cold or nearly so."

The small woman looked suitably humbled.

"All right," said the Inspector, "let the ambulance men through please. Suppose everybody gets back to where they were, except, say, Mr. Gooseboote and Mr. Keast."

"D.O.A.," said a young doctor as he straightened. "Dead on Arrival. He's nearly gone."

"I'll stay. Keep the party going, Mark," said Keast.

They watched people shamble off and the ambulance men expertly convey Percival away.

"The local police will want the contents of his pockets, doctor," called Inspector James. He turned to Eldred Keast. "I'm just pinch-hitting for the locals. Did this barrel contain sherry—we can save a bit of time."

Keast's long finger pointed at the etched three palms as he nodded. "There's a history label on the underside, unless it has come off. It is sherry, a very good one. We get these sample casks, sherry being a blend of wines, and we keep them in cask until we get round to bottling it and sampling it around a few of the trade. They are kept up on the hogs." The Inspector peered at the vast barrels secured upon wooden chocks.

"They are put up manually," said Keast, "a firkin being capable of being handled. It's an art practised by men who spend their lives stacking barrels. The firkins are about eight feet up and I would not guarantee how secure they are. Old Percival was a tall fellow; if he reached up and meddled with the sherry it might have crashed. I presume that is what happened."

"It's unbroached," said the Inspector, looking at the barrel.

"We get a bit of pinching. Of course, they are all adept at taking a pint or so and putting the bung back. We take every precaution and they are generally an honest lot. It's a question of thirst, you know."

"There was plenty of grog around tonight," said Harry.

"But lightish. I'd say he would want something harder than table wine. I imagine that he grabbed and the cask came down on the poor devil."

"Excuse me, Mr. Gooseboote." The Inspector drew Keast a few feet away. "Now, sir, we know that Mr. Hanna slipped him a tenner yesterday."

"I know nothing of that," said Keast.

"I'll make a deal, sir, in that I shall not interrogate Mr. Hanna until morning, leaving you time to talk to him. Percival said he heard you and Hanna talking behind the vats over there."

"We used to meet," said Keast quietly. "Stigg, Hanna and me, because with that dirty fat swine having a passion for bugging and tape-recording your soul was not your own. Yes, Percival approached Hanna who gave him a tenner."

122

"That'll be all, and thank you. You will find that I am a co-operative kind of man to those who play fair."

He smiled at Mr. Gooseboote as he watched Keast disappear into the darkness. Gooseboote wiped his forehead, but with aplomb. In his time he had turned men in to the Gestapo and the even nastier little men in Haiti, but a cellar *and* policemen tended to make him perspire. In fact Harry had heard of him. In his peregrinations around Gracious Living Gooseboote heard things and passed them on and although he was not on Harry's personal informer list you did not treat informers badly.

"Did you know the dead man, Mr. Gooseboote?"

"Not from a bar of soap. What Keast said was right. A lot of liquor workers get a craving for the stuff."

"And Botting?"

"When he died I was doing a fancy job of work in Rome, Inspector. Check all you like. But he was a villain, I'll tell you that. Once he wanted a favour from me and went about it in a very unpleasant way. Just hinted at something I wouldn't want bruited about. I mention this because we have mutual friends." He mentioned names.

"No idea who did him?"

"A man like that! Oh, dear, no. I'm afraid you'll find a wide field."

They always talked as though it was a horse-race, thought the Inspector, even the most intelligent not realising the simple laws of logic when it came to crime. He took Gooseboote by the arm like a brother and led him back to the party. He noted with inward rage that Honeybody was pawing a lady journalist—the profession for some reason brought out the worst in the Sergeant. At that the party was dying, Bill Stigg quietly notifying people that cars were awaiting. Unobtrusively crockery was being piled up. He left Gooseboote to his own devices and waited until three men from the local station came in. He took them into a corner and dictated a statement. The senior man was a sergeant, the inspectorate being employed at other things at the moment, which in a way simplified things. He ordered photographs and finger-prints and the barrel to be taken for examination. Altogether just tiresome routine, but in return he would see that Gooseboote's statement was taken in London. He supposed he would have to attend the inquest, another useless day out of his life.

"Oh, Inspector, I'm Mrs. Hanna." He looked up and saw a big lady. "I hear from my husband, the Director, that a sad occurrence happened below."

"A man named Percival, which was his first name I imagine, got hit on the head by a small barrel, enough to kill him."

She nodded. "He stuck on labels in that rather gruesome bottling department. I gather he was old. Had he any relatives?"

"I rather gather not."

She made a non-committal noise and moved away; he wondered why she had approached him, then remembered the tenner bribe. If she knew, and she looked a formidable lady who found out things, she might wish to ascertain whether the dead man had any relatives to whom he might have spoken.

As it turned out old Percival had relatives. The Inspector collected Honeybody and they drove out, the Inspector at the wheel, to the lodging house where Percival had lived. It was a superior class of house with a nice old landlady. They went up to the dead man's room. It had some personality, the odds and ends of a life-time including a boomerang which looked the real thing, old fishing gear and an ancient box camera. On the dressing-table was a set of Jack London. There was one suit, old but originally better than average, shirt, underwear and a pile of letters, the most recent four months old. Percival had a son named Albert, himself now sixty and a grandfather. He ran a 'mixed business' in New South Wales. The Inspector made a note of the address and said goodbye to the tearful landlady. She knew nothing of the dead man except that he was a good tenant. They drove to the local station and did the paper work.

When they had finished a constable got coffee. "I'm sorry about misleading you over Smart. Once again apologies," said Honeybody.

"In the end you might have done me a good turn for otherwise I might not have thought of this." He pushed over one of his notes and the Sergeant whistled.

"Trouble is that at the moment it could be anyone and it'll need some very discreet snooping. Innocent and friendly prattling. I think I'll try that new man, Pope. He looks as though butter wouldn't melt in his mouth, but he had a good reputation on the vice squad." He sighed, "As far as tonight is concerned anybody could have killed old Percival by nipping down the other steps. I don't think we'll ever prove what, if anything. But this other represents a cocksure somebody making a great mistake."

II

"A GREAT MISTAKE," Mrs. Hanna had made coffee and they were seated in her large drawing-room, "giving a man like that ten pounds. He would have leeched on you for the rest of your life. Fortunately he has no relatives or somebody would be round asking you to be a father to them." She sighed.

Hanna was frightened of his wife more than he really cared to admit. And the children favoured her. Not for the first time he made a vow to really establish a sizeable private fund. Feller he knew had done damned well out of an English-type pub in Torremolinos. Freedom and no damned nine to six hours. He might specialise in, say, Welsh rarebit.

"There's the door, dear," said Noni with her usual unnecessary emphasis.

He groaned as he went down the hall. Eldred had told him the police knew about the ten pounds but would not question him until tomorrow. He saw from his watch that it was twelve fifteen. He paused to comb his black hair. Surely they did not practise such continental devilries as yanking you in for questioning at those hours when resistance is weak? He peered through the spy-hole he had had installed after his wife's unpleasant encounter with Nigel Heavan and through the little cylinder saw the eye of Harold Stiggins seemingly fixed directly on his. "Christ," said Hanna sotto voce.

"Here's Harold for a midnight chat," he called gaily as he ushered the little man into the drawing-room.

"I couldn't face sleep," said Stiggins, "went for a drive with all the windows down and saw your lights on. I hope there's no intrusion?"

"Do have coffee." Mrs. Hanna poured. "If it stops you sleeping just leave it."

"Nothing stops me from sleeping, my dear, but when my brain is working I don't like shifting it into neutral."

"Thinking of anything in particular?" asked Hanna, sinking his bulk into one of Noni's big chairs.

"Mr. Stigg. At that party I didn't like the way he was talking to the policeman. Kind of guilty, he seemed. Nobody notices a little man like me as he moves around. And he was talking peculiar, most peculiar. I suppose he couldn't have done it?"

"Surely the point is that almost anybody could have done it. An unlocked-room mystery," said Hanna.

Stiggins tapped his fingers on his knee. "I'd as soon not have him Managing," said Stiggins. "We'll need a merchant bank eventually and those boys want everything simon pure. I've known them beat a hasty retreat because of a bad adultery among the board, let alone violence."

Noni shrugged massive shoulders. "You heard Nefer's thoughts this afternoon. Unless Nigel changes his mind then Bill must be Managing. On the whole I'd prefer not to badger Nigel. In his unstable state God knows what the outcome would be. Himself perhaps."

"Ah," Stiggins drank his coffee heartily as Noni listened with distaste. "As I was going around I heard some talk about a tenner." His sharp eyes shifted round.

"My husband for good reasons gave it to the poor wretch who brained himself tonight with a cask. We are glad it may have eased his last hours."

"Oh," Stiggins sounded a little deflated and conversation drooped to a close.

"I hope that won't be mentioned at the inquest." In the silence of night a whining quality in his voice became more evident.

The door bell rang again and Mark Hanna went gladly to answer it, thinking even more of the pub in Torremolinos. How much would he need? One good coup perhaps.

It was the Inspector. Hanna stared aghast.

"May I come in?"

"It's terribly late. Oh, well," Hanna weakened. "Please do not worry my wife."

Inspector James bowed gallantly at her. "Normally I would not be here, but, well, you realise we keep a general eye on everybody. Sheer routine. The fellow who was on to Mr. Stiggins was about to go home when he saw him drive out here. He followed and then phoned in. So I thought that if there was a conference, I could nip in and ask a question."

"What question?" Noni's voice was hard.

"An odd thing happened," said the Inspector, leaning against the mantelpiece. "An attempt was made to pin this on to your Mr. Smart, indeed a very clever attempt. The main thing that saved him was that one Jasper Smith was whitewashing all morning, so he swears, outside Smart's room. So we can argue that the killer was somebody who did not know that Smith was scheduled to start whitewashing that old building that morning. As it happened Smith did not enter Smart's office, but he could have. Thus we can eliminate a lot of people. First, who gave him orders?"

Hanna gave a short laugh. "Oh, Smith is a useful man if not too pleasant. His schedule was drawn up monthly by Smart in fact."

"Did he change it about?"

"I would say not. He is not the sort of man to change a schedule. And Smart is the old-womanish type to raise piercing cries if time-tables are abandoned. Between the two of them there is not much question of that."

"Was this schedule on public display?" said the Inspector with weary disappointment in his voice.

"Botting had a board over one wall in his official office—the one in the new building—on which every blinking happening due to take place was listed. He took umpteen spot checks always, you know. I remember that whitewashing business is always stuck on it. Mind you, I can't remember when I last saw it. But it was for the seeing."

"Did people drop in on Botting?"

"He liked privacy. No, there is a telephone in the tiny anteroom.

127

If you wanted to see him you phoned and it was either 'yes' or 'no'. But a number of people did go in there in a month. I'll try to get some sort of schedule drawn up for you."

"Thank you, sir. I suppose the cleaners went in nights?"

"One of his idiosyncracies was to not have cleaners in there. It was full of dust-resistant processing and he had a little vacuum thing with which I presume he occasionally did a chore."

"That's interesting. And of course most of the workers would know what their mate was doing?" The Inspector sounded sly.

Hanna laughed with some humour this time. "You're a nice fellow. We try to help you and then you in turn try to limit suspicion to executives. In fact Mr. Jasper Smith is a mate to nobody. I suspect his fellow wage-slaves loathe his guts."

Noni seemed to have lost interest. "I think I'll go to bed now. I don't suppose you'll be long." She hefted herself to her feet and acknowledged the "good nights".

After she'd gone, Stiggins sat a little forward on his chair. "There was a ten-pound note mentioned tonight, Inspector."

"I may as well say," said Hanna, "that I gave the man who got crushed a tenner yesterday. He came up to me in the yard and said he had heard Keast and me in the cellaring discussing Botting in bad terms." Hanna moistened his lips with the cold dregs of his coffee and took hold of himself. "It was a foolish action on my part, but I'm freely admitting it with no dodging."

"He'd have bled you."

"Dammit, only until you chaps get the killer. I talked it over with Keast and we half decided to ask Mr. Stiggins to arrange a pension."

The Inspector laughed in high humour. "We find people do foolish things. Good night."

"I'll come with you," said Stiggins. "Good night, Mark."

Hanna nodded.

"A funny thing," said Stiggins as they gained the fresh air, "but as I was going round the party tonight I heard young Bill Stigg talking very curiously to you."

"He was trying to pump me," said the Inspector patiently. "In fact if people don't make these clumsy efforts we think it suspicious. Good night, sir."

128

He watched the twinkle of Stiggins' rear-light before getting into his own car and presently into the room which he shared with Honeybody.

"Anything doing, guv'nor?" The Sergeant sat up in bed as Harry undressed.

The Inspector ran over what had transpired. "All trying to cut each other's throats," sighed the Sergeant. "It would have been nice to pin it on old Smart, but too many things are agin it."

"Smart had a very distinguished three years in the War, and he now supports a couple of orphaned kids out of what I imagine to be slender resources."

"Which if threatened by Botting might have led him to kill. I've seen these model citizens take to violence, Harry, for what they consider perfect moral reasons. Anyway he's out of it. Good night, looks like being a stinker."

It was. The Inspector, who inclined to sleep badly in strange beds, seemed to spend his time listening to Honeybody's gentle snoring and then watching a formidable red sun come up. He dropped off and was aroused by the Sergeant shaking him. "It's seven thirty, sir, and the water in the bathroom's piping hot. You wanted an early start."

It was nevertheless nine when they reached the police station, where plainclothesman Pope politely attended Harry. "So you see," the Inspector concluded, "I wanted to check who went into Botting's office and any other information as to who knew about the whitewashing."

"I suppose it was premeditated?"

"It could have been a brilliant sudden idea," admitted Harry, "but I incline to think not because of the three-litre bottle. Somebody had to locate it and have it placed handy. I think there was a time-factor and Botting had to go that day. Anything you come across that might be useful!"

They arrived together at Heavans and Harry and Honeybody went in search of Jasper Smith whom they found in the actual cellaring, but this time sucking a foul old pipe as he stood up his ladder. He was a trifle more polite this morning.

"Have you a copy of your schedule?"

"What? Oh, this crap." It was greasy with whitewash as Jas eased it out of one buttock's pocket.

Harry checked it. On the morning of Monday, the seventh, Jas had been scheduled to be outside Mr. Smart's office.

"Do you ever change the routine?"

"What would be the point? Sometimes wine gets spilled over a wall, but it's only half an hour for me to scrape off and give it a coat."

"This did not happen on the morning of the seventh?"

"No," said Jas sulkily, "I've took my oath on it so to speak."

"And do the monthly lists vary considerably, I mean by the day? You do not do the same job on the first working day of each month etcetera?"

Jas scratched at his long, unshaven chin, then said deliberately. "To do the whole job takes three working weeks plus one day, plus me holidays, plus public holidays, plus sickness to be worked in. You could work out what will happen on one day next month, but you'd have to be a bleedin' mathematician which neither Smart nor me is."

They went up and into the new building, noting that Stiggins was hard at work within his glass office. He did not look up. They passed by the girls at their machines and gained the black-partitioned office that the chart from the local police said had been Botting's office. Harry produced a labelled bunch of keys and opened the door. It led into a windowless little cupboard of a place. He switched on the overhead light. There was a coffee table upon which reposed a small black telephone and a calendar and an uncomfortable-looking chair.

"According to the notes from the locals he only saw staff and executives here," said Honeybody. "There's a posh modern inter-view room which he and the other Directors used for seeing callers. He had his own ideas about organisation, not encouraging people hanging about gossiping. No secretaries, but a typing pool of two very competent ladies working from tape."

The inner office had a small window from which Harry could see the front gate. It was completely featureless and utilitarian. There was no ashtray for Botting had given up smoking. A big square clock face, of the kind which flipped over the hour and minute in the form of cards, faced the desk. There was a tape-recorder and a couple of baskets plus cabinets. It was a featureless place. On one side wall was the large clipboard to which were attached a couple of dozen schedules—travellers' journeys; staff holidays; regular repeat orders to fulfil; a schedule of all visitors from the previous month and their purpose and finally there was the now familiar sheet marked 'Whitewashing'.

"Nowt here," said Harry. "I should say he liked to be rather a cruel man."

"His lady friend had no complaints."

"He was probably all right to women," said Harry. "It was men he had it in for. His Army record, by the way, states that as a lance-corporal he got the M.M. for holding a position for three hours until a counter-attack was launched. But he was very unpopular with his mates; that was noted twice on the report which asked was he officer material. Not specific but you could read between the lines."

"A bit of a let-down, all the others having been pro Service officers in their time and now led by a lance-corporal."

They gained the anteroom. "One of the difficulties is that we've got three men, four counting Smart, who have proven nerve and training on the suspect list. We'll lock up and see Smart first and then a final burst at friend Stiggins. If I'm not mistaken he is no luxury."

There were sounds of activity upon the top floor and from the voices the travellers were in. Presently Smart appeared, not particularly pleased to see them and looking worried.

The Inspector sat down on the one guest chair and Honeybody stood.

"Yes, of course I make out the whitewashing list with Smith," Smart presently snapped. "No secret about it. It takes half an hour on the last working day of each month. It is so routine I could type it in triplicate myself in around eight minutes, but Jasper Smith likes to make a ceremony of it. My copy is kept in this second drawer in a file."

"Thanks, sir," the Inspector made as though to get up but sank back again. "You're looking worried! Your job in jeopardy?"

Smart stared and smiled. "Frankly not now. I wonder how you

knew? Of course, his habit of tape-recording was notorious. A month ago he came into my office. I stood up. He remained standing looking at me with his round eyes. 'What is it exactly that you do, Mr. uh?' I listed my multiple duties, things that the machines can't do such as pacifying old customers. He said, 'It all sounds fearfully unimpressive, Mr. uh,' and walked out. If you think I fear to lose my job you are very right. On the other hand I could never commit murder."

There was a considerable dignity about the old-fashioned gawky man. To cover his embarrassment the Inspector said as lightly as he could. "But you did look worried."

"Somebody stole my keys. Three personal keys which I keep in my top drawer."

"The drawer is locked?"

"I think I did lock it, but it was unlocked this morning."

"Excuse me," the Inspector peered. "You know, given the necessary knowledge one could open this with a nail file in about fifteen seconds; a stout piece of suitable bent wire would cut the time in half. What were the keys?"

"A spare one to my house, one for the private filing cabinet I have (not very private at that) and the key to my private bin." Mr. Smart said the words a trifle proudly.

"I didn't see you at the high jinks last night."

"I haven't been asked for years," said Smart. He was going to expatiate further but the words did not come.

"I would guess it's common knowledge where you keep the keys. Somebody could have nipped up the stairs and forced the drawer although I don't see the point of it. Are the contents of your bin valuable?"

"I have a few rare bottles and some curiosities, but, no, say a couple of hundred pounds if I had to sell. Perhaps less, sales are unpredictable."

"When did you look inside?"

"Six days before Botting's death to collect my weekly ration." Smart emphasised the words as he looked at Honeybody who stared back with his bland smile.

"We'd better take a look a your little hoard," said Harry and led the way to the cellars. Mr. Smart's private bin, totally protected by stout wire, was in the old part. The Inspector flashed his torch on the wire door, in the lock of which was a key.

"I swear . . ." began Smart.

"No need," interrupted the Inspector. "Another mistake! Unless interrupted sneak thieves always carry the key away to dispose of later. This is cute thinking—'old Mr. Smart must be doddering,' was the desired impression."

"I see," said Smart dubiously. "Shall we take a look?" He opened the gate and Harry squeezed in behind him.

"This is just a curiosity—a burgundy of three years before the vine disease hit the area. We'll never know what wine then tasted like. I always fancy rather higher in sugar content. Here are my treasures from Madeira."

The Inspector admired, then asked, "Nothing missing?"

Mr. Smart took a small book from his breast pocket and checked. "Nothing," he said and started to leave.

"One minute," said Harry, "just check the vacant spaces. There's a very dusty one there." He pointed.

"So there is. Good Lord above!"

"Better come out where we have room to manoeuvre." Smart was shying like a nervous horse.

"Well, really," said Smart as the Inspector locked up and handed the key to him. "It's like that Edgar Allen Poe story of not seeing accustomed objects. Five years it's been, dear, oh, dear." Then he said crisply. "Five years ago there was a runner attached to the Directors named Pocock. This was a practice going back at least until when I joined the firm. I say runner because whoever it was was older and somewhat better educated than an office boy, capable of doing various kinds of clerical work, gathering records together and carrying out confidential assignments. They usually spent two or three years in the job and were then promoted, sometimes to the old counting house, sometimes to being junior travellers. Mr. Botting—so I believe—abolished the position just about four and a half years ago, so this happened just before young Pocock left. He was about eighteen, but, you know, my memory cannot distinguish one single feature." He shook his head. "I am sure, however, about his name. One morning he came to me with an oblong brown-paper parcel with what I thought was wood underneath. He said, casually, 'The boss would take it as a favour if you stored this in your private bin for him'. It felt to me, judging by weight, like an encased bottle."

"One minute," said Harry. "Who did you take the 'boss' to be?"

"I was sure it was Botting."

"You did not think it odd?"

"I just thought that they had come to the best man to take care of it," said Smart with engaging egotism. "I thought it was some remarkable brandy or just possibly a port. I placed it there, and to tell the truth it's three years since I thought of it. You will see that it is in the corner where I keep my own curiosities which I rarely inspect."

"Somebody must have nipped down first thing this morning," said the Inspector, making a note. "I wonder whether the old ladies saw anything."

"None of them in, sir," said Smart cynically. "I was told when I got here this morning about old Percival's death and also the fact that the ladies had some kind of wake." He shrugged. "They squirrel away bottles of overspill and stuff they get from broken bottles. When one of the 'girls' has a birthday out come a couple of bottles. But last evening all of the hoard came out. The watchman left a note saying he had got four taxis here at around four this morning to take them home. No work today. Perhaps old Frankly may bring in one or two this afternoon—she is conscientious in her queer way."

"I suppose you knew Percival?"

"Oh, yes, when he came I was more or less in charge of the permanent casuals. I remember that he was a friend of Mrs. Frankly and I thought older than he said. That was no problem as the job carried no insurance worry for us. You know, only a certain type would have liked the job and I spotted him as the one. He was with us a good few years which vindicated my judgment."

"We'll get a statement from you later," said the Inspector. It was no good pressing Smart too much. If you did that he would become unco-operative. Most probably, thought the Inspector, the thought of opening the package would not have occurred to him at all. In any case there would probably have been some sort of seal under the outer wrapping to preclude prying. It would not look good in his report—("Mr. James's cases have too many loose ends," a snuffly old critic had gurgled during one of the periodic work appraisal sessions)—but, Christ, you could not start by peering into every nook, cranny or wine bin looking for you had no idea what. Nevertheless it wasn't going to look good in the report.

He walked moodily up the stairs and into the new building. Stiggins was in his glass box and saw them at once, pointing to the glass door with his forefinger.

"To see me, I s'pose," he said as they entered. "Take chairs, gentlemin, I'm sure. Well?"

"I'm sorry we've been so long in getting round to see you, sir," said the Inspector, riffling through the clip of papers compiled by the local police.

"I don't suppose anybody really wants to see a policeman," observed Stiggins with conscious shrewdness, "eh?" His small face cracked in two with the grin.

The Inspector smiled back and at his side a little foam of false mirth, like hastily poured stout, trickled across the Sergeant's plump lips.

"That's a fact, sir. Now the locals have you as being unable to account for your movements on the morning in question."

"Indeed." Stiggins appeared to chew on something. "I was in, out and about, in this building mostly. Although I nipped out around ten to the pub over the road. As you probably know we own it and part of my sphere was to keep an eye on the books."

"It was a spur of the moment call?"

"Oh, dear, no. I was working all day on Saturday—the Joshua's Ales bid called for figuring piled on figuring. Never mind, I like it! Sometime I called up the Manager and said I'd come over on Monday morning when I could make it."

"As far as my notes go," said the Inspector, "Botting was in on the Saturday morning until noon. He spent the morning in his office on this floor and the afternoon and evening at home. At one o'clock he had a sole at a pub not far from his apartment and he dined somewhere on steak."

"That'd be Botty," said Stiggins. "Sole and steak were all he

135

ate, those and a bit of cheese. Dreadful cramps in the gut he used to get if he noshed fancy. Me, I can eat old tires and not whisper a belch."

"You did not see him on the Saturday morning?"

"I think he was here when I got in at nine thirty. When he went at twelve he nodded through the glass, the last time I ever saw the poor devil."

"You'd been together over the years?"

"Kids," said Stiggins shortly, "chalk marks on the pavement, hopping in and out the lines. That's how I first remember Botty, a big, overweight kid he was."

"And you worked together on many occasions?"

"Six companies altogether, including this."

"That doesn't take into account the book-making affair. A man named Georgie Krock."

Stiggins' head gave the impression of freezing in mid-air. He shook it slightly and smiled a little. "That would be the new computer wouldn't it, the big new one you've got?"

"Something like that."

"I suppose I support it in theory," said Stiggins, "but, Christ, it is the welfare state gone barmy—big brother computer. Ah, well, you know the facts. The fellow who died, Georgie Krock, was a crook—if you could find out exactly what he was doing crooked which you fellows never did. Apart from the illegal book-making he was hand in glove with the Warren Street mob. But that did not concern me. He used to hand me sheets of figures and ask me to put them in a certain way. There was an income-tax return among other things. Times were hard for me and then I was about to marry. Five nicker a week he paid and damned useful it was. The evening they killed him I was with Botting in his flat; we were working for a holding firm, him as assistant manager and me as accountant. But I gave all that to the police at the time."

"Could Botting have killed him?"

"He didn't know him and he was with me, apart from fifteen minutes when he went out to see somebody at a pub. But surely that's under the bridge?"

"Unsolved murders just bob about near the shore. Forgive me for bringing it up, but it is a curious item."

"I don't suppose the average man has any contact with one murder, let alone two," said Stiggins, "but you know that the figures do run oddly at times."

"In confidence, sir, and reverting to book-making, who would you make favourite for the who-done-Mr. Botting stakes at weight-for-age?"

"I never knew a man who made such enemies," said Stiggins. "Truth to tell Botty positively enjoyed getting them down and then putting the footie boots in. Relished it he did. Afterwards he always had a funny look, like the saints in them old pitchers. Transfigured as you might say. Knowing we'd get round to that, I made a little list. Here." He whipped a hand into a drawer and drew out a foolscap page. The Inspector glanced at it and put it in his pocket. "And," said Stiggins, "as a saver I'd have a little on Bill Stigg."

The Inspector gave a long whistle. "I remember your words last night, but his wife's the second largest share-holder."

Stiggins held a finger against his nose. "If my wife is right, which bless her she often is, the lady's tiring rapidly. I've often noticed how women quickly tire of red-headed men. All right for novelty, but for the long road, no, unless they go bald. Stigg is worse than penniless and untrained, he's got ye olde family tradition of luxury at other people's expense. He'd find it difficult. I did hear," Stiggins lowered his voice and his small eyes seemed to recede further into his head, "that madam would not find it hard to find cause."

"Then Botting's death does not solve anything for him."

"Perhaps Botty had something on him that would have really sent the balloon up. As it is little Nefer might well give him a small pension, for services rendered as you might say, which would not come off if she really got her dander up."

"But nothing concrete."

"Nothing concrete."

Harry thanked him and went into the fresh air with the Sergeant.

"Anxious to help somebody into a cell, isn't he?" grunted Honeybody.

"He just wants it cleared up so that he is free to get on with whatever larcenous schemes one small head encompasses."

A police messenger parked his motor bike and gave Harry a packet. "I'm told there is no reply, sir."

It proved to be a summary of all that could be gleaned concerning the death of old Percival and its total evaluation was nil. The firkin which split his head open had no discernible finger-prints on it, in itself not suspicious as the oak staves were poor carriers. Among the butts between which the little barrel had rested there were likewise no prints, but there were large patches where fairly heavy dust had been disturbed and cleared, such as might have been made by somebody climbing around. On the other hand workmen did periodically do just that in order to check the condition of the barrels. Further tests would be made for cloth fibres. As at the time of writing none of those people at the wine-tasting so far available for questioning had seen anybody with dust smears.

The Inspector showed it to the Sergeant and shrugged. "The Directors have a private changing-room-cum-shower block. It would've been easy to nip in there and clean yourself, or even put on a duplicate suit. However, it can only be opened by a key."

"Ah," said Honeybody, "I've known the ladies, bless 'em, strip down to their undies before committing a crime, the detective books tell 'em about dust and minute blood splatters. With what they wear now it only takes a second. Then on with the skirt again and quite immaculate. Bless me, there was that fellow who went naked upstairs to kill his old lady."

"True," said Harry. "I'm going to London for the weekend; there might be an end there. The way I see it we might as well let things stew. They're getting nicely on each other's nerves and we just might get a statement. Do you want to come?"

"I'll carry on here, Harry." The Sergeant wagged his great head. Happily married, the Sergeant had been wedded a long time, and although his wife, Dodo, was an excellent woman in most ways she had a certain intolerance towards alcohol. "No, I'll hold the fort," said the Sergeant. "You know where to ring me. Love to your little wife. One thing," he glanced up into the pale blue shining sky, "it won't rain."

12

"**I**T NEVER RAINS but it pours," said Superintendent Hawker, in his new room in Victoria Street, a huge functional oblong in which he rattled, as he said, like a pea in a colander. Outside the sky had opened sending gouts of warm rain on to the heated concrete. On his desk a dreary file grew higher and higher with each incoming messenger boy.

"And I've only got ten outlets from the computer," the old man mourned. "I swear they promised me sixteen, but there's nothing in writing. I must have been plied with an extra brandy. Taking advantage of an old man is just like *them*! Well, here's your report back. I must say that losing the sealed package out of the locked private bin doesn't look particularly good." His hooded eyes grew large and cold.

"I . . ." The Inspector stopped.

"Two years ago you'd have bashed my ear for half an hour," crowed Hawker. "You are learning, but nevertheless *they* won't like that bit. When you write the final report play it well down. I want you to be very sure of this one, laddie, because the Heavan family are wealthy and their dear husbands come of influential families, cousins popping up in all kinds of establishment sinecures."

"I wish that darned computer would do the job for me."

"I'll be pretty much at that stage next year," said Hawker. "If they give me more leads from the bloody thing. Feed all the facts in is my idea, and get out a kind of racing sheet listing the odds on or against everybody concerned. Anyway I've got you annotations on that list from friend Stiggins and the ones culled from Botting's tapes. Some cannot be traced, some are dead, but there are seven runners. About this dead bookie, Georgie Krock, what's left of him is over there."

The unfamiliarity of the new room combined with memories of the former one—with battered brass spittoon, used as an ash-tray, which Hawker had retrieved as a souvenir from the old Tombs prison in New York, and ancient worn carpets—combined to make the Inspector start. He remembered that unsolved murders were one of the old man's specialities and that at odd moments you would always find him having a browse over some unavenged corpse. "No need to get him out of the file," said Hawker, "I remember it well enough. It was on a dirty foggy evening he got it. His flat was a mixture of luxury and squalor, vintage champagne and half-eaten tins of cheap sardines, a silk-covered divan scuffed by his boots, and the best part of one closet stuffed with dirty silk socks, size nine. He wore 'em until they were as stiff as boards and then put them in the cupboard. Stank like a cheese cellar at high noon. His business had a lot of ramifications, all twisted lines which apparently led nowhere but up the creek. Do you think your Botting might have done it?"

"Stiggins was his creature, his puppet. If Botting demanded an alibi Stiggins would have given one. When Botting got his big break clear of the field he took Stiggins along. That is not in character. When a man ceased being useful to Botting that delightful feller enjoyed booting him off the ladder. Stiggins had no experience of the big league stuff Botting was going after. Why take him?"

"Sentiment, boys together," said Hawker with a crocodilian leer.

The Inspector put his little finger in his right ear and rolled his eyes at the ceiling.

"Well," Hawker looked at his watch. It was ten o'clock on the Sunday morning. "How is your wife, she should be near her time?"

"Elizabeth is sitting up and giving cheek," said Harry. "I asked her ghastly female doctor who shrugged and looked as if I'd robbed her kind by coming out of an egg."

"If you want to be taken off it . . ."

"No," said the Inspector, "it'll be all right."

In fact he welcomed work to take his mind off it. He had not liked the way his wife's doctor, a misogynist in reverse named Florence Hollybotham, had looked at him.*

His first three calls were negative. The first was in hospital a week after a hernia operation, the second had been in the cells (the only real alibi, as judges have observed), and the third had died a week ago. He did two of these by telephone and blessed his luck. Too often you had to career from one end of London to the other. The fourth sounded important and was at home. The traffic imprisoned even the tycoons, thought the Inspector, in their concrete London cages in August. In the City itself the driving was not unpleasant; he had managed to get an open sports car from the pool. The man lived in a bit of architect's Tudor stuck in a pleasant suburb of bewildering dead-end streets. The maid showed him into a book-lined room. Very impressive if you didn't know what he knew.

"Yes, yes, the Inspector, you did not make yourself quite clear." A seer's deep-set eyes raked him alongside a great Roman nose.

"Well, Doctor," the Inspector seated himself, "we talk so much in our game that the keen edge does get blunted."

The good doctor was on the way to making a fortune from interviewing prospective employees on behalf of directors so palsied that they had become incapable of finding, let alone assessing, staff. Anything from an errand boy to a managing director could be found and vetted (the full treatment included wives, children and relatives as remote as you cared to pay for, plus full psychiatric reports). The only trouble was that the Doctor's LL.B. and Ph.D. were entirely assumed. According to one of Botting's tapes there was indeed a doctor of that name who had dropped out of sight, presumed dead, for some years, a man with no relatives or friends save the bottle. Botting, who knew strange people, had run into him, bed-ridden, but screeving ingenious begging letters from a rooming house in Brixton.

The Inspector looked at the old fake behind the massive desk.

"Cristobal Botting was killed Monday."

"So it was reported in my paper. Murder?"

"Yes."

"So you come to see me!" The deep-set eyes showed amusement.

"We found that you had proposed him for his two clubs"—very snooty ones they were—"and was one of his referees when old Nonsuch Heavan engaged him."

"A very good brain," said the Doctor, "a top-rating power of organisation. I did Heavan a good turn in recommending him. As for the clubs he proved an impeccable member, not that he used them much."

"He was an old friend?"

"I knew him for ten years. Perhaps you'll come to the point."

"Where were you on Monday morning between nine and noon?"

"I am at the office on alternate Sundays because on that day we get a great many enquiries. Directors, possibly with Saturday night indigestion"—the deep-set eyes twinkled man-to-man and the leathery jowls shook a trifle—"become worried about staff problems. So after breakfast they phone my office. It is very necessary with these people to reach agreement while they are enthused. Anyway I am adamant that I do not attend the office on alternate Mondays, a slack day generally. Last Monday, as usual in summer, I arose at seven, took the old station wagon and drove into the Cotswolds. I parked and walked in a great circle for three hours and got home around four."

"No witnesses?"

"I had beer, bread-and-cheese and pickled walnuts in the saloon bar of a pub. It was, however, very crowded and I doubt whether they would remember me in particular." He was still twinkling.

"Do I gather that deceased was a personal friend rather than somebody you met through the employment exchange?"

This time he brought a slight wince to the Doctor's old wrinkled face. The employment exchange had a very sonorous and impressive title.

"I forget where I met him. Possibly at some dinner. He became a valued acquaintance. We were friendly, but not close friends. I rarely saw him of late."

"So your relationship was quite amicable?"

"Of course," but the Inspector's experience could detect a slight, queasy sickness in the noble face opposite him.

It was nothing to him. Superintendent Hawker had calculated that nine per cent of people with degrees had faked them one way or another. It is no crime unless used for fraudulent purposes or false pretences. The Doctor operated a genuine parasitical business

142

likely to get him a mention in the honours' list. "Can we have a look at the car?" he asked.

Normally citizens hummed and hawed, a natural reaction, an automatic defence of property rights, and the Doctor's ready acceptance produced a wry inward grin. 'Modern Master of Psychology' a trade press interview had dubbed the old Doctor, but, then, when a copper called Freud fled out of the window. They went out into the sunlit garden.

The Doctor pressed a button and one sector of the covering of the four-car garage slid up. There was a Bentley, a Triumph, a sedate Volks and a station wagon by Fiat, oldish but well preserved. The clock showed fifty-eight thousand miles.

"When was the last oil change?" asked Harry.

"I don't know," the Doctor was slightly flustered. "I think my man Jarvis keeps a record." But the Inspector was already opening the door and taking the neat service record book from the glove box. He glanced at it and slipped it in his pocket. "It'll be returned to you within a week. People are always trying to fiddle alibis by faking service records so our counter-measures are infallible from practice. This shows the car was serviced last Friday and has done seventy miles in the interim. Not enough mileage to get to Heavans, sir, or to Banbury Cross even. That settles it unless you did something cute like parking the car and getting a cross-country bus. I do hope not, because we always catch cute people."

The old man looked bent and shrivelled as his white handkerchief caressed his eyebrows.

"I suppose," his voice was a base rumble, "that Mr. Botting kept records."

"He was the completest bastard for keeping records I ever came across. However why should you worry, Doctor?"

The old man forced his shoulders back. "Of course not."

The Inspector drove across country to one of those outer suburbs which for some reason were blasted as far back as their genesis in the early thirties. Various quirks outside the promoters' control—roads and transport among them—had left it looking still half finished. The upswing would gradually embrace it in the bosom of commuterhood, but now there were unfinished-looking lanes with 1932-type bungalows that hadn't fared very well in life. It was at one of these that he knocked.

An old lady showed him into a room. It was comfortably furnished, but old-fashioned, not antique or plain with-it quaint but just dully old-fashioned with good 1925 Bon Marché furniture. A man sat behind the desk and did not get up. "Sit down, take a cigarette if you want."

"You know that Cristobal Botting was killed last Monday?" said Harry, crossing his shins.

"It couldn't have happened to a nicer person," grated the man. Looking at him the Inspector saw a head like a parchment-covered skull with great pain-lines graven from the mouth.

"You knew him?"

"He blackmailed me twelve years ago, ruined me as a result."

"You are under no obligation to say anything, you know."

"What have I to lose? My son had got married. The girl had a criminal record; she'd done six months for embezzlement while a trustee. She had gone through this one year of madness, so it seemed. Botting got to know. It would have ruined the boy professionally."

"He got money from you?"

"I was a Director of a manufacturing business which used essences. Botting was Manager of a company which imported them, mostly from Holland. He'd gambled very heavily on some kind of new essence, it doesn't matter what after all these years. The new product proved in practice twice as expensive as the one it was due to supersede, due to the fact you had to use two-and-a-half times the quantity and at that results were variable, one thing that condemns an essence. He came to see me and laid it on the table. Either I signed a contract to take that essence on terms which gave his firm a profit—oh, God damn his soul if only it had been cost!—or my daughter-in-law's past became known in certain vital quarters. He had photostats, the lot. I betrayed my trust and placed the contract.

"It finished me, of course. I was right in line for the Managing Directorship. I just had to keep my division floating nicely and it was a foregone conclusion. As it was it became painfully apparent I had either been bribed or lost my judgment. Most people were

144

charitable enough to take the second view. The result was much the same, I found myself proprietor of a struggling one-man agency. I still do a little by telephone."

"Where were you last Monday morning?"

"Here!"

"Witnessed?"

He shrugged. "The old lady comes in from nine until four every day. I can't bear to be interrupted in the mornings—force of habit. She puts my bit of lunch on the dumb waiter outside the door, always a bit of cold meat and stuff, and I go and take it when I'm peckish."

"So you have really no alibi."

"What?" The man was genuinely astonished.

"I mean you could have killed him."

The man rolled round the table. What the Inspector had cursorily taken for granted as a conventional chair proved to be a wheel-chair, manually propelled. And the subject of his interrogation had no legs. The Inspector found himself staring at the neatly pinned trousers.

"I'm sorry, but I thought you must know. Egotism, I'm afraid. It was eighteen months ago when a taxi turned over. It will be another four months until they have a go with the tin ones. The only reason I can afford a roof of my own was the compensation I got." He wheeled himself back to his original position. "It would have been a long way to propel my only vehicle!"

The Inspector admired his courage. "What manner of man was Botting?"

"Oh, him," his voice was rather absent as if the thoughts behind it were far away. "I knew him when he was the Sales Manager for this essence firm. It was a small one, third generation, with the survivors immensely experienced and curiously devoid of brains. He was a very intelligent man . . . you felt it. A great moon face and rather goggling eyes plus a eunuch's voice. But he could talk very well and there was a kind of . . . rawness? I can't get the exact word, anyway personality could flow from him when he wanted it, though next minute he could be tight and buttoned up. I happened to know the Directors very well, nice fellows in their ineffectual way. Botting had his way with them and they made him Managing Director. It was between the two jobs, when he became General Manager, that he blackmailed me. He didn't muck about or finesse, just put his hat on my desk, got a manila envelope out of his brief-case and said 'unless etcetera' in that high voice of his, goggling at me with those nasty eyes. Ah, well, I suppose you'll ask me if I have any suspicions. I haven't. I believe you reap as you sow and the late Botting was some sower one would imagine." He cocked an eyebrow.

"A compulsive blackmailer, not for money but for advantages," agreed the Inspector and bade him goodbye.

His penultimate call was to a strange man who was working this Sunday at the largish shop he owned—or so some people said—and managed. The Inspector stopped his car outside the soberly painted front. In gilt letters the simple word *Earth* was inscribed over the façade. Within the double-fronted window was a bucolic farm-scene. Beside an old-fashioned midden a nineteenth-century whiskery effigy bent in the act of feeding several fowls. A basket filled with brown eggs was beside him. Vague primitive farm-buildings were the back-cloth with bee-hives arranged in front of them. Somebody in the window was rearranging small piles of jars. Earth had a steady custom from people with a yen to get back to the typhoid and ptomaine belt in the matter of eating. That its products emanated from the usual battery establishments and jam factories had perturbed the Yard. Was it passing-off or even false pretences? But the staff of Earth were rigidly trained to adeptly side-step searching questions regarding the exact origin of the produce they sold so dearly.

The Inspector got out his warrant, pressed it against the plate glass and tapped sharply with his signet ring. Presently he was ushered through the cool air-conditioning of the carefully lighted shop to the long store-room behind. Fat Auntie, the alleged owner, was always careful to avoid unnecessary concealment. His nickname was self-explanatory. Over-plump buttocks stretched the green corduroy pants that were his affectation, a sweaty, round bland face dripped chins over the turtle-necked red velvet sweater. Little green eyes looked playfully at the Inspector as he introduced himself.

"No secrets around here, my dear. Over there is a consignment of deep frozen Danish chickies being thawed, a tiny weeny bit at a time under a little lamp system poor me designed himself; there we are garnishing those lovely choice taties."

Bags marked 'Produce of Spain' were being spilled on to a moving wire belt. Two men dexterously splashed them with a mixture of earth and water as they travelled along. A young signwriter held up a placard, 'Dug with loving care by human hands', and Fat Auntie nodded approval.

"I buy those pea plants special from a real farm," he said, nodding at a pile, "and we break them up to put among the Channel Island peas. Oh, yes, that's South African honey, dear." Two girls scooped it out of a blackened metal container into amateurish looking ceramic jars.

"It's only window-dressing, love, I always say," said Auntie, "and I do trooly think you should see Mr. Bogg my solicitor, dear, who is so clever at explaining these things."

"It ain't about the grub," said Harry.

"Oh," Fat Auntie turned very business-like and led the way past the troughs where the marketing board stamp was being chemically removed from eggs. They went into a small aggressively neat cubicle.

"Well?" The usually merry little eyes were emerald hard.

"The late Cristobal Botting and where were you Monday morning?"

A pudgy hand massaged jowls. "I'm a right lucky bleeder," said Fat Auntie, "a right lucky bleeder. I went into smoke all Monday. When I saw that old Botty had been paid what he owed I was sweating like a filly over five furlongs I can tell you. Sweatin' from the pores and my doctor says he's never seen so many as I got. An abnormality. At eleven I was leaving an address in Tottenham, my mind on several things and ticking along quick, and I nearly ran into young Donald, the chap as writes me signs and tickets. I was wearing dark specs and a hat pulled right down and not me usual clothes, so I shrank back like and let him pass. Next day I sat in this chair reading my paper and there it is. It occurs to me that the gents I was seeing the day before would watch me go down for life without saying a word; in fact they'd deny they ever knew me. And I know Heavans."

The Inspector frowned.

"Born near there. Damn it, a feller has to be born somewhere. It was in the council cottages as they were then and I was one of the kids that didn't get taken off while young with the summer trots or the dip. There was a World War One air raid shelter outside Heavans. We used to light candles and boil apples in tins," Fat Auntie sighed for lost innocence. "There was a strange kid named Nigel, one of the Heavans, who was always naggin' away at a recorder. We used to fight. Ugly little cuss he was and used his knees if you let him. So there we are. Oh, well, get on with yer work, I says to meself. I look at the Monday staff list. Sure enough Donald had phoned in at nine saying he had a slightly sprained ankle.

"I took a long shot. I asked him in, and let him stand sweating while I made up the day book. Then I said sharpish, 'For a boy with a twisted ankle you was nipping right smartly along de Graves Street yesterday morning.' He blushed and said 'I hoped you hadn't recognised me.' I said, 'I have eyes in the back of my head and two sets attached to me arse. What time was it you saw me?' He said it was five past eleven, so I ticked him off fit to take a layer of skin off and let him go."

"Just get him in," said the Inspector.

"He's an honest lad, Inspector. He was at art school until they had this sit-in and he lost his head and squirted paint on an alderman so now his figure studies are confined to my tickets."

"Get him in!"

Fat Auntie hoicked his buttocks from the close embrace of his chair, stuck his chins through the door and shouted.

Donald was a nice boy with good bone structure underneath his shoulder-long hair.

"I am a police inspector. Did you see this gentleman on Monday morning?"

The youth's eyes sought Fat Auntie, but the Inspector smartly stepped between them.

"Yes, sir, at five past eleven in de Graves Street not far from my home."

"How was he dressed?"

"Hat pulled down, sir, dark glasses and an old blue suit."

148

Harry thought he was telling the truth. It just might be something fancy, another man pretending to be Fat Auntie, but people rarely went in for these double-bluff alibis. He asked a few personal questions. Donald's father was a solicitor's clerk, two brothers were in a bank, and he had a place at art school until there was 'a bit of bother' and he lost it. He confidently expected another place in the near future. The Inspector wondered if he really didn't know he was blacklisted, then realised that the boy would not admit it. He dismissed him.

"Well," he said, seating himself, "you're out of it."

"And how, but, God, I had a nasty quarter of an hour."

"Let's see, when you knew Botting you were using some stuff to doctor stale fish, buying it cheap because it was starting to get itchy and 'freshening' it by patent process. Only the chemical, used in treatment of antiques, was a bit toxic to humans and you were up for all kind of offences against the pure food laws."

"Statute barred," said Fat Auntie, "or so my mouthpiece, Mr. Bogg declares. How did you know?"

"Botting kept records."

"I should have known that. Howsoever, Botting knew what I was up to. In fact I'd paid him seventy-five nicker for advice as to what to use. Mind you it freshened the fish up lovely, but made it a bit on the poisonous side. I used to buy the goo from his company. He made me give him letters in which I purported to be in the antique way. Cor! He was thorough, the effer. One day, after it had blown up in my face, and only the fact that I'd kept in the shadows saved me . . ."

"An old woman died after eating doctored halibut," said Harry.

" . . . I won't talk about that. Well, one day he said he wanted a favour. The old man who was the boss of Heavans—can't think of which one he was—was ninety per cent set on engaging Botting as his General Manager at a fat increase over what he was getting. Now, Botty was a man who checked and double-checked, so he came to see me. No 'please' about it. It was 'you will.' Nice fellow! There was a very prominent city gent who owed me a favour and somehow Botting had smelled that out. This chap had some slight acquaintanceship with old Heavan and belonged to one of the posh clubs that Botty had weaselled his way into. Not that I'm jealous, fish-and-chips and flies comfortably open being my style. I was to see that my man came by when Botting and Heavan were in the club. He'd greet them both and have a drink. Then Botting would make an excuse to go. Naturally old Heavan would pump my friend. Botty had provided a very clever script, very subtle indeed, but you got the idea that Botting was just about the cleverest, loyalist chap this side of eternity. He got the job. To tell the truth I was always expecting him to march in my door, saying 'You will . . .' but he never did. I never saw him close up again."

"Where did you meet him?" The Inspector was curious.

"The 'right place' was near the Deauville desert in those days, great Victorian wastes all around and cold as buggery even in summer with the north wind clawing at yer kididdleys but that was *the* place in those days if you wanted to meet the wiseheads. Not crims necessarily, though there was quite a few years inside represented when I was there, but the wise ones. There were two or three vast, run-down old hotels where you climbed marble steps to get yerself on the throne and bidets—cor, I tell yer ignorant me thought they were drinkin' fountains until I was tipped off by a chambermaid who saw me. A very funny scene! I was looking for somebody who knew something about cutting cement with a filler, so I went there and met nobody in that line of country, but I did bump into Botting. Nobody knew him much except that he was 'all right'. This food-refreshing thing came up. He was a very impressive character was this Botting, Inspector, and, bless me I'm sure, you found yourself unburdening to him while he wagged that great cropped head of his like a Dutch uncle. Well, that's all over. I'm in health foods permanent."

He led the Inspector out into the shop where there was a display of coconuts. Two girls were rigging a mock-up which showed a scrofulous family of naked pygmies picking them. 'Untouched by Progress(! !) Nature's Bounty is Sealed within the Nuts' said the headline.

"A luv'ly biz, luv," said Fat Auntie as a benediction as he let the Inspector out.

Harry drove some way along Warren Street before jinking down two side streets. Where he stopped was a half caff, half club. The big, gloomy old room was probably almost exactly the same, apart from the espresso machine, as it had been when it opened one sunny day in 1876 before the joys of the motor car had descended on the land. In those days a foreigner—they were mostly German or Polish—could get an all-in quote of one shilling and sevenpence which entitled him to sit there during the twenty hours of the day it remained opened and receive Continental breakfast, three-course midday dinner and supper of herring or chicken liver, plus three coffees and as much water as a man could drink. Newspapers hung on sticks. Now it opened only eighteen hours a day and the habitués often spoke recognisable English. The man he saw was known as The Foot or Feeto, whichever was preferred, and from ten a.m. until three p.m. seven days a week he was to be found in the caff, which incidentally had no other name. Apart from the periphery of large jewel robberies in which his name idled like a piece of driftwood in the stream of evidence, The Foot had no criminal record. He had a dubious birth certificate from Malta, but some people thought he was a Greek from the islands. He spoke English with a Manchester accent. He was seated at the wide marble-topped table reading a folded newspaper when Harry paused before him.

"Nice to see you, Inspector," he said without looking up. It was his inevitable formula. "Have a coffee?"

"Thanks. How's with you, Foot?"

The cadaverous man put down his newspaper, folded, Harry noted, at the chess problem—chess was played surprisingly often at the caff—and beckoned the waiter, a blond hairless egg of a man who had been there as long as Harry had known the place. "Struggling along, struggling along," said The Foot obedient to his ritual. "And you?"

"Struggling in re the late Cristobal Botting."

The cadaverous man's leathery face, perpetually set in a half-droll half-quizzical expression, looked round and waited until the waiter came with the coffee.

After he had gone, Harry said, "I know that nine years ago he had something on you. The Haliburton emeralds it was; for once you'd got too closely involved. He had a statement from old

Haliburton's clerk that you had bribed him to get the combination of the wall safe."

There was a disconcertingly large intelligence behind the vacuous mask, as if a Grimsby cod professed philosophy. The Foot said in his low, colourless voice, "The clerk died five years ago. Oh, natural causes! The rest of Botting's evidence is equally valueless."

"I have no doubt," said the Inspector. "I know you too well, old fellow." He wondered how old the man was. Fifty? Seventy? There was no telling. The dubious birth certificate said fifty, but he doubted it.

"It was on the cards he'd die violently," said The Foot. "I was here by the way. It was a busy morning with about twelve people, three respectable in a modest way, seated at various times where you are."

"My dear Foot, since when have you ever indulged in violence, personally I mean?"

"I did get mad and do somebody over in 1933," admitted The Foot, "but not since. I didn't like the way my heart started to beat. Botting, Botting! He was quite well known, you know, in a way. Nobody had the slightest thing on him. An ugly customer if roused was the verdict. They said he had some kind of business. In those days there was a dollar black market, you know, with premiums between seven-and-a-half and fourteen per cent. He must have got through eighty or ninety thousand a year. One of the fleas by the name of Little Darkie used to do the running for him. I think he wasn't above taking a monetary share in a caper, though *you* know that that side's difficult to get the truth about. He made a good profit and that's a fact, say two thousand pounds a year in notes after expenses. A better hobby than stamps. He came here to see me one day and came straight out with the Haliburton robbery bit. He never finessed, by the way, just threw the heavy stuff up front. He wanted me to put somebody out of business, a rival firm I suppose. Their lorries were to break down, deleterious stuff poured into the product, stuff that wasn't insured smashed or sent off. He had it blue-printed." The Foot gave his rare laugh, dry as a desert. "His jaw dropped when I told him to piss off. I had to explain that I can't afford blackmail. If I pay once the pack springs on top of me. So I would have to have him killed. You remember the Trio?"

The Inspector did. One used the piano wire, the second, an ex-butcher, did the cutting up, and the third, a cashiered pilot, dropped the weighted packets in the Channel.

"I told him it would cost me two thousand guineas," said The Foot. He sighed. "Funny how that's the only thing which has gone down under the present Government. The ruling rate is five hundred quid shot through the skull and buried in lime on a farm. Anyway I told Botting that's what I'd have to do, that I wouldn't like it because of the personal risk, but that I could see nothing else for it. Plus the fact that if he shopped me anonymously I'd know where it came from and that the last thing I'd do before sentence was to give a friend a cheque for two thousand guineas. He just took up his hat and went smartly out of the door leaving me to pay for his coffee. Hum. I never laid eyes on him again; some time later I heard he'd dropped right out of things."

Harry finished his coffee while The Foot considered his words. "He was a man who got his kicks from ruining people, you know," the man said at length. "The black itself was not enough; in the end he had to drive them into the gutter if he could. There were one or two cases. He screwed the mark not for money but for favours they gave them, but when he could he kicked them fair and square in the crutch. I'm glad he's dead."

"Of course you knew Georgie Krock."

A slightly startled look came into the doll-like eyes. "Christ, it's years since I thought of him. You always had to keep to the windward with Georgie. Expensive aftershave fought against sweat and at best it was an uneasy draw. I'm damned, you bringing him up!"

"It's unsolved."

"I never had much to do with him except a couple of times we were mutual investors in a job. I have never known a man who would haggle for hours over a pound or break down and weep over a fiver as Georgie would. Strange fellow About his killing, it wasn't any of the boys who were around. Georgie was very much 'in' with the heads of those days. But being a refugee he had a lot of foreign contacts, sailors mostly. That stuff's sheer poison and some very tough boys are in it. The drum said that Georgie might have had an argument and . . ."

"Did he know Botting?"

"I wish I knew what you are fishing for," said The Foot. "Not as far as I knew. He was killed a good two years before I ever heard of Botting. I think I previously remarked that the latter is better dead."

That was pretty much Botting's epitaph, thought the Inspector later as he strolled along Whitehall. He had returned the police car to find that Hawker had knocked off. He had nearly two hours before he could visit his wife in hospital, and rather than hang around, with the faint possibility of being nabbed for an emergency job, he strolled aimlessly along, hands in trouser pockets. Even so his police eye—he always said it was his left and that the right one, a civilian, merely watched girls—saw Eldred Keast loping towards him.

They stopped a yard away from each other.

"Is this what is called shadowing?" Keast grinned.

"I never thought you would penetrate my disguise. I was trying to look intelligent. But it is a small world."

"I take Nord and the children up here most Sundays. We have lunch with her best female friend, then she takes off for the Zoo or something improving while I look up friends. At the moment I am clubwards bound. Care for tea?"

The Inspector thought he might as well and presently was in a long comfortable room with punkah-type fans, operated, he hoped, by machinery rather than Indians imported for the purpose of doing it by cords attached to their big toes, although it was the type of club where you could not be quite sure about such things. He sipped tea and ate Gentleman's Relish on buttered crumpets. There seemed a surprising number of men in the room. Keast met his gaze and shrugged. "It puzzles me, too," the tall, thin man said, "why they should be here, I mean it's like Thackeray's favourite theme, how club life ruins marriages. However, we're here. How are you going by the way?"

"A nasty case of dead ends, I'm afraid. Between you and me there were many people who had a grudge against deceased, so many that I doubt whether we could ever find the total."

Keast grimaced. "I found his conduct strange. No need to mince matters off the record, but I found his insane hatred so suddenly revealed of Stigg, Hanna and me abnormal."

"He liked tramping on people's faces," said the Inspector, "for no rational reason. It is not uncommon, we find. A lot of thugs are quite miserable if they aren't commissioned to break an arm occasionally. The protection racket drives them up the wall. They are paid not to break anybody's arm and the tension becomes overwhelming so that they do something silly. That's why we eventually get the protection gangs. Botting had to break somebody occasionally."

"Queer fellow. Only thing is that we feel it hanging over our heads."

"I gather that Mr. Stiggins was not particularly close to the Directors, other than Botting."

Keast cradled his jaw in one hand. "I suppose I always regarded him as a little shadow appended to Botting. If we wanted anything he very quickly and efficiently did it. He was very close-mouthed; sometimes he'd say a few words and then clam up. Yet I think recently little Stiggins was getting ready to cut the umbilical cord. I noticed that he spoke very little to Botting and was faintly hostile." He smiled. "The others noticed nothing, but observing such things is part of my make-up from the days when I chaired a simply horrible inter-services standing committee. You had to watch faces so that you could step into the ring before the Navy started clobbering the Air Force and the Army crept up behind both! At that last Board Meeting, the one where we resigned, I could feel hostility coming out of the little man. Once Botting asked a question of him and was bloody well ignored. He threw back that great head of his as though a gnat had sprouted fangs."

"Did your intuition signal the wherefore?"

"Oh, I guess Master Stiggo had another, better job laid on and no longer troubled to soil his lips around the boss's brogues."

Conversation petered to an end and the Inspector against his better judgment seconded the suggestion of more crumpets. Presently he was summoning energy to cart the weight in his stomach as far as the cloakroom so that he could wash his greasy hands when Keast, who had the elegant art of crumpeting without splatters, dabs of Gentleman's Relish round the corners of his mouth or even soiled fingers, said, "About that whitewashing schedule, I knew, at any rate I thought I knew when Jas Smith was to whitewash the old house. I'm afraid I'm by way of being a mathematician of sorts. In the Army I was called Computer Keast, the mathematical man, not altogether enviously. I'm afraid my weakness was to ignore the human element. However, the whitewashing is done on a rigid day-to-day schedule, over and over again. If you have the kind of brain to memorise the sequence and the time taken per stage, plus taking into account the day the cycle began, number of days in the month and the holidays, if any, you can pinpoint where Smith will be on any given day. I do these calculations with half my mind. It is really a kind of therapy when I'm apparently listening to some fearful bore from the trade. Only thing is that I had Smith pinpointed to be white-washing outside Smart's office on the Saturday, not the Monday."

The Inspector used his handkerchief to wipe his hands and mouth. "What had happened?"

"I was only mildly curious because of the shock of Botting's death, but when you brought the subject up I gave it some thought."

"I suppose the incidence of half-day holidays comes into such a calculation?"

Keast grinned. "It appears that friend Smith can whitewash as much in a morning as in a day if he wants. He is a creature of habit and half a day would put him out. Therefore he merely works quickly on a half day and at his usual pace on a full day. Oh, it had not escaped Botting's eye, but he wanted to keep the place lime-washed and old Smith is one of the few dodos who really understand the stuff. Botting investigated the possibility of spraying on, but it was no good. As it was Smith was a standing irritation to him."

"I suppose the solution is that Smith took a day off."

"Must be, I think. He would probably have made it up over a week's period, so it must have been, say, the Thursday or maybe the Friday." Keast shrugged. "I suppose the staff in general could have known, but Jas does not, but does not, mix much with his fellow wage-slaves who regard him as a snake, besides which he

156

often spends his days slapping lime on in remote parts of the building. Perhaps the gate-keeper knew, certainly old Smart did. Botting had a rule that all absenteeism was notified to Smart by all departments by nine thirty. Smart drew up a list and sent it to Botting who pinned the sheets to his clipboard. At the end of each month, and quarterly, Smart made some kind of dissection so that excessive absenteeism could be dealt with and the people concerned culled. You might say that anybody could have known. I didn't but I very well could have done."

Harry sighed. As so often happened the brilliant clue was rapidly becoming duller, the diamond ending up as useless quartz. He stood up to go.

"When will you be coming down?" asked Keast.

"I thought about nine tonight, there's a train at a quarter past."

"Tell you what, I'm collecting Nord and the kids at nine. There's plenty of room if you care to settle a picking-up place."

The Inspector hesitated, then agreed to take a taxi to the address Keast gave. He thanked him.

"Not at all, only too glad to get you back down there. We don't want this hanging over our heads."

13

"HANGING OVER OUR HEADS," said Noni, "and our children's heads. They whisper about them in the playground. I was talking to old Mr. Smith and he has a cousin who was once secretary to the present Commissioner of Police. He offered to see that a *word in season* was passed on."

She was in her pompous mood.

It had been cold supper at the Hanna house for the Stiggs and the Stiggins, and Nigel Heavan, although it was impossible for Noni to provide a simple meal and crayfish tails and pheasant largely featured. It was Noni's habit to retire to her drawing-room exactly half an hour before the gentlemen who she always hoped would circulate the port but who usually preferred a little brandy.

Noni thought it was part of the general decline of morals within a permissive society.

"I doubt whether they will ever nail anybody," said Nefer, sharply. "Activity will gradually become less, then one day the last policeman will have been withdrawn and the affair will gradually be forgotten. Don't worry about the children, dear, because they are objects of envy not derision from their chums and playmates, but even then it will be a nine days' wonder."

Noni clicked a thumbnail against her large front teeth. "So inconsiderate of Nord to fly up to London."

"She's been doing it, barring sickness, every Sunday for eight years that I remember," said Nefer, "and it's about the only time she can get Eldred off the seat of his pants when he's home. To disrupt routine now would disrupt the kids even more."

"Yes, I did insist mine went for their riding this afternoon," said Noni in tones of one trying to be fair. "Still it must be a traumatic experience."

"Kids like murders, dear," said Mabel Stiggins comfortably. "I caught my eldest reading a book about executions with illustrations. I must say the men who work the guillotine are funny little fellows."

"Foreigners!" said Noni contemptuously.

"Anyway," said Nefer, "Nord and Eldred are rather out of it. I mean it's Bill, Harold . . . and Mark," she hastened to say after a small pause, "who *are* the firm."

"Harold was saying that there are too many Directors," said Mabel innocently, "or there will be."

"It will be a rather unwieldly Board," said Nefer. "Mark, of course, will be Deputy Chairman. That is by Harold's wish as he feels it necessary to have someone of great dignity and experience to support him. Although I am afraid the net result of all this is to expose some dead wood."

Noni had looked faintly pleased at the reference to her husband, but now her large face slipped into impassivity.

The ladies sat in silence. Noni and Nefer had brandy, but Mabel crooked her little finger as she supped a large slug of banana liqueur. She had explained that brandy 'did things to her.' Noni had merely looked and seized the banana bottle from the back of a cabinet. Now Noni leaned forward and refilled the coffee cups, giving Mabel the small dash of warm milk she required. They drank in silence, which if not precisely companionable was comfortable enough. Mabel strolled over to the big open window. A breeze stirred the open curtains. Presently she came back, hesitantly.

"I say, I'm not a nervous kind of person, but I did think I saw a torch flash somewhere in the garden."

"One of the children . . ." began Nefer, but Noni was already waddling towards the door. She was gone five minutes. When she returned she said, "One is asleep, and the other two are in the bathroom. The staff are in. Should one inform the constabulary?"

Nefer glanced at her diamond-studded watch, rather big for her wrist. "The men will be with us in about ten minutes. Let them relax over a drink until then."

In fact relax was hardly the word to describe the gathering round the brandy tantalus. Harold Stiggins had set himself out to charm and even Hanna admitted that his pawky cockneyish humour had something to it. Perhaps they could even produce and present Stiggins as a character. There had been some odd looks at the wine-tasting, although Stiggins' new rank had not then been announced. "Keepin' monkeys, dear boy?" had asked one scarlet-faced doyen of the London West End trade. However, apropos of some quite innocent discussion of possible exports to America, Bill Stigg had come out with a suggestion, no doubt the product of sleepless nights, of such monumental stupidity that Stiggins had hurriedly buried his beak in his glass and even Nigel's lop-sided face had worn a peculiar expression, half compounded of alarm. Hanna had exerted all his considerable personality to by-pass it, and now Stigg sat with his young-looking face in sulky lines.

"The new Board will be a bit top-heavy," said Stiggins, "with five of us. If you like we'll cut out my wife."

"No, no," said Hanna.

"She's a sharp little thing and will pull her weight. The point is that we should shop around for one—two'd be better—professional Directors with strong merchant bank connections. Not now, but within the year and when we have shoved anything nasty under the carpet."

Stigg's face had brightened. "I suppose poor old Eldred is the obvious one. Nord is the minority shareholder."

Stiggins had looked at Nigel while he was speaking. "Any comment, Nigel?" he probed.

Nigel laughed unpleasantly. "Eat each other as you will but avoid indigestion. I suppose you *can* dump Eldred?"

"What do you mean by that?" said Bill Stigg puzzled.

"You alibi each other. I just wondered whether it was mutually agreed and you drew lots for the, er, unpleasantness. It's a good, staid old whodunit plot. I expect Agatha thought of it originally."

The silence was nasty until Stiggins said, in a high voice, "I don't think we should talk like that gennelmin, even in fun, you know."

"Just wondered," rumbled Nigel's basso.

"I assure you we can dump Eldred," said Bill Stigg with an assumption of dignity.

"Oh, I don't mind as long as the old firm's shipshape so that I can eventually ease out of it. But I always had some respect for Eldred's brains; if anybody had planned Botting's death I would have suspected him. He was a very young planner during the War, y'know, and had the reputation of being quite a master at misdirection."

"I don't suppose," blurted Stigg, but shut up as he met Hanna's black glance.

"I'll fix it." Stiggins had the air of a lion tamer. "You see we'll have to have our own export drive and that means Aussie for spirits and top-quality cream sherries, Canada ditto, and the new brand lines Botting was bringing for the States. It can be tasty, gennelmin, very tasty, but there's an element of luck. Above all I want turnover. Nothing looks better in a prospectus nowadays than a million quid's worth of foreign turnover and the small investors don't trouble to work out margins even if the information is there. The man for it is Keast. Oh, I can provide the drive, gennelmin, and the whip if it should be necessary, but Keast has the brains and the charm. I believe he has friends all over?"

Hanna nodded, looking amused for the first time that evening. "He has more acquaintances in all parts of the world than any man I ever knew."

"Well, then, we relieve him of his Board seat and give him the title of Vice-President in charge of overseas sales. It's the kind of title that would go well in the U.S. And we'll point out to him that owing to the travelling it would be better to resign from the Board for the present. We would leave his emolument unchanged. In fact, with the usual fiddle on the old swindle sheets, he'd be better off."

"There's his wife," said Nigel.

"Oh, they've been married for a long time," said Bill Stigg, "and Nord's got all those arty hobbies and the kids. Besides Eldred likes travel as long as there's somebody to order his taxis to meet him at the airport."

"It would probably work." Mark Hanna felt more depressed than a man who has been told he is to be Deputy Chairman should be. "Eldred enjoyed the Army, but I'm afraid the firm has proved rather a bore. You're right about him being the man for the job. People like him and even respect him."

"And, of course," Stiggins shrugged, "if he falls down, well we can just dispense with him in a nice way. The accrued special superannuation fund, plus the tail-end of the contract we'll have given him paid out as a retirement allowance, would be a comforting tidbit I dare say."

"Come in," said Hanna loudly and angrily. You couldn't train Spanish maids not to knock at doors. God knows what went on in their country.

She looked at them impassively with large brown eyes. Carefully she said, "Weeth the cumplimientos of the meestress weel you belong."

"We are coming now," said Hanna, spacing the words and booming them from his head. "We're eight minutes over our time," he told the others. "We'll have to throw Nigel to the wolves and say he was to blame!"

"I'm used to that." Nigel was drinking brandy rather fast.

"Well, well, ladies," piped Harold Stiggins as they filed into the drawing-room. "I am to blame, I alone, but when business is on the table, God bless me I have no sense of time, as my good lady will allow."

"Mabel saw a torch flash in the front garden," said Noni abruptly.

Stiggins frowned at his wife who said, "I saw it quite plainly."

Bill Stigg was already peering out. "We'd better go and take a look-see," he said crisply.

"You'll get no thanks for that," said Nigel, his eyes blood-shot, "plus taking the risk of meeting some scared delinquent with a gun. You'd better phone the police, Mark."

"Yes," said Hanna after a pause. "I'll do that. It is police business."

He was in fact right because an unfortunate constable from the local police force had been meddling with the unfamiliar new-issue torch, a thing capable of infinite variations in its beam, and had negligently touched the 'on' button before Sergeant Honeybody had painfully twisted his wrist.

Honeybody had been notified that the Stigginses and Stiggs together with Nigel Heavan had made their separate ways to the Hanna house. He already knew that the Keasts had departed, ostensibly to London. Equipped with one detective constable from the Yard and one local he had driven out carrying a pair of powerful binoculars. As it grew dusk he had stationed himself and the two others behind the hedge which lined the driveway. Through the open window he could see into the drawing-room quite clearly and wished he could either lip-read or was equipped with one of the beam-listening devices favoured by the Americans. He said so.

"Would it be legal?" said the man from the Yard.

"There has not been any ruling," grunted Honeybody. "I was under a Sergeant once who had deaf parents so he could lip-read fluently. You'll find a lot of things are planned in crowded bars where the noise's so great nobody can hear more than a foot away. He used to sip his stout and read lips. Not admissible as evidence, I don't think, but in any case the Serge didn't want the crims to know how he got them."

He peered through the glasses. "The dollies are a bit tensed like," he said, "I suppose nobody's confessed and the men are thinking of ways to hush it up! Too much to hope." He put down the glasses to wipe the eye-pieces of sweat.

When he took them up again he saw that the gentlemen were now with the ladies. He watched Hanna dial and speak into the telephone. "Another invitation?" wondered Honeybody and felt excitement in his spine. Perhaps the murderer would walk right up the path. "Get concealed all of you, and quick." They all three went into the acrid smell of the shrubbery and crouched motionless for a quarter of an hour. Honeybody heard footsteps on the gravel and strained his eyes in the gloom.

"Sergeant," said a slightly familiar voice. The Sergeant cursed inwardly. Not for the first time in his career some heavy footed booby from the local station had come blundering in and ruined things. "Over 'ere," he hissed resignedly.

It was Senior Constable Fright whose house in the village bore the brass plate 'County Police'. If a stoat could have had laughter wrinkles it would have looked like Mr. Fright. He gave the Sergeant the benefit of his recent meal of stout, cheese and strong pickled onions as he whispered (unnecessarily), "Mr. Hanna phoned that there were intruders in the garden."

"That's you, playing engine drivers with that bleedin' torch." The Sergeant took out his spleen on the abashed constable. "All right, nothing to it but to brazen it out. You two chaps stay here and me and Constable Fright will go up to the house. Here, mind me binoculars."

"I'd be grateful if you'd do the talking," confided Mr. Fright as they walked up the long drive.

"That bloody young idiot with his torch!" grumbled Honeybody.

"The wife reads a lot of psychology in her women's mags," said Fright, "and she says torches are phallic symbols. I mean women don't particularly like torches, but you give one to a man and it's switch on, switch off, point there, flash here. Significant, the wife says."

"Ar," said Honeybody as he rang the doorbell. "I can think of arguments against. For instance . . ." but the door opened and Hanna peered out. As he saw the Sergeant he slipped off the safety chain.

"I think there's something to it, Sergeant," he said as

Honeybody with slight mendacity said that he had been "on the spot" when the complaint had been made.

They went into the dining-room, the stout, bland Sergeant and the lean, sharp-faced constable. Nothing much missed their eyes, even the fact that Noni was aching to go somewhere private and divest herself of her stays. The Sergeant said quickly, "No need to worry, ladies. I have two men in the front garden and when I leave I will station a man all night." That would teach the young effer to fool around with torches, he thought vindictively, all night stint in that stinking shrubbery, besides which the forecast was that the rain was going to reach them during the night.

"Sit down and have some beer," said Noni, memories of comic stage constables stirring in her elephantine memory. "Or," she remembered who Honeybody was, "a whisky."

Both gratefully accepted the double which Hanna poured for them on ice cubes.

"Thank you ma'am," said the Sergeant, "it's been long hours today."

"We shall feel safer with a Constable." Noni gave the noun full capital treatment.

"What exactly did you see, ma'am?" The Constable had reported glimpsing a wiry, carrot-headed female peering out of the window during his second of illumination.

"It was I, officer," said Mabel, rather as if she was imploring the law to arrest her but spare her white-haired father. She sensed that her histrionics, product of generations who had lived in the close, theatrical-minded slums of South London, with their dozens of little daily curbside dramas, were not fitting to present company, swallowed and said in quiet tones, "It's a stuffy old night and I thought a breath of fresh air, such as it is, would clear my head. I was standing looking out of the window and saw a torch beam. In fact it hit me. It lasted perhaps two seconds, then pointed to the ground and I just glimpsed a man's trousers before it was turned off."

"Funny you could see that," suggested Honeybody, "after being blinded by the torch beam."

Mabel gave her thin, not unattractive smile. "It was an immensely powerful pencil beam, Sergeant, such as I never recall seeing before. It did not shine on my eyes, but to be precise on my bust. If I was dazzled I was dazzled there."

Mark Hanna guffawed before being quelled by Noni's gaze. Vulgar she could be en famille; in public never.

"Didn't recognise him?"

"I got the feeling—I cannot analyse it and if I did the impression would vanish—that he was bulky and wore blue pants. I could not, of course, swear to it."

"With the open drive, madam, it might have been someone relieving themselves, begging your pardon," said P.C. Fright, sagely as behoved one whose working life largely revolved around illegal relief. "After a skinful at the Black Dog half a mile away like. Half a mile, we find in the profession, is the crucial moment, the point of no return like. Hold it they cannot, madam, and it's public nuisance or exposure according to the circs."

"Quite," said Hanna.

"I can't see why any of the factory workers who get a skinful in that particular bloodhouse," said Stiggins, "should carry powerful torches. That smacks of a professional job, you know."

"We will search so thorough, sir, that a mouse won't have concealment. Some of the smart boys park a van or car and send a man on to recce for houses where the lights are all out. It probably was one of those if it was a matter of criminal intent. No cause to worry, but in future I would put protection on those windows."

"We have it," said Hanna. "You cannot see the grille now, but it is there and I check that they are all pulled up and locked each night. We put them in after . . ." He went crimson.

"After Uncle Nigel went barmy and cut up rough." Nigel had sat silent in the corner, his odd eyes looking worried. Honeybody saw a tremor in his hand as he lifted a glass. Brandy, thought Honeybody. "Oh, don't worry dears, I'll eventually get used to it. It is something if in my small, humble way I have discouraged burg . . . bulgery." His tongue was unsure of itself.

"Where's Mr. Keast?" Honeybody asked innocently.

"He usually takes the family on a London treat trip on fine Sundays," said Nefer. "Noni thought she would have a get-together of the family remaining." She stopped in some confusion as the Sergeant's eyes became riveted on Mr. Stiggins.

"By adoption only," chuckled Stiggins, but his little eyes remained hard. "Just a bit of a chat. I'm afraid I'm a man with a fixation for business."

"So am I," said the big Sergeant softly, "although my business is murder, which I don't suppose you discussed."

"But we did." Nigel was on his feet, swaying slightly.

"Sit down!" said Mark.

"Mind your own bloody business." Nigel's eyes appeared to burrow into the sides of his long nose. He stood glowering at Hanna until gradually one could see the cause slowly erasing from his mind. He was left with a foolish smile in place of it. "Murder," he said, "we were talking of murder. Mark shaid, I think it was Mark, or you Bill, that they had drawn lots and given each other an ali . . . ali." He fell backwards into his chair and commenced to snore.

The Sergeant and P.C. Fright sat, arms folded, looking at their shoes. A good old dog produced by the hard road, thought Sergeant Honeybody, looking at the Constable out of the corner of his eye; you didn't have to tell him not to frig around with torches. Silence was a technique never known to fail even with hardened recidivists. Women usually resisted longer than men.

It was Stiggins who said, memories of the *Magnet* imbued in the format, "I thought it was just a jape. Nigel suggested it himself."

"A wot?" said Honeybody incredulously.

"I thought he was jokin'," Stiggins said in a small voice.

"Joking about murder with poor Mr. Botting not in his grave," thundered the Sergeant at his Jehovah best.

"Now, Sergeant," said Bill Stigg, writhing under the imputation of bad manners, "it was just a joke in bad taste. Poor old Nigel shouldn't drink, but somehow he got at the brandy. Drink in, brains out."

"And we find often that truth comes out," said Honeybody.

"What the hell do you mean?" blustered Hanna as the women watched.

Honeybody teetered his chair on to the two back legs and saw

Noni wince as something groaned inside the frame. He leered his blandest and said, "Whatever anybody cares to make of it, I'm sure, sir. It's an old Latin adage, sir, in vino veritas, which I understand . . ."

"We all know what it means," said Hanna, shaking his head low like a bull with the lance in its shoulder muscles, "but what the devil . . ."

"I think, Sergeant," said Noni's heavy voice, "that we should make allowance for Mr. Heavan. You surely know his unfortunate history." She shook her head as she glanced at the unlovely, flushed face of Nigel with its open, gurgling mouth.

"It's most unfortunate, ma'am," said the Sergeant, "for these things have a habit of getting bruited abroad. By Friday every public bar will be ringing with it I shouldn't wonder."

"Damn him," said Nefer in a whisper, "why couldn't he stay inside."

"Surely, Sergeant," said Noni, "nobody can believe such a thing. It is not credible for a start."

"People like reading and hearing the worst," said the Sergeant. "Did you ever read a book about nice people, excluding the Good Book," he added with hasty official obeisance to the Establishment, "and I must say some of them were a bit odd, though of course they *were* Jews mostly."

"Noni's right," there was a bleating note in Bill Stigg's tenor, "such a notion is beyond the bounds of possibility. Beyond the bounds."

"I remember a few years ago, sir, at a weekend party at a country house, the old Friday noon until Monday noon effort. You don't often find that nowadays. It was the Sunday night," the room was very still apart from Honeybody's rich voice, "and four men were in the first-floor library playing bridge. The rest of the party, some twelve of them, were downstairs having a scrabble evening. The bridge players for one reason or another all left the library at one time or another. And sometime during the evening a diamond bracelet worth thirty thousand pounds went off. The lady of the house was going to the opera on the Tuesday night in full fig and the family jewels were out of the strong box. Now during the first hue and cry the men decided that it would be simpler to say that they were never out of each other's sight. They were honest, honourable men, three of 'em, and it never crossed their minds that they might be providing an alibi for the thief. It was just that their instinct was 'keep out of it' and besides they were men in the public eye, very busy in spite of that long weekend, and they did not want a session with a stupid old police sergeant." He stopped and eyed his whisky glass. Mrs. Stiggins glided forward and refilled it.

"What happened?" asked Bill Stigg in a flat voice.

"Nothing much for a time," said Honeybody, "except that they got mortal sick of seeing my sylph-like figure hanging around them and their servants. Complain, they did, to the Commissioner, but I was still around. Then one day I let it be known that I'd be willing to have a chat with any of them *in strict confidence*. Two of the innocent men told me the truth, sixty-six point six six, an unheard-of percentage in our business. Lumme if we get two-and-a-half per cent truth we dance with glee," the Sergeant undulated his hips so that his stomach bounced. "Six years the culprit got and his fence five. We caught him handing the bracelet over on the tube. Ah, well, thank you for the whisky. I don't often taste that quality, ma'am."

"We own a very small distillery, have done since 1820," said Noni with pride.

"Well," said the Sergeant, getting out a square of pasteboard and scribbling, "sleep easy now. There'll be a vigorous young constable about the grounds the night long. And, just to make sure," he put the pasteboard on the mantelpiece, "here's the telephone number at my local lodgings. Come any complaint or worry you can cut the red tape and get on to me. So we will be wishing you goodnight, all."

Hanna took them to the door, but did not speak.

The Sergeant allowed himself the pleasure of assigning the transgressing constable all-night duty until eight a.m., and took P.C. Fright and the Yard man to the car. He dropped the latter off in town and drove back with Fright. "Do you think they'll call, any of 'em?" said Fright.

"No loyalty among them, except husband-and-wife kind," grunted the Sergeant, "and they are all on edge, did you feel it?"

168

"Like poachers on a dark night with the ferret out and a badly bitten finger on the cards," grunted Fright.

"The big woman—Mrs. Hanna—is loyal to something, probably the firm's name," said Honeybody, saying goodnight.

To his surprise he found Inspector James already in their room, stockinged feet doubled under him as he squatted on his bed and read the Sunday papers.

" 'Allo, Harry, never expected to find you back so soon."

"Ran into Keast in Whitehall. I travelled back with the family. Three kids to be amused! Gawd!"

"And your own good lady?" asked the Sergeant with the tactlessness of an old friend.

"Moribund. Yet I do not like the way I was looked at. I caught a probationer staring at me and when I glared she lapsed into some kind of nervous hysteria."

"Your magisterial eye, Inspector, just as we see suspects quail when you look at them." Agile despite his bulk the Sergeant dodged the flung pillow.

"I'll tell you my day first," Harry James got off the bed and carried two rickety chairs over to what had once been a washstand.

Presently he said, "So it all boils down to the fact that the London end is very dead mackerel, barring the kind of fluke that doesn't much happen. But it was interesting psychologically, firmly placing Botting as the man who simply did not like resting on his ill-gotten advantages but persisted in trying to ruin his victim."

"Not uncommon," said the Sergeant, his thoughts telescoping the sordid years. "Many of them get into the dock for that very reason. I never knew a blackmailer who wasn't a bit of a sadist. Fear stops a lot of them, but a percentage has to follow right through. O' course, sometimes the victim, being smashed and ruined, has nothing more to lose so he goes to the police at long last. A nice feller, eh?"

"I think with Botting there was something else besides sadism. The South London police turned up the bare bones of his family. There was a paternal grandfather from southern Europe, a fruit packer in Covent Garden, who was probably suffering from what we would now term a persecution complex. The father took to one of the gloomier religious sects in a very strict way; young Botting was reared on stories of blood and damnation. I think the ruining part of it is kind of sacrificial. He offers a victim and is thus temporarily a better man himself."

"They should keep religion for the upper classes who know how to use it," grunted Honeybody with conviction. "Like pot and all that it does the nobility no harm, but Joey Bloggs just can't wear it without there being trouble. I bet there's not a bishop in the country who don't agree with me if the truth was known."

"Quite," said Harry reflecting on the large number of middle-aged policemen who went in for the homespun philosophy bit. "Another thing, I am inclined to remove Keast from the possibles to the remotely possible list. A lazy fellow, I think, who might fight if his family was threatened but not for much else. And I cannot see that that happened. His wife's money ensures that they're comfortably off; his wife is a dilettante lady but very kind-hearted. No rumours of domestic uproar and they both dote on the kids in a sensible way. No, I can't see it. Okay, Serge, let me hear the worst."

"First thing, Mr. James, is that the laboratory made nothing of the cellaring where Percival got his head bashed in. No lint on the barrels, definitely no prints that should not be there. Inquest on Wednesday and the Chief Constable won't oppose an 'accidental death' finding. He asked me over the blower whether we wanted to use the inquest for cross-examination, so I stuck my neck out and said 'no'."

The Inspector nodded. Using an inquest for a fishing expedition without judges' rules was occasionally useful though nowadays frowned upon. In the last century, indeed well into the 1920s, you could positively torture a witness, but the public stomach was more fastidious today and the Sunday papers had to rely upon the bread-and-milk of the police courts for their fun.

"The P.C., I'm mentioning him in the report, did a good job with the workers, sir, a very good weasel he'll make and with his innocent look a natural for Vice. Yet it is very thin, sir, very thin," the Sergeant looked down at the sheets of paper before him. "Botting was a remote kind of Boss. He'd ask questions and that was that, but he wasn't particularly unpopular in spite of a faint contempt in his manner. He was quite aloof; if he saw an employee in the street he might barely nod. He wasn't the one to stand a pint down at the pub, and the other Directors had the chore of fronting up at the Christmas parties. He left the women and girls alone and nobody ever saw him tight . . . Mark Hanna, now, sometimes has a list to the starboard and a couple of times one of the van drivers has driven him home, protesting. They like Hanna, an open-handed gent. Bill Stigg they have pretty well placed, but he's a gent to the manner born and polite in an officerish way. They grin behind his back, but not maliciously. There are jokes about Mrs. Stigg, the bouncy little lady, I'm afraid. Keast is more complex. He's got a malicious kind of wittiness which makes 'em writhe, you know, but he's also authoritative and approachable. Anybody with private troubles sees Keast if he can. Stiggins, well he's an unknown quantity to most of them. The office staff think he's extremely efficient, not very human, and, as one of the young ladies said, no gentleman. Of the ladies, I've told you about Nefer. Mrs. Keast doesn't come to the business much, but they say she's a nice lady. Noni they are in awe of. They understand the type, the old matriarch in the corner bossing everybody. Grandma Buggins to the life."

"Summed up with shrewdness, Serge, I couldn't improve on the assessment."

"Now as to the movements of Jas Smith, Mr. James, in the first place he had the Thursday off before Botting's death. He ran a nail into his foot when helping his wife to clear out the loft; we checked with the neighbours. The wife is a talking machine and everybody who would listen got a blow-by-blow description. This was on the Wednesday evening. He went to the doctor and got tetanus and other shots and a certificate to take a day off. He gave the certificate on Friday to Smart who filed it and phoned the pay clerk not to deduct his day's wages. Botting was quite ruthless about that sort of thing. No certificate, no pay. Now as to knowing where Smith was, you might say that sublime indifference prevailed. Nobody speaks of Jas without some nasty word attached. He's known as a boss's pimp, sir, and is strictly a non-unionist, not that there is any union trouble here. Botting adhered to the law and trade union agreements down to the last letter; nevertheless old Jas is regarded as poison. I expect people had a fair idea where he was each day, but nobody wanted to know except to look around to see he wasn't near if anything confidential required to be said." Honeybody shrugged and turned over the pages.

"The mysterious parcel that got swiped out of old Smart's precious bin did exist, so it seems. You remember that it was given to him by a young clerk who shortly afterwards left? One Pocock, which is a common name around here. He was in lodgings here and the landlady has moved. Me and a constable phoned or visited thirty-five Pococks, and fluked his auntie forty miles from here. There's a beer house near here and he knew the publican's son who remembered he had this auntie. He joined the Army, poor young devil. He read one of these Service ads, where they'll teach you leadership until you're retrenched at forty. You know, a young bloke with a mush telling troops to go plunging into the jungle— taken in film studios so they say, us not having jungle any more. He fell for it and is fourth in charge of the puttees warehouse near Swansea."

"Puttees warehouse?"

"It's never been off the classified info list, Mr. James. Twenty-eight million puttees, that is fourteen million pairs, the Lloyd George Gu'ment having awarded a twelve-year contract they were unable to get out of. Young Pocock, I say 'young' though the report says he looks twenty years older than his chronological age, got silverfish in the two bays he commands."

"Silverfish!"

Honeybody nodded. "Over the years they had eaten five million puttees, the odd number making it worse. Since they have got rid of their worries east of Suez, the War Office have been concentrating their energies on the puttees. They had to strongly resist a scheme of the Big Feller to give them to the Biafrans just to prove he wasn't taking sides. Then the silverfish were discovered. Cor! Generals running round like schoolgirls, sir. If the Select Committee got hold of it, God knows how many poor old devils would get reduced pensions, sir. So they've retooled an ordnance factory at the cost of seven hundred and fifty thousand quid and are working three shifts seven days a week. M.P.s who get nosy are told it's a secret weapon. Cor!"

"Seven hundred and fifty thousand nicker wasted!" snarled Harry.

"A bagatelle, sir, if it didn't go on that the frogs would con it out of them in a phoney aircraft deal."

"Get to the point, Sergeant!"

"Mr., I should say Lieutenant Pocock's wits have been professionally addled by the training. It took the local Inspector who saw him four hours to get a total recall. Pocock finally said that the big round-faced man with the funny hair—he couldn't remember the name—had given him the package and instructed him just to say it was the 'Directors' wish' that Smart should put it in his wine bin. But no kind of a witness, sir, trembles like a leaf if spoken to harshly."

"I suppose there is no doubt that this man Pocock *did* collect a parcel and deliver it to Smart?" The Inspector was tired and his tone was sharp. Honeybody always embarked upon these orotund and dubious anecdotes late at night; the only thing to do, the Inspector knew from experience, was to grind him down to facts.

"Yes, Harry, the Swansea chaps have no doubt about that; there *was* a packet sent across."

"That is the corner stone," said the Inspector, "and the motive. In it was incriminatory evidence, I imagine, something so nasty that time could not dull the sharpness of its edge. Therefore hardly adultery or the odd bit of slanderous talk. But black-mailers . . ."

Honeybody wagged his head. A considerable proportion of 'unsolved' murders and murderous assaults in Superintendent Hawker's files bore the little red paper star which meant 'victim was suspected blackmailer'. Many were never likely to be solved because the dead man or woman had such a plethora of enemies that it was impossible—if the killer had normal luck—to isolate a handful of prime suspects. Harry remembered a fat old disbarred solicitor, strangled with nylon cord in a palatial hotel near Nice, whose cryptic notebook indicated that he had three hundred paying 'clients', as the pros called their victims.

"Two other things, sir. P.C. Fright was checking through his notebook, which he does each Saturday night, and found that he'd taken the number of Botting's car about 1 a.m. on the

Monday morning. It was parked just down a lane a quarter of a mile from the Hanna house and a matter of eight miles from Botting's apartment. The P.C. checked his missing cars bulletin, saw that the parking lights were on and it was parked right on the verge and got back on his bicycle, but he noted the number."

"Another one of these straggling, dead-end leads," said the Inspector. "The evidence is quite clear that he did go out and perhaps came back in a state of agitation. If he went to meet anybody it was probably in reply to an outgoing or incoming phone call. At least you hardly make an appointment for after midnight, or not a business one! He was sitting down with a bottle of extra good wine, preparatory to nuzzling it in comfort before hitting the cot. I found the half-bottle with one glass missing. So either he gets or makes a call or else a thought strikes him so sharply that he has to get out of the flat to think it over. Sometimes anxiety catches people like that. They have to go for a walk or a drive, even to the cinema, to think it over. The familiar four walls become intolerable. He might have been sitting there in the lane alone with his thoughts or with somebody."

"The killer?"

"Damned if I know. About that lift shaft, y' know, I guess it was pretty well known. I telephoned a wine merchant I know while I was waiting at the hospital. The Heavans and their eccentricities are part of the folk-lore of the trade. It's rather proud of them. Most of the stories are apocryphal, of course, and there is a legend of the huge old house, filled with letter-presses, commodes, ancient clerks, bibulous partners with amazing habits and a lift groaning under the weight of endless bottles of port and game pies."

"But wouldn't the voice have been known to him, and well known, too? You just don't poke your head into a lift shaft for anybody," said the Sergeant.

"Well," said Harry, "if an unknown voice cooed 'Pray come and stick the old loaf in yon lift shaft', I don't suppose there would be any reaction. On the other hand if it menacingly hissed, 'I've got you to rights, you murdering bastard. Come here and listen,' you probably would stick your head in. Although I agree it is odds-on it being a familiar voice, and by extension the voice of somebody who might be expected to be on the premises. That leaves us with too many suspects!"

Honeybody grunted. "I softened up the barmaid in the pub opposite Heavans. Four pounds on expenses and half an hour's ride in the police car. It's amazing what a smart girl hears over the bar, although it's mostly in one ear and out t'other. Oh, she knew about Bill Stiggs' ladies and Mark Hanna's disastrous speculations—he still owes a packet to his bookie, but he always pays in the end so nobody worries much. Keast she likes, but puts him down as a man with a talent for fading into the wallpaper. A careful listener, she said. She rather liked Botting as an open-handed man who was a witty talker although with moody days. Stiggins, well she just laughed and made a joke I won't repeat. At one time he had a drink three or four times a week with Botting, but for a few weeks before the murder they were never there at the same time. There was also a feeling around the office staff that Stiggins wasn't more than civil to Botting. They thought that maybe Stiggins was on to a better job, putting him down as a chap who wasn't over civil unless it paid him. And now, sir, we made a muck-up tonight. We found the Heavans and the Stiggins were meeting at the Hanna house, so . . ."

When he'd finished the Inspector laughed. "Trust you to turn adversity into advantage. Do you honestly think one of them will call you?"

"I pressured them as well as I knew how," said the Sergeant modestly. "And I would think that Stiggins might turn the screw a bit more after I went. Mr. Botting's faithful hyena has turned into quite a bity little lion, sir."

The Inspector looked at him for a long moment. "You'd better take a day off tomorrow and stay here just in case."

"That was my idea, Harry. Some beer in quarts, paperbacks from the Women's Institute Library, guaranteed pure though a few did seem to have crept into the shelves by mistake, you could pick them out by the thumb marks. I'll rest my great feet for a change and do a bit of routine work over the blower."

The Inspector took his coat off and yawned. "I've got that feeling. Tomorrow will be the start of the long path to a lifetime in quad for somebody."

14

"I T W I L L B E a long path, gentlemen, but a successful path. We can look forward to the House of Heavan being in the ascendant."

Harold Stiggins sat down. It had not been a bad speech, thought Keast, and God knows he'd sat through enough of them in his time. He glanced round the table of the private banqueting room of the Good Queen Bess. There were only twelve for this, the monthly Directors' lunch. It was usually held in the kitchen of the old house, but late the previous afternoon Stiggins had telephoned Stigg and suggested they used the pub. It had been a commonsense decision and in any case the pub always did the catering. Besides three Directors, Nigel Heavan and Stiggins there were six guests and—hardly in that category—Inspector James, unexpectedly the life and soul of the party. On impulse, because the man was unassuming, likeable, and, Keast thought, perhaps a little pathetic when you envisaged him against a background of tough, ruthless cops with granite chins and upward-thrust chests of steel, Keast had asked him. Stiggins had thought it a good idea when told early this morning. "It'll scotch any malicious rumours," the little man had declared, "when it gets around that the Yard are wining and dining with us. Keep your eye on him and see he gets the best of everything—perhaps you might get 'em to turn on caviar."

"The menu is already planned; caviar would look vulgar," Bill Stigg had said sulkily.

"Very well, very well, but *keep his glass filled*."

In fact, thought Keast, the Inspector was capable of keeping his own glass filled. Traditionally, these lunches, where sometimes confidential matters or *sub rosa* trade gossip were exchanged, had a minimum of servants. Stigg acted as wine steward and two waitresses entered briefly to serve and take away used dishes. But as it was today served in the pub, it had been thought better to abide by normal service and the jolly old wine waiter hovered over the Inspector more assiduously than the other guests. In between courses the Inspector entertained his fellow guests from a seemingly limitless store of anecdotes concerning bygone crimes and scandal in the wine trade. The Cromwellian vintner who ran brothels under the cover of frequent sherry tastings; the strange case of the Holborn bottle-maker who kept seven wives and periodically murdered one of them as his scruples would not let him take an eighth; old Higgins who chopped up wealthy customers and concealed the bits in his famous casks of Spanish brandy. These, embroidered by many a comic detail, tripped off the Inspector's tongue; his face became flushed but his tongue remained nimble until the brandy was reached. Thereafter he remained silent until old Cark, a giant of a man but not renowned for tact, asked in the shrill, querulous voice known to three generations of bibbers—Cark on white Bordeaux was unsurpassed—"When are ye going to take up the feller who brained poor Botting?" Cark's pronunciation and use of words were faintly Georgian.

Keast estimated that the Inspector had a third of a bottle of brandy in him, but he raised his head and said, with the pedantic, hair-splitting of the sloshed, "Take in, rather than take up, the local station having no stairs, it being found that drunk and disorderlies tend to break their limbs if steps are provided. We have a clue, my dear sir, a vital one."

There was an avid silence as the Inspector's glass was refilled. He spun the glass between finger and thumb, gazing into it as though into a crystal. "I can tell you this much, but no more, because more would be under the Official Secrets Act which I am sworn to uphold. There was a certain package, I can tell you that much. It was purloined, which means swiped in lay language. But Mr. Botting diseased—I should say deceased—had the habit of duplicating everything."

"Systematic man, Botting," said a wizened Dutch gin man who dabbled in Tokay as a sideline. "System makes the man," he hiccoughed and lay back in his chair blinking profoundly.

"You were saying," said Mark Hanna, gently.

"Eh?" said the Inspector, focusing his eyes by dint of a villainous squint, "Oh, yes. By dint of rat, ratio, much thought I have alone deduced the approximate area of concealment of the duplicate. Every hope, gents, every hope for a quick arrest. Click,

click, the darbies well on and before a local magistrate. Bail strenuously opposed." He solemnly crumbled a roll and cut off a piece of cheese.

There was a hum of conversation. Only Nigel Heavan, who had toyed with his food, said nothing and drunk great quantities of Vichy, continued to look at the Inspector with a faint, sickish smile.

At a nod from Hanna, Stigg, as the official host, arose and began the business of dispatching guests. Without exception they had hire cars awaiting them, prudent precaution these days at trade get-togethers. One of the first to go was Inspector James, his eyes looking straight ahead, his speech slow and sparse, and his steps deliberate.

When the room had cleared Keast said to Hanna, "I hardly like the thought of the Inspector driving himself home."

Stigg sniggered.

"He'll be all right," said Stiggins. "When did you read of a cop being lumbered for pissed in charge, eh? They look after their own."

Nigel Heavan, who was by now looking human, started to say something, but abruptly shut his mouth.

"Probably sleeping it off in the back seat by now," said Hanna as they prepared to leave.

In fact the Inspector was in one of the toilets off the loading bay over the road. He hung his coat up, and swallowed the contents of a tiny bottle. After forty seconds he was spectacularly sick. He straightened, squinted at a tiny capsule he produced from an envelope, and took it. He cleaned up, leaned against the doors and waited the prescribed five minutes, after which there was only the slightest, muffled knocking in his head. He knew that in ten minutes' time he would feel normal. He turned his coat inside out. Strapped inside the right breast was a soft leather flask of cured goatskin. It held three-quarters of a pint. From the top was a short rigid tube and a curved funnel. It had been invented a hundred or so years ago by the pimps and rollers along the waterfronts who were forced to 'drink' a great deal in their activities. A few hours' practice and you could secrete your hard liquor even when facing a victim. The only trouble was that there could be no air holes and there was usually a delayed 'glunk' as the drink was swallowed into the flask, so that the practitioner talked loudly and laughed a lot. The Inspector disconnected the piping and put a screw top on the flask before placing it in his hip pocket. A very fine brandy, just under half a pint of it, which he would put away for his wife who preferred it to liqueurs.

He continued to wait for a quarter of an hour, put on his coat and cautiously went into the bay. A couple of men were loading a truck and did not even glance at him. Separated by fifty yards, the new office building and the old house looked down on him. He did not look at them. He hoped, he very much hoped, that behind one of the windows a pair of eyes were watching him. He walked very slowly and carefully towards the entrance to the old cellaring. The foreman cum manager was immersed in a pile of invoices and only looked up to nod very briefly.

He wandered around, looking vaguely at things, until he reached a spot where the barrels towered thirty feet above the ground. Ladders and scaffolding gave access. He saw great hooks attached to the beams of the ceiling. They used slings and tackle to get them up. He took a closer look. A notice hung on one of the bottom-most barrels. Nothing was to be moved until a date set four and a half years from now. Probably Madeira, he thought, by the markings. He had known that he must find a set-up like this somewhere in the cavernous cellars, but his search was ended. He stood, very carefully memorising the exact location, and then walked on until he came to the bay where Mrs. Frankly and her staff were bottling. Nothing had changed, not even their clothes, but this time they were on port.

"Afternoon, ladies." The Inspector, flushed by his grammar-school successes in amateur theatricals, had once thought of training for the stage until his father had put his foot down. Now he achieved a thirsty, bibulous leer and the faintest tendency to stagger sideways. "What is this galaxy of beauty that meets my eyes?"

"Full as a country dunikin arter a Methodist picnic," hissed one old lady.

"Ar, proper pissed," agreed a less poetic neighbour.

"Wine and beauty is the toast," said the Inspector with the

179

slightest of belches as he ogled the rich red stream emerging into the bottle from the nearest lady's hose-pipe. "Ere, luv," she adjusted the cloth cap she wore, peak on the nape of her neck, reached under her chair for a soiled pint glass, and squirted a generous tot into it. "We 'ave to up'old the honour of 'Eavans when the p'lice is effing investigatin', eh, Mrs. Frankly?"

That lady merely grunted as she watched the Inspector wander about the various barrels. When he turned round the glass was empty. Another lady, clad in a voluminous football jersey, squirted it half full.

"The reason why I have to keep my strength and health up," confided Harry, mysteriously closing one eye, "is that I am on the scent of a vital glue, congealed, I should say concealed, among the barrels down here."

"Wot is it, the budget secrets?" barked a cynical woman. "If they tax the stuff much more we'll all be out of jobs."

"A clue to put somebody inside for the rest of his or her natural life," said the Inspector, bending to examine the doubled end of a length of hose.

"Wot's an unnatural life?"

But the Inspector had picked up the hose, the doubled end snapped straight and a gush of port wine narrowly missed the lady with the cap. " 'Ere," said Mrs. Frankly, moving fast, but the Inspector obstinately hung on and not until a fine porty rain had moistened most of the bay did the head lady bottler succeed in wresting it away and expertly cutting the flow. "Here," she picked up his half-filled glass, "you take this and bloodhound arter your clue, sonny boy, afore you get yourself drownded in this fine old fruity."

For a few seconds they watched the Inspector weave off until Mrs. Frankly said in a cutting voice, "They pay us to bottle, girls, so up and away."

The Inspector 'lost' his glass and went up the old way into the kitchen where the wine-tasting had been held and thence to the loading bay.

"Like a lift home?" It was Eldred Keast, his nose twitching a trifle as he saw the port marks on the Inspector's suit.

"Many thanks, I'm sure." Harry made heavy work of entering

the low-slung car and remained silent and breathing heavily until Keast dropped him outside his door. He stood there trying to find the door bell until the motor of the car died away in the distance. Then he straightened and rang.

"Christ," said the Senior Constable Fright, "you stink like several distilleries."

"Thought I might as well do the job well," said Harry. "Did you get the stuff?"

"Spread over the dining-table."

"I'll sponge this suit and take a bath," said Harry, "I feel as though I'll never face a drink again."

"That feeling never lasts," said Fright sagely.

"Where's Honeybody?"

"Went up to his room for a siesta."

"No need for him to be mixed up in this," said Harry as he collected a towel from Mrs. Fright.

The P.C. laid a calloused finger against his sharp nose.

Honeybody was asleep, head cradled on one massive forearm, and the Inspector smiled affectionately as he got into his dressing-gown and took his soiled suit along to the bathroom. When he came back he put on dark slacks and a beige turtle-necked sweater and tennis shoes. He checked a small but powerful torch with a variable beam. Sticking his wallet in his hip pocket he went downstairs. Fright was standing looking down at a musty, stained old plan. "Fortunately I was at school with the surveyor. It was a rare old job to dig this out. The old tunnel was dug in 1916 as an emergency exit when people sheltered in Heavans' cellars for fear of zeppelins. It was checked in 1940 and the shoring and pit props were still okay. Heavans was never used as a shelter last time because there were no raids hereabouts, though Heavans itself went up when a sneak raider got himself lost and jettisoned a land mine. It's had barbed wire on the exit which comes out in a field at the back of the business premises, but you can't stop the kids playing around and getting in They worry and worry at the wire until they've made a gap. I crawled through a year ago and it's quite dry and safe, with the woodwork thoroughly creosoted; I put in a recommendation that the entrance should be filled with hollow concrete slabs, but that was just to cover myself if there were an accident. Nothing was done, o' course."

Harry looked at his watch. It was four forty-five. "I'll doze in that easy chair," he said. "If it suits you we'll take off at around half past eight."

The Constable nodded and the Inspector, sweating in the stillness of the little room, dreamed uneasily that Mrs. Frankly was forcing home-made wine down his throat, including the cockroaches which she said improved the flavour. Eventually the Constable tugged at his arm.

Fright was in plain clothes and surprisingly smart and with-it. In uniform he contrived to look around fifty, but in civvies he was his real age of thirty-five. "We'll stroll across the fields, Inspector. It's cow and orchard country and quite pretty seeing it is quite close to the city."

The Sergeant had 'nipped out' for a drink, reported Fright.

It was pretty, with that particular drowsy quality which seems unique to the remaining grassland of England. The Inspector began to wish he could call the whole thing off and have an early night. Murder and its ramifications just did not fit into this landscape. The last hundred yards was through an apple orchard, then over a stile into a weed-covered field of perhaps an acre.

"Bad neglected soil," said the Constable with a countryman's concern. "It was turned up during the war for allotments—food for the creepies and crawlies was all it ever produced. But it's zoned as farmland, that's why Heavans haven't extended over the laneway. Lot of nonsense, this," he scuffed his foot, "is no kind of farmland at all unless you poured money on to it. They do some strange things. Well, here we are."

It was a mound with an open brick entrance covered in barbed wire.

"Why didn't they have a door?"

The Constable shook his head. "Doors are likely to get jammed if there are explosions near and in case of a direct hit they accentuate the blast effect. And if we put one on now those kids would fiddle it off its hinges in three months. Here," he touched the barbed wire and a section, large enough to permit the ingress of an agile young body, flapped down. "Cunning as monkeys," said the Constable with a trace of local pride as he produced a glove and a small wire-cutter from his hip pocket. He snipped and pulled for a couple of minutes. "There we are, sir, ample room."

The Inspector flashed his torch into the cavity. The shoring looked in good condition and the sloping earth floor was free from tell-tale stones.

"It slopes down for about twenty feet," said the Constable, "then there are thirty very broad stairs—almost a stepped ramp. comes out about the middle of the old cellaring."

From the map Harry had judged that the entrance would be near the massive cask behind which Keast, Stigg and Hanna had been driven to discuss their grievances against Botting.

"The cellar entrance had some empty old crates pushed against it last time I saw it," said Fright. "Not much trouble or noise to move them, but just the chance they may have sealed it with full barrels in which case you're unlucky. You know Bert, the night watchman?"

Harry nodded.

"He used to have my job for a good many years. I'll have a word with him—we're old mates—and tell him not to mind if there's a a a bit of noise from the cellaring. I suppose," he hesitated, "I could easy come along with you, Mr. James, not being on duty until midnight."

"Thanks," said Harry, "I appreciate it, but I'm not certain of my ground. It could be that Heavans could charge me with trespassing; it's a slippery legal point, and besides . . ."

He did not need to go further. H.M.'s judges disapprove and M.P.s eloquently denounce anything smacking of a trap, of the sinister Continental-type *agent provocateur* and un-English listening at keyholes.

"So," said Harry, "you please forget this. If anything goes wrong you know nothing. And if Honeybody asks you where I am I'm eating with the Chief Constable." He nodded, bent his head and went into the shaft. He pulled back the lever which made his torchlight into a wide, flat beam. Under foot it was smooth and easy, and the stairs immensely broad when he came to them. The air was fresh with none of the dampish, mouldy nose-tickling which he associated with tunnels. Superb natural drainage, he thought, tribute to the perspicacity of the founder of the firm.

The topography repeated itself, up a broad stairway and then a gently rising shaft. He shone the torch at the archway. There were old crates stacked up, but he thought there was something else behind. He shoved and the centre remained rigid. A couple of barrels, he thought. The right was equally obdurate, but to the left there was a movement. He heaved and eventually the cases at the top fell back. There was one barrel pressing against the bottom half, but at the top was now an aperture three feet by two, its bottom edge four feet from the ground. If there was anyone already in the cellars, thought the Inspector grimly, they were alerted now. Standing sideways he put his head, left shoulder and arm through the hole, jumped and clawed sideways at the barrels for purchase. There was the sound of ripping cloth and a rasping at his ribs as he fell through and down, his clutching fingers gaining a hold on a barrel top, taking the strain as his shoulder thumped against the dusty floor. A kick and he was sprawling there. He got up and felt his ribs which gave no pain as he pressed. He felt blood on his cheek and traced it to a continuous drip from his left ear. He cursed and clapped his handkerchief against it, flashing his torch with the other. As he had thought the entrance to the tunnel was behind the great barrel. He went round it and stood getting his bearing and waiting for his ear to cease bleeding. When it eventually did, he pocketed the handkerchief and got out an old envelope; alternatively peering at this and flashing his torch he walked zig-zag towards the new part of the cellar, where the stacked barrels were high among the ladders and scaffolding. His nostrils caught the odour of port wine and for a moment he thought that his earlier encounter with it still clung, but it could hardly have survived a bath and fresh clothes.

This would do nicely; he picked the spot he had seen earlier and climbed twenty feet up. Once you got the hang of it it was easy to walk on the sides of the barrels, and for the rest the curves of two barrels made an admirable avant-garde-feeling seat. He put down the torch so that the light dribbled and bent as if in deep calculation. He slid from his hip pocket the heavily sealed foolscap envelope that he had prepared first thing that morning. Straightening, he gave a little triumphant whistle and leisurely put it in his breast pocket and commenced to turn, but then found himself without strength, falling forward. A strong hand caught him and broke his fall, so that he lay paralysed between the barrel tops.

As he bent over the detective, Mr. Harold Stiggins kept his face out of the torch beam, as agile as a squirrel and, Harry knew now, with wire and whipcord around his lean frame. There was something white in his left hand.

"I did pore old Krock with thât," smiled Stiggins. "A spanner with abaht a hundred feet of tape wrapped rahnd it. I 'ad to finish pore Krock when he came home unexpected like, but that was Lambeth tap, as my old dad used to teach us, wiv just the right force be'ind it so that the john is paralysed for fifteen minutes like a black beetle on its back. It don't leave no mark." His little white teeth gleamed as the edge of the torch beam caught his mouth. "I won't keep you long, old fellow." He groped inside Harry's breast pocket, took the envelope out glanced at it and very carefully stowed it in his hip pocket, buttoning it down. "That was the only flaw," he muttered, "Botty being given to duplication. I got into his flat when he was in France and found those tapes in the wine bin. Nothing on them abaht me so back they went before he got home. Nothing in that safe of his arter I done him and took his keys. Nothing except that one tape which I recognised because of the code number on it as the one Botty had kept of the interview with the Directors. I'd fiddled the lock on his office door and nipped in later in the day when I knew Botty was out and searched the place and got an earful of the tape."

His own fault, thought the Inspector, as he lay very still. He had expected to flush a civilised rabbit who would run for it and by doing so cook his own goose, or snivellingly surrender himself, or else put up a spiteful little attempt to seize the packet which police judo could easily overcome. Instead he had to get a professional from the London slums—the padded spanner was like a college diploma.

Stiggins had removed a long leather strap from his pocket and was looking at his watch. "Four minutes," he muttered, then bent and looped the strap round the Inspector and under his arm pits. The other end he fastened round his own waist. "We've got to get lower, on to the second tier of barrels, that's about twelve feet down. I'm going to slide you over very gentle and take the strain. If you know what's good for you you'll 'elp as much as yer can."

Stiggins' language had elapsed into glottal South London at its thickest. He slid the Inspector over, clasped the slack of the strap and threw himself down on the barrel tops. The Inspector, unable to move his legs or arms, banged against the barrel fronts, for one moment paused as he was caught on an overhang and finally went down like a rag doll. It was about ten feet above the ground, he thought quite clearly. He must wait and nurse any spark of returning strength to push himself forward and over. Stiggins was sweating as he climbed down and pushed and pulled the Inspector so that he lay face downwards.

"At nine fifteen," said Stiggins, "the watchman nicks across the way for exactly twenty minutes. A man of method. From the window of the public he can watch the gate. I've known for two years, but didn't do nothink. Little fings can prove useful; I learned that from Botty," he cackled, not pleasantly. "My mum's old man was 'anged," said Stiggins, "and three of her brothers did life. Oh, I've known all the lurks since I used to keep cave outside empty houses while me father stripped 'em. But I had this bit of old grey matter and got out of it. Ah, one of the original fam'lies we were. Not like Botty. Blow-ins they were wiv furring blood. I used to protect Botty. Big, fat boy, 'e was and they'd have 'ad 'is blood if I 'adn't intervened because I reckernised the brain box and thought it might be a 'elp. Crafty I always was. Like tonight. The missus thinks I'm spending the night in town on business. I've got the car parked in our garage—did it immediately after lunch and got a taxi back. Tonight I used my key to the Directors' changing- and shower-room and locked myself in the shower until everybody went. I put a ban on all overtime yesterday, Stigg signed it. Afterwards, I'll go up the old tunnel and have a kip half way up until around seven, then into the changing-room and a fresh suit and into my office bright and early. You won't be found until eightish." He chuckled, "After I did in old Percival—the Lambeth tap and the firkin to finish him off—the stupid ol' bastard to hint he'd seen me eavesdropping—I went into the changing-room where I have a duplicate set of clothes, right down to shoes and socks. Not a speck of dust or dirt on me when I went back to the party. Safe as houses, no call for anybody to go in there."

The Inspector had indeed worked out that the killer of Percival would have cleaned up in the Directors' changing-room, limiting suspects to those who had or might have procured keys. He thought he could talk, but decided not. Stiggins was well away on a sea of words; it got them like that, more often than not, just after a crisis, but the wise ones merely talked to themselves.

"Yes," Stiggins looked at his spanner, "this is wot done old Krock. No Lambeth tap for him, mate. Botty and me were speculatin', using the firm's money. It worked out a good thing, but the Guv smelled a rat and smirked at me that he was having a special audit. He made some excuse, but I knew he was getting wise. So we decided to do over Krock's flat. He had four thousand in notes underneath the wall-to-wall carpet—there was a bit that wasn't firmly fixed down. Botty was to alibi me, not that I guessed I'd need it, me being the last person Krock'd suspect, the meek and mild bookkeeper. Cunning old Botty made four telephone calls while he was waitin'—to a solicitor, an alderman and a couple other squares. I got back and told him; 'e 'ad no stummick for murder but he said he'd alibi me. I had to sign a confession that I did it orf me own bat. He took that and this spanner with the prints on it as security. We never mentioned it, but I always had it in me mind. Then there was a kind of spotty-faced runner the Board had. Let's see, begins with a P. Pocock, that's right. I used to be nice to 'im because I could worm a few tidbits out of him as to what was goin' on. He let it out about the parcel and that ol' fool Smart's locked bin. In me bones I knew it was the confession and this here spanner. O' course, I could have pinched it. But so what? I'd only clash head-on with Botty who was looking after me quite well. But I should have known, having seen Botty cut so many throats after getting all he could out of the livin' body. One day he told me I was through; that the deal with the brewery was going through and he had no further use for me. He said with a sneer that there would be just a formal reference—number of years

187

employed only. I told him I was neck deep in property deals and that I'd be ruined if I was out of work for even a month. He laughed and said I could quit on August thirty-first.

"That was five weeks ago; he was so contemp'uous that he didn't even send me a chit. He ignored me after that, wouldn't even see me, so I put a bold face on it and didn't speak to him. Last Sunday night I phoned him, said I was going to the police with a few details of what I knew about him. The upshot was I met him along the highway and got into his car. I swore I'd ruin him if I did myself in the process. I think he might have been taken aback, you know," said Stiggins in a gentle reflective voice, "but it was like a drug with Botty. He showed his great teeth and said he'd turn me in for Krock. He'd say I threatened him into giving an alibi. It might be four years for him, but it would be life—never comin' out, never at all—for yours truly. He had to go. I'd a'ready thought of that lift shaft and made preparations. I said down the shaft, "Botty, the police are in my office about Krock. Did you split, you bastard?" I 'ad fury in me voice and in three seconds I see his great face goggling up like a full moon. I ducked back and dropped the three-litre. But 'e got me in the end the bastard, the effing pig! I knew about the whitewashing, and it was a simple matter for my brain to work it out that Jas would do the stairs on the Saturday morning. A simple maths problem, easy. I never checked—I thought it best not to go near the old house that day. But of course, not being allowed in Botty's office I never seen the absentee list! Effing Jas was absent one day which put his schedule back one. I'd oiled the screws of the partitions and concealed a spanner in ol' Smart's office. I reckoned he'd be the main suspect even if you didn't shop him. Oh, I had some more evidence I'd have produced later. There was that drunken commercial in the next room, but his story might have been disbelieved, but not him *and* the white-washer. So I had to extemporise, a brilliant job I've done when you think about it. I got Nigel back on the brandy—'Not afraid of it, Nigel, are you?' I says. He's got the taste back and I'll see that in a month his brain will have gone again and he'll confess to anything. Well, me boy, time's up.

"A further refinement," Stiggins unlaced Harry's tennis shoes

188

and took them off, "most people think stockinged feet are safest. Nothink of the sort, as my ol' dad told us. They're the slippingest things about. You'll have slipped over the side. Funny thing," the laugh was genuine, "the customs came in this arternoon and prised the top off a hog of port. There's a gang bringing in brandy by floating it on two-thirds of a cask of port—the brandy always rises to the surface. They siphon it off at this end. A lot of money is being made, so the customs are making spot checks. The top's just on loose until the morning when the cooper comes. I'm going to take it off." The man's small face split with laughter, he took up the Inspector's and his own torch and vanished from Harry's sight. The Inspector lay there experimenting, and found he could move a little, but he was damnably weak and Stiggins had his favourite weapon. The little man came back very quietly. "You fall head first into the butt of port. Such a queer accident that nobody'll query it, eh, particularly as there are witnesses to prove you left the luncheon dead drunk. Oh, my, what a brain I've got! To think I wasted years as Botty's backroom boy. I suppose," said Stiggins slyly, "you're feeling better."

Sickness shot through the Inspector's body and he fought gaspingly for breath as Stiggins unexpectedly placed the heel of his right hand near the Inspector's solar plexus and brought his full weight down.

"You have to know the right spot," gloated Stiggins. "My eldest bruvver was a rare expert. 'Ere, stop that 'eavy breathin' or I'll make you wish you was dead!" He waited until the Inspector's breathing grew quieter. "Now, 'ere you go." He raised the Inspector's legs.

Harry James, numb and sick, heard it first, a contralto voice singing none too certainly, 'When Irish eyes are smiling'. His head, flopping over the side of the barrels, saw the wreath of torch light around the head of Mrs. Frankly. In her hand she held a pint tin jug. On her face was a bleary mixture of joy and cunning, as on that of a child who knows the whereabouts of the magic door in the garden fence. She approached the barrel and scratched her head with the jug. "You naughty, naughty girl," she apostrophised herself, "I'd a sworn we put the top back.

Never mind, dear, let's have a good swallow of fruity." She dipped the jug in, and held it, slopping port over the side. She raised her head and stood there aghast, staring at the Inspector's head. Blood dripped down from his ear.

"I know when I'm near the horrors," she said, "and I ain't got 'em. That's a head what I know. Hey, there, head, say summit."

The Inspector managed to put his tongue out and slobber. Seconds passed as they stared at each other. Then he saw Stiggins, half bent, come from the shadows and frantically jerked his eyes left. Mrs. Frankly followed his gaze, seeing Stiggins as he came with a flat-footed rush. Somewhere in her assorted shackings, three with benefit of clergy, the head lady bottler had encountered a wife-beater. Mechanically she side-stepped and threw the jug. It glanced off one of Stiggins' apple cheeks but port wine splashed into his eyes. He rubbed them and cursed, and Mrs. Frankly brought up one stout knee. She was out of practice but Stiggins reeled backwards. Unfortunately she retreated a few steps before rushing forward. Stiggins had gone to one knee, blinking his smarting eyes. This time he held the spanner, misjudged his swipe, but caught Mrs. Frankly a glancing blow. She sat down heavily, jackknifed over. Stiggins gave a brief imitation of a man trying to run in all directions. Reason prevailed and in seconds he was at Harry's side. "So long" he said as he shoved him over the side. The Inspector disciplined himself to breathe out and then deeply in, closing mouth and nose before he dived down into the viscous depths.

Maniacally Stiggins swarmed down a ladder and bent over Mrs. Frankly.

There were sounds of running feet. "You!"

It was the fat Sergeant, thought Stiggins, feeling Godlike and confident. He raised himself on tip-toe to deliver the blow and as though impaled on a moment of time he watched his wrist break and the hand flap back as the hard edge of Honeybody's right hand smashed at it and momentarily glimpsed the professional left rip start towards his jaw.

Afterwards Honeybody swore off port wine for life. Straddling Harry he pressed out a steady stream of red liquid, and when it came to the kiss of life he says, over a glass of bitter, that it made him more light-headed than any kiss he had ever administered. When he'd finished, the Inspector was groaning and retching. Honeybody got up wiping the sweat off his face. Stiggins was rolling on the ground in pain; the Sergeant rightly supposed that his jaw was broken. But indomitable Mrs. Frankly, blood congealing on her cheekbone, was dipping her tin jug in the barrel. "I'll see you get a case of whisky, love," said Honeybody, "but just now skip off to the front gate. If the watchman ain't there just switch the alarm on. I want police, two doctors and two ambulances. Can you cope?"

She nodded and went off at a trot. A game old battler, thought the Sergeant.

As he passed Stiggins he hesitated a moment and drew back one heavy shoe. But he shrugged and passed on, gently raising the Inspector and propping him against the barrel. "Gutsy little sod," he murmured to himself. Two minutes later he heard the scream of the burglar alarm.

First to arrive was P.C. Fright, switching lights on as he walked. Honeybody jerked his thumb. "They'll probably take him to hospital. See he gets a separate room and a two-man guard. He's dangerous. If he is just patched up, book him in for assault with intent to commit grievous bodily harm. Oppose all bail. I've got to see to my guv'nor."

See to him Honeybody did. The admissions officer at the nearest hospital was not the same insouciant young man for some months afterwards; a senior consultant was summoned in the middle of the first grand slam for three years; the Chief Constable gladly left the fag end of a dinner party.

Eventually it was decided that apart from the ritual million units of penicillin by intramuscular injection and a mild stimulant, twenty-four hours of bed, liquid, stewed sweetbreads and regular bowel movements would restore the Inspector to his friends. He sat shrouded in bed, occasionally giving porty belches.

"I never seriously considered that little runt," said Honeybody, eating one of the grapes the Chief Constable had commandeered from somewhere, although he really preferred them crushed, and fermented.

"You said he was a hyena," said Harry, "which made me pause. I remembered that if pressed hyenas will kill their own food and even cope with a lion if it tries to muscle in. If he is to be believed he comes from one of those old pre-1939 South London families of criminals, crooks for generations, and killers according to his boast. A clever devil who managed to confuse the issues without seeming to go near 'em. Cute, of course, and we always find *them* out, but he might never have been prosecuted but for tonight. But how did you come on the scene?"

"You owe your life to Mr. Bill Stigg," said Honeybody seriously. "After I'd come back from the pub he phoned and said that both Hanna and Keast left the room that morning, once together, and that they had coerced him into a mutual alibi. I thought I heard his wife breathing heavily at his side. A nice man, a nice woman. Anyway I asked P.C. Fright. He said you were with the Chief who I got through to. He knew nothing about it, so I threatened and wheedled Fright into telling."

The telephone rang. Honeybody engulfed it in his vast hand. He listened. "Yes," he said, "I'll tell him."

He replaced the handset and said quietly. "That was the P.C.'s wife, Harry. The maternity hospital were on the blower. You are the daddy of twins; they forgot to give the sex."

"This about sinks me for sure," said the Inspector, staring at the ceiling.

"Cheer up, Harry, two don't cost more 'n one."

Harry sat bolt upright. "Can they share a diaper; can they nosh the same teat; do they have one set of school fees; do they wear the same clothes; if girls do they hog into the same wedding breakfast?"

Hearing his bellow, a probationer rushed in bearing a bedpan. She stopped transfixed. The Inspector, thinning hair spreading over his face, was wagging a finger like an Old Testament prophet.

"Never mind," said Honeybody, "the day after tomorrow we can crack *two* bottles in honour of it all."